THE FEDS'
FOLLY

Who Stole $17 Trillion?

BILL BROWN

Copyright © 2018 Bill Brown
All rights reserved.

CreateSpace/Amazon Independent Publishing Platform

Cover Illustration by David Reaves
ISBN 13: 978-1721132003
ISBN 10: 1721132007
Copyright Info

The Feds' FollyCopyright © 2018 Bill Brown

FOREWORD

My first novel, *Money to Burn*, came to such a sudden stop, that I felt obligated to make an effort to write a few more chapters that would carry the Cain/Jones legacy forward. *The Feds' Folly*, continues to chronicle that legacy. A group of men and women spread treasonous corruption into upper echelons of the US banking and financial industry and the US Government, including Congress and the White House.

The Feds' Folly will take readers on a roller coaster trip of highs and lows and give them a front row seat as the drama of white-collar crime unfolds. An elite group of self-serving men and women ultimately pull off the single largest outright robbery, the absolute total heist of American taxpayer dollars by using bank fraud, blackmail, bribery, payoffs, murder, and extortion.

Can they be stopped? Will the perpetrators be punished or prosecuted? It will take close scrutiny by the readers to ascertain the final disposition of these intricate and interacting felonies and relationships.

Read on, America!   Bill Brown

Acknowledgements

Thanks to everyone who bought and read my first book, *Money to Burn*. I appreciate the enormous support and encouragement I've received from a multitude of friends, acquaintances, readers, and reviewers. Collectively, you have given me the courage to write another novel.

Hopefully, you and many others will find time to read my new book, *The Feds' Folly: Who Stole $17 Trillion?*

I would like to thank my friends, who have read my manuscript, provided insight, and helped edit my work.

To them, I shall be forever grateful:

Andrew Stangle, Carol Nelson, and most especially Jane Harvey and S. J. Pace.

"A sin takes on a new and real terror where there seems a chance that it may be found out."

Mark Twain

To my lovely wife, Sandra, my sweet Melissa, my Catman, and all of my friends, new friends, and readers.

Table of Contents

Chapter 1

The No-Fly Zone

The jet was falling out of the sky!

Minutes earlier, the Citation X had cleared Miami airspace, flying southwest to avoid intersecting Cuban airspace. The Miami air traffic control tower had already handed the flight to its counterpart at Owen Roberts International Airport on Grand Cayman Island. The jet had been cruising at its normal altitude and speed. Suddenly, as Mr. Jones reached for his Iridium satellite phone to call Mary, a loud blast erupted causing red lights in the cockpit to blink and fire alarms to go off throughout the plane. All hell began to break loose.

Looking out the window, Mr. Jones immediately saw smoke and flames billowing out of a hole in the left engine. He began to scramble around the cabin gathering his papers, satellite phone, the red Harry Winston box, bank receipts, and the intimidating note. He crammed them into his brief case, made sure it was locked and fastened to his wrist. At that very moment, he realized he had become a target. *I believe they're playing for keeps,* Jones thought.

Seeing flames coming from the hole in the left engine, the pilot hit the SOS button and the distress signal went out. MAY DAY! MAY DAY! MAY DAY! Then he yelled to the co-pilot, "Turn to a new heading. Head southeast. Now!"

The co-pilot responded nervously, "Captain, that'll put us in Cuban airspace almost immediately."

The captain, looking at the radar screen, said, "Doesn't make a damn! Not gonna' make Grand Cayman runway like this. If Cuban jets don't shoot us out of the sky, we might reach Cayman Brac. Set the frigging course now!" The co-pilot did as he was told.

As the crippled jet entered the Cuban corridor, it flew along the southern coast at a low altitude decreasing speed and without lights. The plane was vibrating and shaking violently. *No way can this bird stay airborne very long under these conditions,* the captain thought, *but maybe it can fly beneath Cuban radar.*

Shortly after crossing Cuba's southern coastline, the captain saw the tiny island on his radar screen straight ahead. It was directly south of Cuba. Then looking out of the left side of the plane's windshield, he saw lights coming from the island. He zeroed in on the shoreline and tried to use it as his glide path for landing. The jet was falling fast and quickly losing airspeed. It was not long before it began skimming the breaking waves. Splashdown was imminent.

The captain yelled, "Shut down everything. Turn off all controls, all switches, and prepare for a crash landing!" Mr. Jones tightened his seat belt and buried his face in the pillow in his lap.

The jet skimmed across the sandy shoreline as it hit water on the western end of Cayman Brac. The entire fuselage came to a sudden and abrupt stop as the plane's weight dug deeply into the shallow water and sand.

The plane had crashed. It was horrifying. Fire, bent metal, loud banging noises, things upside down, rushing waters, and acrid smoke, mingled with the fear of imminent death.

Absolute silence hung for what seemed a long period of time. There was only the hissing sound of ocean water lapping the burning engine and hot metal. Fortunately, the engine fire was being extinguished by seawater. Slowly, the flames disappeared. Luckily, the fire never reached the plane's interior.

What is that noise? There. That's it again. What's making that noise? Who's making that noise? Jones thought subconsciously. Groans and then more groans. Sounds implying pain. Real, severe pain. At last a voice. Mr. Jones's voice. As he began to regain consciousness, he slowly tried to open his eyes.

Mr. Jones had been thrown across the cabin during the crash and had seriously banged his right leg. The searing pain was coming from his thigh. His leg was hurting so badly he could barely touch it. Mr. Jones checked to see if any bones were poking through his trousers, but he found none. He knew it would be difficult to walk, if, in fact, he could walk at all. Jones had also sustained a serious cut on his left forearm that he was trying to wrap in order to stop the bleeding. He was in some real serious pain.

"Captain, are you alive?" groaned Mr. Jones.

"Mr. Jones, is that you?" the captain gasped. "Where are you? Are you all right? Answer me, if you can!"

"Can you move, Captain?" Mr. Jones responded. "If you can, try and make your way back here to the cabin. My leg won't let me move yet."

The captain had a severe wound on the right side of his chest, a deep cut from the broken windshield. It was bleeding profusely, and he needed immediate help to stop the blood flow. He was having difficulty breathing and speaking, perhaps due to a punctured lung. After several minutes, he slushed his way into the cabin holding his chest with his left hand. Blood oozed everywhere. He was a gruesome sight. He stumbled and fell in the aisle beside Mr. Jones.

"We've got to get some pressure on that chest wound, Captain," Mr. Jones gasped.

The captain moaned. Mr. Jones ripped a flotilla cushion from under his seat and pressed the cushion against the captain's chest. Then he took the captain's trouser belt and fastened the cushion securely, praying the bleeding would soon stop.

In a broken voice, the captain muttered, "Joe, my co-pilot, didn't make it. He died on impact. Severe gash to his right forehead. He was a hell of a guy and a great friend." Mr. Jones nodded in agreement, as he touched the captain's shoulder to calm him.

Mr. Jones winced again. His thigh was in excruciating pain. He groaned, "We've got to get the hell out of here, right now!"

The captain wounded and badly bleeding, and Mr. Jones, barely able to walk, scrambled to get out of the plane before it filled with water. Mr. Jones still had his attaché case cuffed to his arm. The salty seawater stung their cuts and bruises with surgical precision. *Damn! That really burns,* thought Mr. Jones.

As he crawled out of the plane, Mr. Jones held onto two things-- his brief case and a second flotation device. Luckily, they were in only two feet of water. Both started trudging toward the beach. Mr. Jones put his free arm around the captain and helped him towards the sand. Both struggled mightily.

In the darkness they saw lights in the distance and headed in that direction. Both were still losing blood and strength rapidly. It seemed an eternity before they were able to slosh out of the water and crawl a short distance up onto dry sand. They fell on the shore immediately, exhausted. They prayed they had reached a safe place.

They slowly examined each other's lacerations. Using their belts and parts of ripped clothing, they re-wrapped their wounds and prayed they didn't have life-threatening injuries. If only they could stop the bleeding. Too weak to exert any more energy, they lay quietly, thinking and praying about their next moves.

They realized that rescue efforts would soon begin--ships and planes, and all those things. They decided to wait until early light to lay out their plan of survival. Totally exhausted, and certainly in varying stages of shock, both men passed out right there on the beach.

As early morning light crept over the horizon and hit Mr. Jones's closed eyelids, he squinted, rubbed his eyes, and tried to focus his brain and gather his thoughts. It was barely light, but Mr. Jones remembered *he'd survived a plane crash.*

As he rolled over and looked around, he realized immediately something very strange about the position of the captain's body. It was curled into a fetal position lying on sand soaked in blood. In an instant Mr. Jones realized that the captain was dead, but he reached over and checked him for a pulse or a heartbeat to make sure. He got neither. *Probably bled out during the night from internal injuries,* Mr. Jones surmised. He closed the captain's eyelids and covered his face with his jacket.

Next, he looked to the water, but he saw only half the plane. The once sleek, ivory white, eight passenger Citation X jet, on its side, was crumpled up and blackish in color from the explosion. The remains of the aircraft were partially covered by the sea. *It was a bloody miracle that I survived,* Mr. Jones thought.

Mr. Jones unlocked the cuff on his wrist and opened his briefcase, which he had managed to keep out of the water. He grabbed his phone, checked its power, and clicked on the Google Earth icon. His location immediately showed up on the small screen. He made a mental note of the coordinates, as he called Richard, his stockbroker and friend on Grand Cayman Island.

Surprisingly, Richard answered the call on the first ring, "You're still alive, you bastard? You've got everybody on Cayman looking for you. Where the hell are you? Mary's going crazy!"

"Shut up and sit down, man. Listen very carefully. Get down to the dock and get my Fountain boat. On the way there pick up three burner phones. Grab lots of cash from the slush fund you keep for me. Lots and lots of cash and pesos. Throw in my passports, fake ID's, and some items that Mary and I can use to disguise our looks, when we go out in public. Toss my German Luger in the bag. I'll probably need it later. Don't ask why. Don't tell anybody you've heard from me. No one. Got it? Then crank up the Fountain and come to these coordinates on Brac. Now. Hurry.

"I'm on the western end. Come get me now. Both pilots are dead. I'm hurt, but I'll survive. You've got to get here before the rescuers find me. Don't call Mary, I'll do that." Then he shut off his phone.

Mr. Jones was somewhat relieved. Above all he was alive, He knew Richard would follow his directions. He realized he was damn lucky. No thanks to the Feds, or whoever had been out to kill him. He'd made contact with a friend and business associate, who was now on the way to pick him up. *That was good,* he thought.

Mr. Jones slapped himself and said out loud, "Get real man. Those bastards, those Feds are trying to kill you. They want you dead. You better get your ass out of here to somewhere they can't find you. Gotta put a plan together to fight back. It's your only hope of surviving."

Meanwhile, earlier that same day.....

It had been an absolutely beautiful September morning when Mary Whitmore left the villa at the Breakers for her run. She had mapped out a three-mile jaunt across this Grand Cayman paradise that took her about the island. She could see the bay as she ran under and through a grove of palm trees toward a freshly cut meadow. Mary could feel the morning dew on her ankles. She was in a good place.

Her mind was racing as her feet hit the turf, stride after stride. There were so many things she had to do today before getting dressed and going to the airport to meet Mr. Jones. She was excited and could barely wait until his plane landed at Owen Roberts Airport. Hell, she hadn't seen Mr. Jones in almost four days.

As she continued her jog she began thinking about what she would wear, where they would go for dinner, and at which bar they'd catch a late nightcap before jumping into bed. So many things to decide, so much to do. *Hurry up,* she thought to herself as she picked up her pace.

Mary finished her run and slid into a booth at her favorite open-air cafe, Sunrise. As she removed her baseball cap, her long blonde mane fell to her shoulders. Beads of sweat had popped up on her brow as the result of her forty-five-minute trek. She needed a cool drink and maybe a scone with jam. Yeah, that would hit the spot. When her order arrived, she sipped her iced coffee and took small bites of the pastry while perusing the local newspaper. After completing her breakfast snack, she headed back to the villa. On the way she checked her phone again to see if Mr. Jones had called, emailed, or sent a text. No cigar. Nada. Mary, subconsciously, registered some concern.

Mary's concern was not unwarranted. By the time she arrived at the General Aviation terminal that evening, she was quite upset that she had not heard a word from Mr. Jones. Actually, Mary's feelings were a bit hurt, because he hadn't thought enough of her to let her know when he would be arriving. It was going on eight o'clock at night, and Mary thought *he should have been here by now.*

She waited patiently until nine o'clock before she really got upset and started demanding answers. She had already called Mr. Jones's iPhone several times to no avail. She asked the General Aviation folks about Mr. Jones's arrival or the lack thereof, several times. Around ten o'clock she demanded they tell her what the hell was going on. She sensed they were hiding something.

"Tell me the damn truth, now," Mary demanded. "Quit lying to me and tell me what's happened to Mr. Jones or his plane. If you don't tell me right now, I'm going to call the police," she screamed.

The manager came out of his office and spoke very softly to Mary, "Please calm down, young lady. We're trying to confirm incoming information as I speak. Regarding the jet in question, it is not currently on our radar screen. That does not necessarily mean that anything is wrong. Maybe its departure was delayed. Once we get more details, we'll let you know."

"There's more to it than that," Mary said. "If Mr. Jones's jet left after the Senate hearings, it would have already been here by now. So, where the hell is Mr. Jones's plane?"

Mary was becoming hysterical. She was losing control. The manager guided Mary into his office and got her to sit down. He brought her a bottle of water and asked her to sit tight while he made more calls.

When the confirmation came in, the manager relayed the bad news to Mary, "Mr. Jones's Citation X dropped off radar at 8:13 pm. That's all I know. Search and rescue teams have already been notified, alerted and deployed. Is there someone I may call? Is there anyone here with you?"

Mary started to sob uncontrollably. "No! No! Mr. Jones can't be dead! Please tell me he's all right."

"Ma'am, I can assure you the rescue efforts will not stop until the crash is located. Emergency personnel will do all in their power to find Mr. Jones." The manager was trying his best to offer Mary some hope, however illogical it seemed under the circumstances.

Mary stopped crying, pulled her phone out of her bag and dialed Richard, Mr. Jones's stockbroker who lived on Grand Cayman.

"Hello, this is Richard."

Mary screamed into her phone, "Jones is dead! Can you believe that, Richard? He's dead!"

"Mary, calm down a bit, please. I just saw the news alert on TV. All they're saying now is his plane is no longer on their radar. That doesn't mean he crashed, and it certainly doesn't mean he's dead."

"Richard, what am I gonna do? Help me, please," Mary sobbed into the phone.

"Mary," Richard suggested, "Please pull yourself together and go back to the villa. There's nothing more you can do at the airport. Please go home. Wait and pray."

"All right, Richard, "Mary replied softly. "I'm going back to the villa. Please call me if you hear anything, good or bad. Promise?"

"I promise," Richard responded.

Chapter Two

The Alert

Twenty minutes after Mr. Jones's Citation X logged in with Grand Cayman Island control tower, the Captain hit the SOS button and sent a MAY DAY! message. Unfortunately, five minutes later the jet dropped off the radar screen.

The control tower went directly into emergency search and rescue mode. Their ER codes were transmitted to planes, ships, and the US Coast Guard simultaneously. Rescuers of all types went into motion. Two helicopters hastily left Miami-Dade airport headed due south. Two Coast Guard patrol boats launched at once from Miami harbor. A single engine plane left the tarmac in Key West, and a search and rescue vessel left Grand Cayman.

Their search coordinates guided them all along a fifty-mile swath of water from Miami due south to the southwestern side of Cuba, which is a lonely ninety mile stretch of sand and ocean. However, it was dark, and so far, no beeping emergency sounds had surfaced or been heard.

One helicopter took the east side of the designated search area and headed due south. The other 'copter took the west side of the swath and headed south as well. Both were listening for emergency beeps and looking for some type of light like a flare or burning wreckage.

The two Coast Guard patrol boats split the same routes south on the seas. The boats were equipped with all types of survival equipment. They were stocked with ropes, rafts, life jackets, search lights, major flares, extra blankets, and dry clothes. The boats carried all manner of medical supplies to treat any and all types of injuries. They also had food rations. Hoping for the best, they were prepared for the worst.

The single engine plane left Key West and flew due south right down the middle of the search area. The search and rescue vessel that left Grand Cayman headed northwest to cruise the perimeter of the ninety-mile area. Its main purpose was to stage a base of rescue operations.

All in all, the full force of the US Coast Guard Search and Rescue teams had now been deployed to find this missing, presumably crashed jet plane. Somewhere in the realm of a couple hundred individuals were involved in this emergency operation. They would search around the clock in an all-out effort to locate the crashed plane, and hopefully rescue any and all survivors. These Coasties had trained for this type of rescue operation over many years, and they had racked up hours of on-the-job training finding and saving survivors from all types of water-related emergencies. Therefore, they had high hopes of rescuing any victims.

It was going to be a long, dark, and busy night.

Chapter Three

The Call

Mr. Jones dreaded his next call. He re-adjusted his sitting position, trying to relieve the pain in his thigh. It wasn't because he didn't want Mary to know he was okay. It was because he knew he was now going to have to tell her the whole story, or most of it, sooner rather than later. He also realized that it was not going to be easy. He was keenly aware that she would be very upset, and rightfully so.

Reluctantly, he dialed her number, took a deep breath and waited for her to pick up. Mary answered, "Jones. I love you. Where the hell are you?"

Jones almost broke down but recovered before responding, "Mary, honey, you couldn't have said anything I'd rather hear."

Then Mary screamed, "Are you hurt? Are you okay? What the hell is going on?"

Jones, in a somber tone replied, "Mary, I'll explain later, but please follow these instructions. First of all, pack up all our valuables. Gather up a few clothes. We'll go shopping for what we need once we settle down." *A positive idea,* Jones thought. *Mary loved buying new clothes.*

"Close up and shutter the villa," Jones continued. "Then get over to Veracruz as soon as possible and charter a sailboat. Don't tell a soul you've talked with me, not even your parents. Do not call my phone again. I'll call you back later this morning."

Mary interrupted, "Don't you dare hang up! What the hell is going on? You never called me, and all I hear now is this cloak and dagger crap. Tell me right now! I have to know."

Quietly, Jones said, "Mary listen to me. I'm in danger, real danger, and so are you. Please just do what I've asked you to do. Go charter the sailboat. I promise I'll call you back in two hours." Jones hung up.

Not realizing at this point that he had survived a plane crash, Mary was relieved that she'd finally heard from Jones, but, deep down inside, she was really pissed at him. He'd screwed up all her exciting plans. She went from having great expectations for the two of them to having a feeling of despair and uncertainty. She already had underlying feelings of concern, but now she felt alarmed. She was scared.

She thought about what Jones asked her to do for a few minutes, then decided to get busy throwing a few of her clothes and valuables in her travel bag. Jones's instructions to get to Veracruz and charter a sailboat were a bit unnerving. She didn't feel comfortable thinking about how to do that. Maybe she could call a boat charter company or maybe do it online. She'd think about that later.

Then Mary's thoughts turned to what was involved with closing up and shuttering Jones's villa, and she quickly decided she needed help. She immediately thought about asking his housekeeper, Inez, and maybe the housekeeper's husband to help her.

Mary's mind began to drift off as she poured herself a glass of wine. *Must be more to this deal than I've been told*, she thought. *As I've suspected all along, Jones hasn't leveled with me. He's been holding back. He hasn't been totally truthful. Not really a surprise. What has he done that's so terrible that he doesn't want me to know? Has he murdered someone? No, no way Jones would kill anyone. Then it has to do with the Bank and his job. All this trouble began after he testified before the Senate Banking Committee. Yes, that's the key. That's it. He must have said something godawful at the hearing to start all of this backlash. But what in the world could he have said that was so threatening? Guess I'll find out pretty soon.*

Shortly, Mary snapped out of her daydream. Soon she was busy organizing a plan to do all the things Jones had demanded that she do. First things first, she decided. She got the valuables together and packed them in a travel bag, one she could manage by herself. Next, she called Inez and asked her to come in that afternoon to help her shutter the villa. Mary suggested that the housekeeper bring her husband along to help close up everything.

While she waited for them to show up, Mary opened her computer and started searching for a charter boat company operating somewhere in the Caribbean. It didn't take long before Mary found Caribbean Charters out of Veracruz. Once reviewing their website, Mary picked up her phone and called the charter company's office number.

Upon getting an answer, Mary began explaining what she wanted, "I'd like to charter a sailboat. A sloop with one mast and a fore and aft rig. I need a luxury sailboat. My partner is a very experienced sailor."

"Okay, Mam. We can do that," the charter agent declared. "We have an older model Bermuda 40 Hinckley that was made in Southwest Harbor, Maine. It's a real nice sloop made from fiberglass. It's the perfect sailboat for an experienced sailor. When would you like to leave on your cruise?"

Mary answered, "Okay, that sounds good. One week from today. But, wait, that's not all. I want the sloop fully stocked with provisions, including wine and hard spirits, for at least a week. Tell me how much all of this will cost."

"Mam, it depends totally on how long you keep the sailboat," the charter agent responded. "Well, at least give me an idea, please," Mary said.

"Sure, I can give you a quote right now. This type sailboat charter with everything included runs $15,000 per week," the agent stated. "I'll need a credit card to hold your reservation."

Somewhat surprised, Mary pulled out her credit card, reeled off the info, and said, "Can you let me reserve the charter with my card, but let me pay cash when we pick it up?"

"No problem," the agent replied.

"Okay, we'll see you next Wednesday. Make sure you don't forget the booze," Mary insisted. About the time Mary ended the call, she heard the doorbell ringing. It was Inez with her husband.

"Here we are," the housekeeper said. "Tell us what you want us to do"

"I'm so glad you both could come on such short notice," Mary replied.

Mary continued as she gave them specific instructions, "First of all, you need to shutter all the windows and doors. The storm shutters are in the shed. I believe they are already coded and marked, so you'll know where each one should go. You need to bring in all of the patio furniture and stack it along with the porch furniture up against the inside wall. Completely enclose the porch. Those shutters are in the shed as well. Then cover all the furniture inside with the sheets in the closet at the end of the hall. Unplug all appliances and cut off the water and gas and turn up the thermostat to eight-five degrees. Clean out the fridge and take home what you want and toss the rest. Finally, take off the bed covers and cover the bed with plastic."

The housekeeper said to her husband, "Let's get going. Lots of work to do."

"You're right about that," Mary answered. "The villa must be completely shuttered by this afternoon, because my flight to Mexico leaves today at four o'clock."

"We'll get it done in time, no need to worry," declared Inez.

"You're my angels, for sure," Mary added. "Here's three hundred dollars for your efforts. I hope that's satisfactory. Please keep an eye on everything while we're gone. You have our numbers."

"Of course?" Inez said. "We haven't seen that kind of money in months. Thank you so very much."

Chapter Four

The Search

Within the first hour, the Captain Commander, T. C. McCoy, had launched C-130 airplanes from Clearwater, Florida, plus a MH-60 helicopter. The US Coast Guard search vessel was designated the base of operations enabling Commander McCoy to make key decisions. The Captain then summoned his Lt. Commander to his post at the helm.

"Yes Sir. Reporting as requested, Sir," the Lt. Commander barked as he saluted.

"At ease, Lieutenant," Commander McCoy growled. "You need to make some important contacts. We're going to need help in locating that jet."

The Commander continued, "First, contact Digital Globe in Boulder, Colorado." Commander McCoy was aware that a major consolidation in the imagery business over the past several years had combined Orbimage, Space Imaging, and GeoEye. DG had become the premier satellite imagery provider in the world after its acquisition of GeoEye.

"DG now has as many as three or four satellites orbiting the skies on any given day. These unmanned devices collect up-close, personal, and quality high-resolution imagery. They span the globe in their polar orbits as the earth revolves on its axis. If Mr. Jones's jet is visible, chances are a DG satellite can locate it as quick or quicker than any other source."

"Officials at DG will be more than willing to help us locate Mr. Jones's aircraft," the Commander added. "They are accustomed to getting these types of emergency requests from around the world. They'll record all relevant information you provide them, input it in their computers at their control center, and then program their orbiting satellites with your specific search instructions. In a matter of minutes, DG's eyes in the skies will be looking for Mr. Jones's jet somewhere in or around the Caribbean, somewhere between Miami, Cuba, and the Grand Cayman Islands."

Then Commander McCoy gave his Lieutenant more instructions, "Call Precision Hawk. It's a small, but impressive company located in Raleigh, North Carolina. It's on the cusp of drone activity in the US, particularly in the agricultural sector. Their little toy airplanes with cameras are the perfect tool to use in our designated search area for locating the plane crash."

Two hours after receiving the call from the Lt. Commander, a Precision Hawk company jet was on its way to Miami with three different types of drones on board. The devices would be deployed later in the day to comb the designated search area for evidence of the downed aircraft. Hopefully, they'd spot survivors or a part of the jet or a debris field. Possibly, these drones, little toy planes with cameras, would find something leading to the rescue of possible survivors.

Commander McCoy was well aware of the latest technology available worldwide to assist search and rescue missions, and he never hesitated to ask for help in any circumstance wherever that might be. He was certainly impressed with the immediate response and willingness to help from both DG and Precision Hawk. He was certain their help would once again make his job easier, and their efforts would increase the likelihood of rescuing any survivors.

This search and rescue mission was nothing new for the Commander. He had headed up many similar operations over the past twenty years in these very waters. Many times his team had been called upon to help locate and save Cubans, who continually risked their lives in make-shift floats trying to escape the tyranny of Castro.

Cuban refugees would overload a boat or a raft and desperately try to make it to freedom in the United States, where they hoped to start a new life. Often, many didn't make it very far. Many times, soon after launching, their overloaded vessels would begin to take on water and sink, tossing the occupants into the ocean. Many couldn't swim, and they drowned. Fortunately for some, they were found in time and rescued by the Commander and his rescue team.

Sometimes, Cubans, who actually made it to the Florida coast were picked up by the US Coast Guard, only to be returned to Cuba. Somehow that seemed unusually cruel to Commander McCoy.

One air disaster the Commander would never forget was the tragic crash of Air France Flight 447 from Rio de Janeiro to Paris on May 31, 2009. It crashed into the Atlantic Ocean, killing all two hundred and twenty-eight passengers aboard.

The Commander was summoned to assist the French and the Brazilians in their search and rescue mission for the Air France plane and any survivors. They searched for days on end trying to find the passengers' bodies, the plane debris, or even passenger luggage, but they found nothing. Amazingly, and unfortunately, only fifty bodies were recovered from that crash in 2009.

Two years later, Commander McCoy, working with the WAITT Institute, discovered the partially intact remains of the aircraft's fuselage. It was located by WAITT's AUV's, full ocean depth autonomous underwater vehicles, at the astonishing depth of 2,180 fathoms or 13,060 feet deep. An additional 104 bodies were recovered along with the cockpit voice recorder.

Commander McCoy still remembered how devastating the Air France crash had been for the victim's families.

Bill Brown

Chapter Five

The Rescue

Three hours later, Richard came speeding toward the western shore of Cayman Brac in Mr. Jones's Fountain boat, powered by three, three-hundred-fifty horse power Mercury engines. He drove the boat right up on the shore, wildly waving his arms, hopped out, and sprinted up the beach to where Jones was waiting. Aghast at the sight of Jones's injuries, Richard, making sure they didn't leave anything behind, helped his friend, very carefully and painfully, to slip into the Fountain boat. As soon as Jones was settled, Richard handed him three burner phones and showed him the brief case full of cash. Jones first examined the phones. Then, with Richard's assistance, he took the battery out of his iPhone and tossed in in the ocean. He opened the brief case and saw the stash of cash along with the German Luger. A sly grin slipped across his face.

Jones instructed Richard, "Head southwest toward Grand Cayman. When you get within a mile of the coastline, hang a right and follow the coast until we find a secluded marina where we can slip in unnoticed and refuel. Then on to Cancun. Put this SOB at full throttle. There's no time to waste. I believe someone just tried to kill me. My jet crashed because there was a bomb on board."

The Fountain boat was a godsend. It had enough electronics to navigate most anywhere in any ocean. Richard set the GPS coordinates for Cancun as their destination. Then he thrust the throttle into maximum speed.

Richard began with the obvious, "What the hell happened? What's going on? Who are you running from? Who the hell wants you dead? Tell me!"

"All I did was tell the truth to the Senate Banking Committee hearing," Jones answered. "Must have really pissed off some folks.

Don't yet know who, but I damn sure plan to find out. Mary and I can't exist like this."

"How the hell do you plan to find out, if you're on the run?" Richard quizzed. "If someone is trying to kill you, there are only a few folks you can trust or even talk to right now. You gotta be damn careful."

"We need to slip back in the states from Cancun without anyone knowing. The public at large needs to think I'm dead or at least missing, for a while longer. I need time to layout my plan and make some moves undercover, so to speak. I've got a gut feeling who I should pinpoint and where I should look for answers. It's going to get real messy."

Richard, staring at Jones, stated, "For someone who thinks someone is trying to kill him, you're about as cool as can be. Hell, I'd be a nervous wreck. I'd be out of control, that's for sure. Hell, you didn't even mess up your pretty face or lose any of that glorious mop of hair."

Jones interrupted, "We have more important things to discuss. First of all, once you see us off in Veracruz, I want you to get back to Grand Cayman, so you can do the following things. Sell the Fountain boat as soon as possible. Move it to another yacht basin and then put it up for sale. Use a fake name. Just make one up."

"Jones, never knew you had a Fountain," Richard stated. "A hell of a speed demon. I did happen to notice that it's painted Carolina Blue. Man, it plows through these swells with ease."

Jones replied, "Bought it several years ago. I have a connection with the manufacturer. Reggie, a UNC alumnus and one of my older Deke brothers from eastern North Carolina, has always been a water skiing enthusiast and a speed boat fanatic. Hell, he could ski barefoot when he was thirteen. He won more championships in both categories than I care to remember. He holds all the titles. When he got out of UNC, he founded a boat company in his home town, and the Fountain boat was born. He sold them all over the world. He even sold one to Bush 41, who keeps it up in Maine at Walker Point.

Man, they're not cheap! I ran into Reggie at a party in Morehead City about three years ago, and he told me that he had sold over one hundred million dollars' worth of his Fountain boats and had spent every dime. Can you believe that? But back to business, Richard."

"You need to get legal documents drawn up," Jones continued. "You need my Power of Attorney and Mary's, so you can sell my villa. You also need ID's from both Mary and me so you're able to transact our financial affairs here or abroad. I want you to be able to buy any real items of importance, like another jet or a yacht."

Jones continued, "Next, transfer all my holdings to a tax haven in Europe. I prefer the small country of Luxembourg. I've checked it out, and they have the most to offer. Their tax rate is about 21% and they only charge a 1% fee for moving money in or out of the country. They're totally confidential. You're going to have to go over there to do all this legal wheeling and dealing. Just keep up with all of your expenses."

"I've got to go to Luxembourg?" Richard asked. "You can't be serious? Why can't I do all this by computer? You're nuts?"

"No, I'm not. You're going and that's final!"

"Once there, go to the Banque Internationale a Luxembourg. It's the oldest private bank there. Open two accounts, one in my name and one in Mary's name. Put half of my assets in an account in my name and put the other half of the assets in an account in Mary's name. That way, if they get lucky and take me out, Mary will still be solvent."

"Once that's completed, fly from Luxembourg to London. Then take a taxi to Portsmouth, where you can take the Hovercraft Ferry over to the Isle of Wight. Open two accounts: one in my name and one in Mary's name with Lloyds Bank TBS. Put a million dollars in each account. Then rent a two-bedroom cottage on the Channel in Bembridge. Furnished. Got all of that?"

"I'm totally dumbfounded," smirks Richard. "Hell, y'all aren't even married yet. Are you crazy or something? You really do some damn weird-ass things sometimes, but this takes the cake."

"Richard, listen to me. I've been dealing with you ever since I got in the banking business back in 1977. You've made me a great deal of money over the years, but somehow, I feel you made a little bit along the way, as well. So don't try and second guess me all the time. Just do what I ask you to do to the best of your ability. It's damn important."

"Oh, I meant to tell you to take a million dollars for yourself and your efforts. Does that make things better?" Jones asked.

Smiling ear to ear, Richard snapped, "Hell yes, Mr. Jones. I believe it does."

Jones went to the back of the fast-moving boat, took out one of the burner phones, and dialed Mary.

"Right on schedule, Jones. What a surprise," snarked Mary. "Tell me what's going on, at least just a thumbnail account until I see you. Can't wait any longer for some kind of explanation."

Jones took a deep breath and replied, "Mary, my jet was sabotaged with a bomb. I'm lucky to be alive. Both pilots are dead. It was scary. Don't yet know who's responsible, but we will find out. Soon. It's a matter of survival, yours and mine. They'll be after you, too."

"The only thing I can think to say right now is---who wants us dead and why? Is this for real?" Mary was shaking, and Jones detected fear in her voice.

"Calm down, Mary, please. Panic won't help either one of us. I, maybe we, know details that are making certain folks very nervous. I believe most of the problem has to do with the financial collapse. Federal agency heads are fearful that we may expose what we know about the financial heist, the actual theft itself, of our government's cash assets. It's what I was talking about in my testimony before the Senate Banking Committee."

"Do you really think those guys would try to kill you, us? Are they that scared?" Mary asked.

"Yes," Jones responded, "The other suspects are people in the

Guardian Society, who tried to take over our governmental system or possibly the bank heads. Remind me to show you the note I found in my briefcase minutes before the bomb exploded."

"What in the hell are you talking about? Note, on the plane? I'm so confused" Mary shouted.

Jones continued. "Right now, only you, Richard, and I know where we are at this very moment. Only you and Richard know that I'm still alive. We need to keep it that way for a while.

We need time to figure out what the hell is going on and why. Then we may have a chance of surviving. This is serious stuff, Mary. There was an attempt to murder me by air crash."

Mary started crying, "I can't live like this. This crap's gotta stop and soon. Please come and get me right now. I can't stay alone anymore. I'm terrified. I've got to be with you. Please!"

"I'll work it out as soon as we get back to land," Jones replied. "Please just get a sailboat chartered in Veracruz indefinitely."

"I've already taken care of that," Mary declared. "For your information, the villa's being shuttered as we speak."

"That's great news, Mary," Jones said. "Nothing like progress, don't you think? We're cutting across and headed to the hospital in Cancun now. Got to get my leg checked out. Meet us there. Yes. That's exactly what you should do. Meet us at the Galenia Hospital in Cancun. We'll be there later this afternoon. Be there." Mary's phone clicked dead.

Mary wasted little time in calling the airlines to book a flight to Cancun. Somehow, she was feeling better already.

Bill Brown

Chapter Six

The Crash Site

As night turned into early morning, there were no positive developments in the search for Mr. Jones's Citation X, none at all. This was totally logical because there were no beeps from the emergency transponder, and the satellites damn sure weren't going to make any sightings in the dark of night.

An hour after sunrise, Commander McCoy received an emergency message from Digital Globe's control room in Colorado. It stated that one of its satellites had relayed imagery of a partially submerged aircraft on the western end of the tiny island of Cayman Brac in the Caribbean. They suggested deploying a drone to the area to validate what the satellite imagery was showing. The Commander took their suggestion and ordered a Precision Hawk drone be dispatched immediately to the area in question. Concurrently, he ordered his crew to redirect his vessel to Cayman Brac. *Progress*, he thought.

On the way to the indicated wreckage area, Commander McCoy received a communication that new drone images confirmed a crashed plane at the site, validating the satellite imagery findings. All images showed the aircraft half submerged in water at the shoreline.

Cayman Brac was a tiny, mostly uninhabited, island approximately 156 miles northeast of Grand Cayman and fifty miles south of Cuba. By the time the Coast Guard patrol boat arrived at the crash site on Brac, it was mid-morning the day after the plane was reported missing.

The search crew had been provided satellite imagery coordinates that brought them to the plane's location. With the additional help of close up drone photos, they could see the Citation X lying on its side, half under water from the incoming tide. From the position of the jet, it appeared that the pilots did everything possible to splash down in the shallow water and glide along the shoreline until the plane bore into the sand under its own weight. It was a frightening sight.

Carefully, the rescuers climbed into the cockpit, where they found one pilot dead, still in his seat with his seatbelt fastened. The cockpit window had been blown out. They concluded the co-pilot died on impact as evidenced by the deep gash across his forehead. The rescuers were mired knee deep in water as they tried to maneuver back to the cabin area. The windows had been blown out by the explosion that also ripped a hole in the left engine. The exit door was torn off the fuselage. Items were floating around the eight upright passenger seats. There was no sign of any survivor. According to the flight plan filed earlier the day before, the manifest showed there had been another pilot and one passenger aboard. It was difficult to say if the missing pilot and passenger had been sucked out of the plane when the door ripped off, or if they were at the bottom of the bay, having been thrown from the aircraft on its final descent and plunge into the water.

Thirty minutes after arriving on the scene, Commander McCoy got a call from another maritime responder further up the shore. They had found the captain, dead and curled up on the beach about a hundred feet from the shoreline in a dry area, but there was no sign of the passenger.

Commander McCoy began his instructional dialogue, "Men, it's time to wrap up our initial findings. Let's get the dead men in body bags and aboard the boat. Take photos of all areas of the plane, inside and outside, including positions of the bodies. Stake the area around the entire site in yellow tape and post No Trespassing signs on the perimeter. Write down every single idea about what you have seen and what you think happened. I need two volunteers to guard the wreckage overnight. We'll come back at first light tomorrow and continue our investigation. Got to get the bodies to the morgue."

At the Commander McCoy's instructions, the Coast Guard patrol boat began to back off from the wrecked plane, slowly turned its bow westward and sped away from the island. It would take a few hours to get back to the Coast Guard station in Miami. It was critical to deliver the bodies to the coroner in Miami for autopsies before they deteriorated further.

Commander McCoy was busy writing up his report using data his troops had collected from the crash site, inside and outside the plane, and his own observations. The Commander's impression was that the plane crash had been the result of an explosion in or near the left engine. The black residue on the sides of the plane's fuselage looked similar to sights he had witnessed in wartime during his career. The photos of the crashed plane were very telling. They told a story, one that was not too difficult to read or interpret.

Back in Miami, the body bags were offloaded from the Coast Guard patrol boat, and the Commander went inside to hand over his report to the authorities and to be debriefed. As far as he was concerned, it was an open-and-shut case. Period. Nothing hard to understand here. The plane was brought down by a small bomb. Over and out.

Commander McCoy was informed that the wreckage debris would be retrieved over the next several days, so the National Transportation Safety Board could conduct its investigation. Their findings would determine the exact cause of the crash in undeniable detail. If a bomb did, in fact, bring Mr. Jones's jet down, the NTSB report would confirm the cause beyond any doubt.

Bill Brown

Chapter Seven

The Recovery

Upon arriving at the public dock in Cancun, Richard pulled the Fountain boat into an open slip. After tying off the boat, he very carefully helped Jones to the dock. In no time he hailed a cab, and they headed to Galenia Hospital, the top-rated medical center in all of Mexico.

As Richard was assisting Jones into the hospital, he could not help but notice how absolutely clean everything appeared. It was not just unusually clean, but the hospital staff was efficient, kind and helpful. Richard was most impressed, and he had no doubt it was a first-class medical facility, deserving of its lofty rating.

Immediately, Jones started giving Richard additional orders, "You've got to be real cool. Give the admissions officer a name of someone you know is dead. Tell them I was in a boating accident while fishing off the coast of Cancun. Don't mention anything about Grand Cayman. Tell them I fell overboard in rough seas and must have hit the propeller. Tell them it took forever to get me out of the water, back on board, and brought here"

Richard was able to get Jones triaged to the emergency room under a false name. He repeated to the attendant that Jones had been in a boating accident while on a fishing trip to Cancun. He followed that lie with the others about falling overboard and being struck by the propeller. No other questions were asked. Jones was taken immediately to the X-ray section of the facility for pictures of his lower extremities to determine if there were broken bones or torn tissues. The gash on his left forearm required twenty stitches.

While Jones was being treated, Richard went to the lobby, where he found Mary. She was sitting by the window reading an afternoon newspaper with a picture of Jones's crashed jet on the front page above the fold. It was the lead story of the day. As she looked up from the paper, she spotted Richard and yelled, "Richard, over here." She jumped up and ran to hug him. Then all the questions began. Richard put a finger to his mouth to warn Mary about talking in front of other people in the lobby. She immediately understood and tugged on Richard to follow her outside.

Once through the doors, she unloaded a barrage of queries on Richard. He hardly had time to answer one before she hit him with another. Most of Richard's answers were a truthful, "I don't know."

He tried to calm her down by telling her, "Jones is okay. He just has a badly bruised thigh and a gash on his arm. Other than that, he is fine."

Mary kept the questions coming, "How long will we be here? Two or three days?"

"I don't know," Richard replied.

"Should I cancel the boat charter?"

"No."

"When can I see him?"

"It won't be long," Richard answered. "Damn Mary, please ease up on the questions. Try and calm down. Jones doesn't need to see you like this. Act like a grown up. He'll need your support."

"I am a grown up... and you can go to hell, Richard. Folks are trying to kill Jones, and you make out like nothing's happening. Get a life."

"I'm sorry, Mary. Just trying to ratchet everything down a notch or two. We don't need to draw any undue attention while we're here. That wouldn't help anyone."

Mary sat down on the outdoor bench and asked very calmly, "Why do you think this happened now?"

Richard sat down next to Mary and put his arm around her shoulders and responded, "It has to do with whatever went down in the Senate Congressional Committee hearing, I suppose."

"What did Jones do?"

"Let's just take it easy until we can get Jones discharged, and the three of us can head on over to Veracruz. Jones can answer your questions about this better than I can," Richard replied.

Finally, the doctor came out and explained Jones's medical situation to both Mary and Richard. After answering a few questions, the doctor said that they could go back and see Jones. Mary went flying into the emergency room, and when she found Jones she wrapped her arms around him and didn't let go for many minutes. Their reunion was touching to watch.

Jones got the diagnosis on his thigh, a severely bruised muscle. Once Jones heard the verdict, he insisted that the treatment start immediately, right there in the hospital. He'd need at least two to three days of deep tissue massage, coupled with extensive water therapy. Mary and Richard agreed.

While Jones was undergoing treatment, Mary was never far away. She even slept in his room, and she turned out to be a great nurse. Richard was scurrying about Cancun trying to take care of Jones's other directives.

After two full days of doing all the things that the doctors suggested he needed to do, Jones convinced them he was well enough to be discharged, although he still couldn't walk without a severe limp. He was offered crutches, but he refused. He limped out of the hospital and all three returned to the Fountain boat and headed to Veracruz. According to Jones, going to Veracruz to charter the sailboat was just another cautionary step in staying under the radar.

Jones's Fountain boat was sleek and great for sport fishing and for speed. However, although it was a good-sized boat, it didn't have a cabin, much less a bed. Needless to say, creature comforts were not a top priority.

There was a lot of conversation among all parties on the trip to Veracruz. Richard and Mary peppered Jones with question after question.

Finally, Jones snapped, "Will the two of you shut the hell up! Damn it! You're both about to drive me crazy, not to mention pissing me off. Look, I already told you everything I know. When I figure out who the hell is trying to kill me and most likely Mary, y'all will be the first to know. So let's just all calm down. We need to get to Veracruz and pick up the sailboat. Then Mary and I can head out for the States."

Mary answered first, "Jones, I'm sorry, but I'm scared to death. I've never experienced anything like this before. I just need to know what's going on, along with assurance that all three of us are going to be fine and soon."

"My feelings exactly," added Richard. "Hell, Jones, you're one of my closest friends, and my best client. I'm worried about your safety, and Mary's, and mine for that matter. It's only natural that Mary and I feel this way."

"Okay, I get it. Enough said. How much longer before we get to Veracruz?"

"It's about a three-day trip by boat. Some seven hundred miles, I believe. This speed machine can get up to eighty-five mph, using about a hundred gallons of gas per hour. Needless to say, we'll have to make port a couple of times for fuel and supplies. So, to answer your question, I'd say a good three solid days of boating. Maybe more, depending on how calm the seas are, and how fast you want to go."

Mary frowned and moaned, "Never thought it was that far. Damn, it's gonna be a bitch of a trip. Where's the bar? I need a drink."

On the trip to Veracruz, Jones spent most of the time lying down so as to keep any unnecessary pressure off his bruised leg. Richard and Mary fixed him a pallet on the long bench seat with some towels. It helped a little, but he still had a lot of pain. Both Richard and Mary decided they'd give Jones a wide berth until he was feeling better. That turned out to be a good decision. The flare-ups stopped, and Jones's temper calmed down. Mary's got worse.

To ease further interrogations, Richard decided he'd bore his companions about Veracruz and began by rattling off facts he had gathered from a travel site, "Veracruz is a Mexican state overlooking the Gulf of Mexico. Major attractions are innumerable beautiful beaches. Too bad we won't have time to enjoy them on this trip. Another interesting feature is Pico de Orizaba, the highest peak in the country, but also a dormant volcano. Of course, we don't have time to climb that mountain this time around. Lastly, Veracruz was founded by Cortes in the early 1500's. What else would you to like to know about this Mexican metropolis?"

"That's a damn plenty, thank you, Mr. Tour Guide," Mary said quite forcibly. "You're driving us both crazy with all of your ramblings. Please just drive the boat and shut-up for a spell."

A couple of times Richard tried to convince Mary to take the helm and give it a try at driving the Fountain boat. However, she was adamant that she was not going to have anything to do with the operation of Jones's speed machine. The second time he insisted, she flatly refused, using distinctly colorful language. Richard finally got the message.

About five hours into their trip, Richard suggested they stop in Campeche. They needed fuel, not to mention a good hot meal. A break from their boring boat ride would be a welcome relief. Mary with Jones, limping along, went ashore first and left Richard to take care of getting more petrol. He joined them in the Seaside restaurant inside the Campeche Marina. They spent well over an hour eating, using the restrooms, and stretching their legs. Richard informed them that their next stop would most likely be Ciudad del Carmen, about two and a half hours away. They hoped they would get there before it got dark, dock there for the night, and find a decent hotel.

The sun came up early in Ciudad del Carmen. Richard was up early and was waiting in the Carmen Hotel lobby when Mary and Jones showed up. They grabbed a quick breakfast in the coffee shop, then went back to the marina, where they climbed back aboard the Fountain boat for another five plus hour ride to Coatzacoalcos, where they refueled the boat, took another break, and grabbed lunch. Jones insisted he needed to rest there for the evening. Mary checked them into a small motel. One room for Richard and one for Mary and Jones. They were now about two-thirds of the way to Veracruz.

All three were up at sunrise the next morning raring to get on with their trip. Richard grabbed coffees and donuts, plus sandwiches and drinks from the cafe and headed to the boat. Mary and Jones were waiting for him. They pushed off from the dock and headed toward Veracruz.

To everyone's satisfaction, Jones sacked out again on the pallet, Mary continued reading a book she had picked up in Ciudad del Carmen, and Richard minded the speed boat. Separate but equal and free of conflict. That's the way it was for the last several hours heading into Veracruz at dusk. It had been a long and trying three days. Everybody needed space and soon.

Chapter Eight

The Cruise

Upon arriving in Veracruz, they found the Buena Aqua Yacht Basin. Richard guided the Fountain boat to an open slip, jumped off the bow and tied the lines. Then he helped Jones and Mary ashore. It was a huge marina with luxury yachts everywhere. Thankfully, Mary had been able to charter a classic sailboat through Caribbean Charters. It was an older Bermuda 40 Hinckley, with one mast and a fore-and-aft rig, and multi-colored sails. As Mary had requested, the sailboat was fully stocked with supplies including a full bar. It was ready to board. Ironically, the name on the back of the sloop was The Evader.

Jones turned to Richard and stated, " I've decided that the best way for Mary and me to slip back to the States is to sail this sloop into some sleepy little coastal town along the gulf. I checked on Terraserver and it looks like Cameron, Louisiana, fits the bill. So that's where we're headed. Gotta get back where I can make personal contacts able to help us figure out what we need to do. Can you help me with the bags?"

Immediately, Richard jumped aboard the sailboat with both briefcases. One had lots of cash, pesos, financial documents, passports. and fake ID's. Jones's briefcase had his satellite phone, his bank records, the "note," the burner phones, his iPhone, the red box, and the subpoena from the Senate Banking Committee hearing. Then Richard retrieved their bags and stowed them below on the B40. Checking around Richard found that the sloop had indeed been fully stocked with rations, a full bar, and other necessary items they would need for a four or five-day trip to Cameron, Louisiana. It was also apparent that this would be a splendid and much more relaxing trip for Mary and Jones.

When Richard started to jump back on the dock to return to the Fountain boat, Jones grabbed his arm and said, "Thanks for your help. You saved my life. Believe me, I really do appreciate it. Take the Fountain back to its slip on Grand Cayman. Hopefully no one missed you or the boat. If anyone asks about me, you know nothing except what you read in the paper about the jet crashing. Don't admit seeing me, talking to me, or helping me. Nothing at all. If they ask you where you've been with the boat, tell them scuba diving."

Richard nodded an okay. Then he jumped to the dock, untied the sailboat lines, and gave it a hard push with his foot away from the dock. "Stay safe. Stay in touch with these silly little burner phones," he yelled as he waved his arms in the air. "Don't worry, I'll take care of everything you asked me to do. Watch your back."

With that, Jones and Mary began to maneuver The Evader out of Veracruz harbor. They were heading to mainland USA. They were alone at last. It was time for a serious conversation. It wasn't going to be easy, but Jones knew it had to be done...now.

When Jones finished rigging the sails and had the sailboat headed on a direct course toward the southeastern coast of Louisiana, he uncorked a bottle of Hess Reserve Chardonnay, grabbed two Baccarat wine glasses, and called for Mary to meet him on the bow. Mary appeared, dressed in Bermuda shorts and a pink halter top with her hair pulled back in a ponytail. Jones handed her a glass of wine as she sat down, and he returned to the wheel. He wondered how she had been able to procure this difficult-to-find Napa vintage wine.

Once they finished with small talk about The Evader, including how they'd take turns at the helm now and then, Mary's expression became serious, as she began asking questions. "Will you start at the beginning, before and after the Senate hearing? Please tell me what the hell's going on that would make someone or some group want to kill you. Please explain it in detail, so I can understand."

Jones squirmed nervously before clearing his throat and then answered, "I told the Senate Banking Committee the truth, the whole truth, and all of the truth. My testimony began with my introduction to Peter Hamilton, who was my grandfather, EC's prison cell mate. When I first began trying to get a job with the Bank, Pete introduced me to their counterfeit money scheme. I didn't leave out a single detail about the Bank's subsequent participation with the bogus money. I explained how EC stashed the counterfeit money in hundreds of safe deposit boxes in multiple banks around the southeast and the southwest. Then I explained how I used the bogus bills in all of those safe deposit boxes as leverage in acquiring hundreds of banks, helping move my bank to the top of its industry."

Mary totally confused, asked, "Remember when we had those heart-to-heart conversations in the British West Indies last year about our backgrounds and our pasts? You obviously left out all of the counterfeit details. Hell, that's flat-out lying to me."

"Wait a minute, Mary. I didn't lie to you about anything. I simply didn't think you needed to be worried about all the crap concerning the counterfeit money, the safe deposit boxes, and the bank leveraging scheme, so I just didn't tell you. That's different than outright lying. I didn't tell you about my plan to short sell my bank stock either, because it hadn't yet been done."

"You did a lot of illegal things," stated Mary. "That stuff you did is against the law. Most of it, anyway. Right?"

Jones, squirming in his skin, stood up and started to explain, "Mary, you're right, yes. The counterfeit money scheme was dishonest and illegal, but what the banks were doing was even worse. Hell, what the Feds were doing during the financial crisis was nothing short of outright thievery. Look, I'm not making this up. I was there. I saw it happen on a daily basis. I know they stole trillions of dollars. I make no excuses for my actions; but I felt justified in doing what I did, because I thought using leverage would eventually bring the banking industry to its knees. I knew that a major short sell of my bank's stock would cause further financial pain for my bank and the banking industry. I also wanted revenge for my mom and for my grandma, because of the way they were treated by EC. They suffered too much pain and shame. Along the way, just to make it right, due to unintended consequences or intended circumstances, I became filthy rich."

"Well you were certainly spot-on with that thinking. You didn't just bring the banks to their knees, you virtually broke the entire banking system. Hell, you could have gone to prison for that, and probably still could. Yes, it's fairly obvious you got rich, intentional or not."

"The banks deserve the pain they're enduring, but unbelievably they're still in business. Also it was payback for what happened to my mom at the Bank of Melbourne. She died in that bank heist because of the lack of security. It was past time for major payback."

Mary asked one last question, "Is there anything else you have kept from me? Are there any more shoes to drop? Please tell me the truth. I simply don't know how I feel about all of this."

Jones reached over and put his arm around Mary and whispered, "That's it. You now know everything I've done. Right or wrong, I have to live with what I've done."

Mary scooted away from Jones's embrace, headed toward the galley, and said over her shoulder, "Let's do lunch. I'm starved, aren't you? Want a beer?"

"Yes, a sandwich and a cold beer sound great to me." Jones moved over to adjust one of the sails. *This probably isn't the last time we'll have that discussion*, Jones thought, as Mary ducked into the galley.

After a long thirty minutes, Mary brought out a tray with two beers, two toasted pimento cheese sandwiches, and a big bag of chips. They ate their lunch in total silence. Without saying a word, Mary picked up the trays and went into the galley. After she did the dishes, she went down for a nap.

Later, when Mary returned to the deck wearing a sexy red jumpsuit, tension was still in the air as they began the cocktail hour about six o'clock. Jones had trimmed the sails, and the sloop was just coasting along on a slight breeze. He had already decided that he'd only use the auxiliary motor if the breeze died completely. It was time to break the ice with conversation.

Looking straight at Mary, Jones spoke first, "I'm really sorry that I've disappointed you to such a degree that we can no longer talk to each other. I've leveled with you about what I've done and what I've said, but if that's not good enough, then you'd better let me know. I guess I let my vendetta against EC and the banking industry become such an obsession that it altered my thinking, as well as my values. Obviously, that's wrong, and I do regret that to a certain extent. But, if what I said at the Senate Banking Committee hearings helps bring down all of those corrupt politicians, and all those crooked investment bankers, and if it exposes the remaining Swamp Rats on both sides of the aisle, then I figure I've done the country a service. On that basis, I stand behind what I've done."

Mary got up, poured them both more wine and answered, "Jones, no doubt you're a standup type of guy. I agree your testimony at the Senate Banking Committee hearings will most likely bring on other Congressional investigations. That alone may very well bring some of these crooked bastards down. However, that being said, you did go overboard with your illegal activities in the name of revenge. Now, I'll be the very first person to say and admit that I've violated statutes along the way, as well. Hopefully, not to the same extent as you. So, like the saying goes, 'people who live in glass houses shouldn't throw stones.' However, I believe that everyone should have to pay the piper for their illegal actions, and most of the time payback is hell. I suggest we try and regain each other's trust and respect and move on. It's pretty damn obvious we have more to worry about than who violated which laws. As for me and you, I'm for letting bygones be bygones and for getting back to the business at hand, which is getting our asses back on American soil, soon. Together, we must find out exactly who it is that wants us both dead. Once we learn that, we might have a chance of surviving."

Jones stood up and opened his arms as Mary moved toward him. They embraced for a long time. They had survived this far.

Both hoped they could survive the oncoming storm. They had endured their very first serious disagreement, and they were about to find out how rewarding "making up" could be.

Chapter Nine

The Landing

Four and a half days after leaving Veracruz, Jones and Mary sailed into Bay Cove Harbor in the coastal Louisiana town of Cameron. They were finally back in the States and, hopefully, no one was any the wiser. They were hoping they were invisible. So far, it appeared that they were.

Mary did most of the work securing the vessel. She tied it off and closed the hatch after tossing their limited baggage onto the dock. Very carefully, she helped Jones use an oar as a crutch to get off the boat onto the dock. What a struggle. His thigh was still painfully sore.

"Never thought I'd be taking care of you this early in my life," she kidded. "Something's wrong with this picture, don't you think?"

Jones failed to catch the humor, as he growled back at her, "Don't worry your sweet little ass. I'll be well before you know it, raring to go. Then who will be looking after whom? Is that proper enough English for you?"

Mary smiled and started sprinting toward the marina office. "Going to make arrangements on docking the sloop indefinitely ind get us a cab. Wait right there until I get back."

"No problem. I'll sit right here until you return."

Twenty minutes later Mary came riding up to the dock in a faded yellow car that had CAMERON CAB COMPANY painted across the trunk.

Mary was waving her hand out of the cab window and yelling, "Welcome home, amigo. Hope you had a safe trip. Come on, I can't wait to introduce you to my family." The cab driver seemed amused.

Jones very carefully stood up and grabbed a bag. Wincing, he growled, "I could use some help with this luggage."

The cab driver jumped out of the car, ran to the dock and told Jones, "Sir, get in the car. I'll take care of your bags."

Once in the cab, Jones instructed the driver, "Take us to the best used car lot in town. Now. Let's go."

"No problem. I know just the place. It's called Joe's." Then he turned the cab around and headed to Front Street in downtown Cameron.

They drove right through the middle of town. It was a quaint little seaside village with lots of weather-worn buildings, only one traffic light, and probably less than two thousand residents.

Mary spoke up, "Can we get a bite to eat first? I'm starving. Know any great local places, Mr. Cab Driver?"

"Sure. There's a fabulous little seafood restaurant a couple of blocks from here. It's called T Boys. It's right on the water. Sound good?"

Jones responded, "Hell yes. Let's go. I'm in the mood for a large fried seafood platter, hush puppies, and sweet tea. What do you say, Mary?"

"I'm thinking about fried flounder with fries and coleslaw."
"Damn," the cab driver said. "You're making me hungry, too."

Ten minutes later the taxi turned into the parking lot of T Boys restaurant. It was right on the water, and it looked like an old fish camp with a covered terrace for outside diners. Actually, it was a genuine Cajun-style establishment. There were maritime-related relics hanging on every wall. Finally, all three were seated in a booth in the restaurant waiting for their orders to arrive. That's when the cab driver started asking way too many questions, "Where're y'all come from? How long did it take you to get here? Why did you come here? Where are you headed?"

Without answering, Jones interrupted sharply, "Hey man, we're from Naples, Florida. Just helping our boat captain by sailing the sloop over here. He'll pick it up later this week. We need to head to Joe's lot as soon as we finish eating to look for a nice used SUV."

The cabbie fell silent. He got Mr. Jones's message from the tone of his answers. All three directed their attention to consuming their fried seafood dishes. It turned out that the cabdriver had a North Carolina connection. He was born and reared in Durham. The military had taken him to Louisiana years back, and he never left. He made Jones homesick for Chapel Hill.

Jones and Mary were dropped off at the used car lot where they immediately started checking out the inventory. Jones really liked a late-model black Mustang convertible. Mary, taking a cue from Joe while Jones was in the restroom, convinced Jones it had been wrecked. *How the hell does she know that,* thought Jones.

"Check out this Tahoe," Mary instructed Jones. "Looks like the best deal on the lot to me. What do you think?"

"Not bad," Jones answered. "Not too many miles and great tires. Let's buy it and get going."

"Sold," Mary said as she banged her fist on the hood of the SUV.

Even though Mr. Jones paid for the car in cash, it seemed to take forever to sign the papers, get the temporary tags, and all those things you have to do when buying a vehicle.

Finally, two hours later, Mary and Jones were headed towards New Orleans in an unusually clean, pre-owned Tahoe SUV. It was shiny black with a beige interior, a 2009 model with only seventeen thousand miles on the odometer, and it had a new set of radial wheels. A deal for sixteen grand.

After stopping to buy a map, Mary agreed to be the navigator and began her job by directing Jones, "Here, take Interstate 10 straight to New Orleans. If we don't plan to spend the night in New Orleans, then we need to say on Interstate 10 or get on Interstate 110 heading for Jacksonville, Florida. Probably need to sleep over in Jacksonville. Tomorrow we can take I 95 north to Savannah and then over to the Highway 17 on the coast and up to Charleston for more fine dining. Sound O.K. to you, Jones?"

"Hell, yes. Let's get going."

Chapter Ten

The Itinerary

The black Tahoe pulled into a Motel 6 parking lot soon after entering the city of New Orleans. You know, the one where 'they'll leave the light on for you.' Jones and Mary decided they'd like a night in this Cajun Country city. Might even try a little jambalaya. They checked in, got a room, and hauled their bags inside. They were not in any hurry, so they took a nap.

About six o'clock, Mary got up and started getting cleaned up. "What are you doing?" quizzed Jones. "Come back to bed."

"No way. Not going to miss a night out on the town with you in the Big Easy. Get up, sleepy head. It's time to rock and roll. Time to hit Bourbon Street, have a few drinks, and grab some seafood Cajun style. Come on. Start getting cleaned up. You should wear your baseball cap, and I'll wear my sunglasses so it'll be more difficult for anyone to recognize us. Tomorrow we need to buy disguises, like a wig or two for me, and more hats for you, maybe even a fake mustache. We can talk about our travel plans at dinner."

"Okay. Let me know when you're finished with the bathroom. Then I'll get moving. I'm always ready before you are."

"Don't think I agree with that statement, but it's all right for now," Mary sighed.

"Okay, I'm going to wear a pair of old sunglasses," Jones added. "You can wear the hat or cap. Probably don't need to be seen in our natural state with all the plane crash publicity."

"We need to hide the briefcase with the money," suggested Mary. "Don't need to leave it on the bed for someone to pick up and walk out of the room. Where can we hide it?"

"Here, let me put it behind the ceiling tile over the bed," answered Jones. "There, it's done. This is where we should hide this briefcase, wherever we stay."

It was after seven-thirty when they jumped into a cab and headed to downtown New Orleans. Jones told the cabbie, "Drop us off in the French Quarter." Turning to Mary he added, "Then we'll head over to Bourbon Street."

The driver replied, "No problem. We'll be there in fifteen minutes. Sounds like you guys got a big night planned, no?"

"Yes", answered Mary. "A real big night. We're celebrating."
"That's great. What are you celebrating?"

Jones spoke right up, saying, "We're happy to be alive."

The cabbie seemed dumbfounded. Ten minutes later Mary and Mr. Jones were in the French Quarter.

First they hit the famous Pat O'Brien's. Jones had a Jack Daniels and water. Mary settled for a daiquiri. Forty-five minutes later they continued bar hopping, as they walked into the Cat's Meow. Jones stuck with Jack and water, and Mary ordered a dirty Grey Goose martini. So far, so good.

Then it was on to Fat Tuesday's for another round of libations. Jones ordered a shrimp cocktail which they shared. *The cocktail sauce certainly has a fair amount of horseradish,* Jones thought.

Mary asked, "Where do you want to have dinner, Mr. Jones? We don't have reservations, so it may be difficult getting in any high-profile places."

"Let's try and talk our way into Antoine's first. If we don't make the cut, we'll try SoBou. Sound like a plan?"

"Whatever you say, Mister Silver Tongue. Let's see if you still have it."

The stars and planets must have been aligned because they got a super table in Antoine's. Of course, Jones didn't tell Mary he slipped the maître d' $200.

Once they were seated, Jones suggested, "Maybe we should switch to fine wine. Does that suit you?"

"I was just thinking the very same thing. All great minds think alike, or something like that."

Mr. Jones beckoned the sommelier. He responded immediately, "What may I bring you? Do you have a preference? I can recommend great reds, or if you prefer a Chardonnay I have the very best. Most are from France, of course, but we do carry a few California wines."

Mary butted in and said, "Sir, surprise us. Make it special, please."

Jones, grinning, grabbed Mary's hand and gave her a soft kiss. "It's going to be a great night," he murmured.

Mary responded with a severe roll of her eyes. Then they both started laughing.

They settled on a favorite Valley of the Moon Chardonnay that reminded them of their time in Sonoma Country. It paired well with their seafood dinner entrees. They started off with the house appetizer, a giant order of soft shell crabs, and they were not disappointed. The crab plate was incredibly delicious.

Antoine's was everything they'd ever heard about this circa 1840 old world grand dame of fine French-Creole dining. According to legend, it was also the birthplace of Oysters Rockefeller.

Once they began their dinner, their conversation moved toward making an overall plan of where they might go for their own security and peace of mind. They needed an out of the way spot, where they could hide from the rest of the world, a remote place where they could figure out what kind of danger they were exposed to and from whom.

Jones declared, "I think we should head toward the northeast. There are so many places to get lost up there, but we'd still have access to existing connections we'll most likely need later. Also, if they think I survived, I don't think the northeast would be the place they'd think we'd go."

"Jones, you don't know all that stuff. You're speculating, just making that up. Let's get specific and map out our trip to a final destination. Let's agree that the plan is totally fluid and can be changed at any time based on circumstances."

"Sounds like high-priced legalese from my favorite barrister. Of course, I concur with everything you just said." Jones poured more wine into both glasses.

"I'm not trying to practice law, just trying to be reasonable, Jones. This is scary and serious. We have to use our combined brain power to devise a plan that'll help us survive any more attempts on your life and mine. I have a great idea as to where we should land for a month or so."

Jones wiped his mouth with his napkin, stood up and said, "Time out. Got to go to the men's room. Be right back."

Smiling, Mary leaned back in her chair with her wine glass in hand.

As Mr. Jones returned to the table and sat down, he mused, "This may very well be a tourist trap, but all I can say is, so far, their food is divine."

Mary nodded in agreement as she continued, "I think we should head for Nantucket and hang out there until late November. Nothing like being there in the fall when the people we know probably won't be there."

"Why and how do we get there?" asked Jones.

"Here's my suggested travel itinerary," Mary began. "We leave here tomorrow and drive to Jacksonville, Florida. We can decide when we get there whether to stay over or drive on to Savannah. Remember, gotta be fluid. Then after that, just north of Savannah, we can take Highway 17 and hit Charleston. Then it's on up to Myrtle Beach, where we can cool it for a couple of days."

Jones interrupted, saying, "How'd you come up with all of this? You've been thinking about this for how long? Sounds logical, so far. Continue on, my dear travel agent."

"Come on, Jones, cut out the bull, okay. We've got to get this right. Now, where was I? Oh, yeah. Here we go. From Myrtle Beach, we stay on Highway 17 North to DC. For obvious reasons, I don't believe we should spend any time there at all. If you agree, maybe we could drive on to Annapolis, Maryland."

"Now you've got my attention. If we can spend time together in Annapolis, sign me up. I know just the places to go."

Mary sighed, "That's what I was afraid you'd say. I have no interest in reliving your sexual memories with old flames. Count me out."

"Okay, let's move on. So, then what do we do?"

"I'm getting to that," answered Mary. "Here's the real deal. We can go to my brother-in-law's family cottage on Nantucket. You know. You've been there before in 2000. First Light, remember?

I know where the key is, and we can stay there for at least a couple of months. They're not there and won't be showing up until Christmas Stroll, which is the first weekend in December."

"You mean skip New York? How can we do that?" Jones demanded.

"We don't have to skip it. We can stop by the New York Federal Reserve Bank, if you like. Maybe they'd shoot you on the spot," Mary laughed

"Don't be silly. We need to be on the same page. I like what you just said. Great plan. I agree. You're too damn smart. Want some dessert?"

"No. We can share a candy bar back at the motel. Time to go home."

When they arrived back at the Motel 6, Mary quickly began undressing. Jones was glad they'd left the lights on, because he saw what was going on and got interested real quick.

"Turn off the lights, Jones," Mary ordered.

While Jones and Mary we're enjoying their overnight romp around New Orleans, Bill Baker at the Federal Reserve Bank in Washington, DC, and Kurt Lane at the American Bank Corporation in Charlotte, North Carolina, were in constant contact. They were discussing Mr. Jones's dead or alive status and his possible location.

Baker called a friend at NTSB to request any information the agency would share with him relative to the plane crash. The only answer Baker got from his contact was that the jet was indeed brought down by a time-detonated bomb device. They were trying to determine its origin. *Not much help there,* thought Baker.

Meanwhile, Lane was pushing the Medical Examiner in Miami for updates on autopsies of the two jet pilots. The Medical Examiner was trying to convince Lane that there was very little data that suggested anything other than the plane crash itself that had cost these men their lives.

The only abnormality was an excessive amount of an anxiety drug that showed up in the co- pilot's blood. *What in the hell does that mean,* Lane wondered.

Lane's mind continued to race. *My local "fixer" didn't get the job done. If Jones's body is missing, the SOB's not dead. I should have contacted Rocky "The Rooster" in the beginning. Killing that bastard is number one on my list. Must let the others believe he may or may not be dead to protect myself.*

Chapter Eleven

The Trip North

Jones and Mary slept late the next morning. They were not too excited to see sun rays peeking through the blackout drapes. Both were hungover.

Jones got out of bed first. He made a pot of coffee and hit the shower. In no time at all, he had dressed, retrieved the briefcase from the ceiling, grabbed all of his bags, packed them in the SUV, come back inside, poured a cup of coffee, and turned on the TV.

Mary pulled the covers over her head and begged, "Please turn the volume down."

Jones obliged. He got up and poured another cup of coffee, handing it to Mary. "Get up," he urged. "It's time to hit the road and get out of the New Orleans. We've got people to see, things to do, and places to go. Hurry up. I'm going to checkout and pick up a newspaper."

When Jones returned to the room, he was glad to see that Mary was up, dressed, and ready to go.

He tossed the newspaper on the bed and said, "Check out the story below the fold of the front page. We've made the news again."

Mary picked up the paper and scanned the front page until her eyes fell on the headlines that read,

CAYMAN BRAC JET CRASH
PASSENGER STILL MISSING

Although Mary's name did not appear on the plane's manifest, the article read as if the authorities were considering that possibility. In the body of the story, both Jones and Mary, his companion, were described as missing and presumed lost at sea. It also stated the US Coast Guard was still actively searching for survivors, and there were photos of both. *Oh, no, I'm on that list, too,* she thought.

Mary tossed the paper back to Jones, saying, "It's like reading your own obituary. Not something to enjoy. It's the photos of us that bother me."

Jones grabbed Mary's bags, opened the door and suggested, "Let's get going. It's about an eight-hour drive to Jacksonville, Florida."

"It can't take that long, can it? I didn't think it was that far."
"Afraid so. Maybe we can take turns driving," Jones added.

Once on the road, Mary grabbed the map and directed Jones to take Interstate 10 East toward Jacksonville.

About an hour into their trip, Jones cleared his throat and spoke, "Mary, I really want us to drive to Melbourne. Maybe we can cut the cabbage and drive a little more southeast and go through Melbourne on our way to Jacksonville. I want you to see where I grew up and where Mom and I lived, until she was murdered in the Bank of Melbourne.

Three armed gunmen stormed the bank looking for cash to buy drugs. One robber, spooked by a teller reaching for a buzzer, started firing and killed my mom, who was in line to purchase a money order for my birthday. It was a bank robbery that went horribly wrong, as there wasn't a single security guard on duty. Not one single armed security guard was anywhere on the bank property. That's totally irresponsible on the bank's part. They knew better. A bank with no security policy in place to protect their employees or their customers in case of an emergency. Unthinkable! Since we're this close, it's proper for me to pay my respects to my mother. I want to visit her grave."

"I understand," replied Mary. "I'd love to see where you lived and grew up. By all means, we should take the time to go to Melbourne. I'll find a route that'll get us there in the quickest amount of time."

"As I remember," Jones said, "it's about a hundred and eighty miles south of Jacksonville, or about a two-and-a-half-hour drive. Not too far. I need to go."

Once they got into Florida, Mary found a shortcut they could take that would get them to Melbourne around four o'clock. They'd have time to look around a little, find Jones's old neighborhood and maybe his old house. Then they could go by the Melbourne Memorial Cemetery, where his Mother, Anna, was buried.

Once in Melbourne, Jones's whole attitude changed. Mary could see both the sorrow on Jones's face. He had adored his mom and he still missed her.

Jones found his old neighborhood and showed Mary the small bungalow where he grew up, two blocks away from the water. "This was a great place to grow up," sighed Jones. "I loved living here with my mom all of those years. She was such a wonderful mother, an incredible person."

At the Melbourne Memorial Cemetery, they found Anna's grave. They both paid their respects with soft words and prayers. Jones introduced Mary to his mother. It was emotional for both of them.

Jones kissed his mom's headstone and then tearfully whispered, "Goodbye, Mom. I'm glad I got to visit with you once more. Say goodbye to Mary. I'll love you forever. Let's go, Mary."

The drive up to Jacksonville was quiet and somber. It was dusk when their SUV passed the city limits sign. It read: "Welcome to Jacksonville, Florida. Fifth Largest City in the US, Based on Land Mass." Both passengers let out sighs of relief.

"We need to get a motel room right off I-95, check in, go back out for a quick, easy dinner, and go to bed. I'm exhausted. Agree?"

"No objections from me," Mary replied. "It's been a long day."

They found a Red Roof Inn, checked in, and without much conversation they went straight to a Ruby Tuesday close by. They both took advantage of the enormous salad bar. It was stocked with most every vegetable known to man. It had several choices of lettuce, numerous meat items like chicken, turkey, and ham, not to mention the different salad dressings. The rolls were delicious. It was a feast for the starved travelers. Then it was their bedtime.

The next morning, they grabbed egg and cheese biscuits and coffees from a Hardee's drive-thru and headed north on Highway I-95. Mary informed Jones, "It's only two hours to Savannah. Only three and a half hours to Charleston, and only five and a half hours to Myrtle Beach. We'll have to take a detour east to get over to Highway 17 to Myrtle Beach. What do you think?"

"Why don't we just take the shortest route and drive straight through to Myrtle Beach. Stopping at all of these places is going to take too long. We need to get on to where we're going, the quicker, the better. Anyway, with our photos in lots of newspapers around the country, we need to more careful about where we go in public. We need more disguises. We'll pick some up in Myrtle Beach. We can have dinner at a spot I know, that shouldn't have many diners this time of the year."

"Okay. We can do that."

"Mary, you're the best, and I still love you."

"That's good to know. Great to hear that I'm still loved, albeit the criminal I have become. Just call me Bonnie, and you're Clyde."

"Get serious, Mary. You have not done one single thing against the law. Quit being so negative."

"I believe they call it aiding and abetting a fugitive. Now that's serious business in my legal opinion."

"Oh, so now I'm a fugitive, although I've not been charged with one single crime. You do realize I'm on the run because someone is trying to kill me. Like Kurt Lane's wanting an eye for an eye."

Mary changed the subject.

Jones was really pushing the SUV as they bypassed both Savannah and Charleston and then started the two-hour drive to Myrtle Beach, South Carolina. The trip from Charleston to Myrtle Beach offered little to see other than miles of undeveloped land and lots of trees and marsh. As the landscape offered very little to talk about, Mary and Jones came up with their own topic of discussion: the ramifications of the Senate Banking Committee hearing.

During the next two hours, because of Jones's testimony, they talked almost exclusively about the Federal agencies he accused of fraud including the Federal Reserve Bank, the US Treasury Department, and the Federal Deposit Insurance Corporation. It started out being a pretty general conversation, then quickly became specific.

Mary asked, "Did your banking career give you special insight into how these agencies work and why?"

"Yes, it did."

"Did you actually interact with different agency heads from time to time?"

"On more than one occasion," replied Jones. "It would have been impossible to do the kinds of mergers American Bank Corporation completed over the years without having numerous meetings with agency heads. It just simply couldn't have happened."

"So you've actually worked with players at the top of our financial institutions?"

"Most of them, over the years," Jones answered. "As unlikely as it was, I started out negotiating with the FDIC's head honcho, Ms. Brand. She is a career government employee with lots of connections, is very straightforward and suffers few fools. She never married, and I don't believe she liked having to deal with so many men. However, we managed to have a good working relationship. "I met her years ago when American Bank Corporation was doing RTC deals in Texas. My Bank appreciated her generosity, since we basically received an outright gift from the FDIC. We got clear title to the assets of many Texas savings and loans in Texas from our government, thanks to Ms. Brand. Believe it or not, our government took all of the bad debt attached to those assets. Hell, we couldn't turn that down, and we didn't. Those transactions were mostly responsible for my Bank's entry into the upper echelons of the banking industry."

"What does that have to do with today? "Mary asked.

"Very simple," Jones responded. "She's still there. It shows how inept she was relative to the nation's financial affairs. It proves how little she knew about resolving a complex and difficult monetary problem. She had way too much power and authority, but not the slightest idea of how they should be deployed."

"Damn, you don't like her a bit do you?" stated Mary. "Glad I'm on your side."

"It's not a matter of liking her or not," Jones replied. "She simply wasn't and still isn't qualified to hold that office or position, period."

"Tell me what you really think about your old boss, Kurt Lane" Mary quizzed. "Other than being your current nemesis, what is his deal with The Bank?"

"Believe it or not, I think he is a good fundamental banker. He's well-qualified, and he has the training and experience. However, he is in no way comparable to his predecessor, Harold McNair, who was one of a kind. McNair is the one who pushed ABC to the top of the industry. When the current CEO, Kurt Lane, moved into the top position at The Bank, he found out immediately that he was lacking the leadership skills to master the office. He was in way over his head. I believe they call it the Peter Principle. So, Kurt turned into a "bully" administrator, not exactly the best way to get the job done. Other than that, he has two major flaws. One is his insatiable greed, and the other is his intolerable arrogance. Not good attributes for a guy running the largest bank in America today."

"The guys at the Federal Reserve and at Treasury are real mysteries to me," Mary said. "Put me wise as to who these men really are and tell me how the hell they got such incredibly powerful positions in the nation's financial infrastructure."

"That's not too difficult to understand. As you'd expect, those positions are mostly political, regardless of which party is in power. In most cases, the powerful are part of a small clique that continues to look after its own, even after they're gone. Most all are Ivy League college graduates that network from the very day they graduate. Most have a law degree, and most are highly knowledgeable about financial matters. As for the ones in power now, most meet all that criteria; but due to the length of time they've all served in their respective positions, they have decided that they're above the law. Also, many of them believe they have been chosen to decide what's best for our nation, and they feel completely justified in whatever decisions they make."

Jones continued, "Bill Baker at the Federal Reserve and Ted Gomer over at the New York Fed, and Peters at Treasury are like three peas in a pod. They think alike, and they are basically inter-changeable in their responsibilities relative to our nation's financial health. In 2008, Gomer, acting on behalf of all three agencies for the US, went to Europe at the height of the financial crisis for no ap-parent reason. Folks who know believe that's when the plan for the 'governmental cash heist' was formalized. What Gomer agreed to while he was over there would be extremely explosive reading."

"You told me about that last summer. Since then I've tried to figure out in my mind what happened that convinced these Federal agency heads they could misappropriate and distribute trillions of dollars to whomever they chose," stated Mary. "How the hell did they think they could get away with such an outright theft of tax-payer dollars out of our country's Treasury?"

"There's probably not a single reason, but more likely a series of events that, coupled together, gave these men the idea that it could be done. You must remember that during that time, the Feds were printing billions of dollars a month. These billions were being funneled into the country's monetary supply in hopes of stemming the tide of what seemed like a certain and total financial collapse. It was easy for them to see that they could divert millions upon mil-lions of dollars over a sustained period of time. They realized they controlled the power to divert funds, not only to their personal ac-counts, but also to accounts of whomever they deemed necessary in the US and around the world. It was easy for the Feds to keep their heist under wraps."

Why was it so easy for the Feds to keep their crimes hidden?" asked Mary.

"The Federal Reserve Chairman and the Federal Board of Governors are appointed by the President and approved by the Senate. They report to no agency, not to Congress, not to anyone. The Fed's mandate is to maximize employment, stabilize prices, and moderate long term interest rates. Additionally, they regulate and supervise most privately-owned banks."

"Sounds like they can do as they damn well please," added Mary. "That's a helluva lot of financial power in the hands of just a few folks."

"You're absolutely right, Mary," Jones replied. "There are 17 Federal Reserve member banks spread around the country. There are seven members of the Federal Reserve Board of Governors and twelve regional Federal Reserve Bank Presidents. They only have to file an annual report to the Speaker of the House. In essence, the Federal Reserve Bank, our central bank, is basically an independent instrument of the government, because their monetary policies don't need anyone's approval, and their funds are not appropriated by Congress. Hell, in 2015, the Federal Reserve made over one hundred billion dollars and transferred almost ninety-eight billion dollars to the US Treasury. So, it ain't like the Feds don't have access to billions of dollars."

"Jones, do you just lie awake at night and dream this crap up or are you simply the brightest bulb in the chandelier?" quipped Mary. "Can any of this be proven or are these white-collar thieves going to get away with this staggering robbery?"

"I have no answer for that question, at all," Jones replied. "It'll probably depend on how deep this economic crisis goes, both here and around the world. However, as is the case in many criminal situations, one person gets caught or arrested and starts talking in hopes of a lesser sentence. Then before you know it, more of the villains are incriminated. Maybe, that'll happen with this ordeal."

Chapter Twelve

The Feds Meeting

While Jones and Mary were scrambling around the country, hiding in plain sight in disguises including sunglasses, wigs, hats, and baseball caps. However, rumors were swirling in New York, Washington, and elsewhere. They hoped they were back in the States under a cloak of anonymity. The powers that be had all heard each and every rumor. The newspapers had documented Mr. Jones's departure from the country in his jet and the crash. Two pilots had been declared dead, but Mr. Jones had not been found... dead or alive. Speculation on his survival abounded. Nerves were fraying.

Bill Baker, Chairman of the Federal Reserve Bank in Washington, called an emergency meeting. He ordered Ted Gomer from the NY Federal Reserve Bank, Harry Peters from Treasury, Ms. Brand over at the Federal Deposit Insurance Corporation, and Kurt Lane, the CEO of the American Bank Corporation in North Carolina to report to the Federal Reserve office in DC immediately.

The meeting started twenty minutes late. Ms. Brand from FDIC was the last one to walk into the SCIF, the Feds Sensitive Compartmented Information Facility, supposedly their top secret and impenetrable office in the bowels of the Treasury Department building. There were no windows. The door was three feet of solid steel that made a threatening sound, when it clunked shut. The room contained a long conference table and a dozen soft back leather chairs. The telephones and computers, along with all other tech devices were secured by tech specifications established by the Intelligence Community Standards. The narrow room was lit with only recessed lighting. The SCIF was specifically designed to accommodate all communication between individuals with secure access in other SCIF's, which may or may not be permanent or mobile.

Ms. Brand looked around the room and made eye contact with Ted Gomer from the NY Federal Reserve Bank, then with Harry Peters from Treasury, and on to Bill Baker from the Federal Reserve Bank. She fixed her eyes on Kurt Lane from the American Bank Corporation and said, "I'm sorry I'm late, but I just got an interesting phone call from our office in New Orleans. There has been a reported sighting of Mr. Jones and his girlfriend, Mary, I believe her name is, on Bourbon Street. Seems they were possibly spotted having dinner at Antoine's. Just the two of them, alive and well, right there in New Orleans. Don't know how certain we are of this information, but we've got people checking it out. Odd, however, for a potential spotting at such a high-profile establishment."

"Got to have more definitive information than that to put any credence in that type of report," suggested Harry Peters. "I don't think we should waste our time on 'rumors' without more substantial evidence."

Ted Gomer chimed in, "Let's talk about the business at hand. First, we must figure out if there's a mole in one of our agencies. Second, we must identify which agency the informant has compromised. Third, we must identify who the informant is, and just how much information he or she may have transferred to Jones. Fourth, we must eliminate the informant.

Disgusted, Kurt Lane piped up and said, "I can't believe it has come to this. We're all running scared. We don't really know anything beyond the fact that Mr. Jones had to have someone feeding him information. It had to come from one of your agencies. The problem we share is, does Jones know who and where we directed all that money to go? If he has possession of those details, we're in real trouble. We need an immediate plan of attack."

Bill Baker took a file out of his briefcase. He could feel the tension in the room, and the smell of fear was prevalent. *Better get a handle on this now,* he thought.

Baker, who had remained as Federal Reserve Chairman with the new administration, knew he'd better clean this mess up and soon.

He passed a typed agenda around the conference table. It had a list of ten items. Some capitalized, others not. One line simply read, "What does the President know?"

After nervously shuffling his papers, Baker cleared his throat and began talking, "We all know the facts. We know what has transpired in our country. We know the gruesome financial repercussions. Most importantly, we all know what we must unanimously agree to do, as a way out of this mess. However, the financial manipulation of $17 trillion that we are privy to and actually participated in, must not be made public to the American people. Now, if there is a person or persons in any one of our agencies, who had access to this information and did indeed pass it to Jones, then unfortunately, we have but one choice of action. We must eliminate the spy, if we're to suppress that data and survive."

Before Baker could continue, Harry Peters jumped up from his seat and raised his arm above his head, he shrieked, "No. Do not go there. We can't do that. No, I won't agree to that. Please!" Then he sat back down.

Ms. Brand spoke up harshly, "Harry, settle down. Fear will get you nowhere. This discussion is headed in the wrong direction. There must be further actions we can discuss, both civil and legal, that would take care of this urgent matter. Let's try and broaden the scope of any potential resolution. We must make a genuine attempt to curtail further damage that may be caused by agency leaks."

"Leaks?" Ted asked. "That's a mighty weak description of what a mole has possibly given up. Hell, if Mr. Jones got the names of all of the people and companies, both here and abroad, that were on the receiving end of the $17 trillion WE stole from our government, it wouldn't just be the end of us, but it could also lead to the total downfall of our country."

Baker resumed, "That's all total speculation. We don't need to waste our time on hand wringing, but rather we must be decisive and call a spade a spade. Be honest with yourselves. The only way we'll survive and the country will survive is to keep that financial data from getting to the public. If Jones is alive, then the only fail-safe way to assure that result is to eliminate Mr. Jones. That's right, I'm talking about locating and eradicating Mr. Jones and most likely his woman, Mary, too!"

Total silence fell over the room. It was deafening. Nobody made eye contact. They all stared at their hands.

The person in the room who seemed most upset, got up, walked around the conference table and stood behind Baker's chair and declared. "I'm on Baker's side. I knew Jones was onto us after the Senate hearing. Elimination of the problem is the only solution. Yes, Mr. Jones must go," said Kurt Lane. *The note and the bomb I had placed on his plane didn't do the job,* thought Lane. *This time I must have him eliminated for sure.*

He continued, "That SOB has made a complete fool out of me with my major shareholders. I can't believe what he told the Senate Banking Committee about the counterfeit money scheme that EC Cain, his grandfather, hatched up. He told the Committee how he uncovered and unleashed millions of dollars of counterfeit money, not only from my bank, but also from hundreds of other banks in the southeast. Mr. Jones then divulged how his scheme benefitted the American Bank Corporation."

Kurt continued, "Many of my largest investors are after my ass. Mr. Jones has made a mockery of the American Bank Corporation, and he seriously tarnished the entire banking industry. Then, as if that weren't enough, he tricked me into buying Wide Country Mortgage. That purchase turned out to be a total disaster. Next, he shorted millions of our ABC bank shares, based on inside information, and it made him a fortune at the expense of all my other shareholders. His short sale caused my bank stock price and value to fall to an all-time low. It caused ABC bank to lose billions of dollars." Ted Gomer started to interrupt, but Kurt cut him off by saying, "Wait. I'm not finished. Hear me out before you say anything."

"I'm no killer, but I know folks who can take care of Mr. Jones once and for all. No one will ever know. Here's something you need to remember. As of today, most people among the general public believe Jones died in the plane crash. Many think he is already dead. Let's make sure they keep believing he's dead by NOT going public about trying to locate him. If we play our cards right, he can be terminated, and no one will ever know that he survived the crash. So all I'm saying is we must locate Jones, if he is alive, find out where the hell he and Mary are hiding and give me the information. I'll gladly take care of the problem. I can promise you that."

Ms. Brand and Harry Peters were both shaking their heads, when she said, "I'll have no part of this madness! You're talking about murder. Are you crazy?" Harry nodded in agreement.

Bill Baker stood up, looked at Kurt, looked back at the other three and said firmly, "We got a deal, Kurt. I'll make sure we find the bastard, dead or alive. I'll get you the information you need to put this matter to rest forever. This meeting is adjourned." With that declaration, they all walked out of the room in total silence.

Kurt Lane went directly to the airport, climbed aboard the Bank's jet, and headed back to North Carolina. He was positive that he and Bill Baker had made the right decision, regardless of what the others might think. He was damn certain that he'd keep up his side of the deal. *Mr. Jones is going to pay,* he thought.

About that time his sat phone rang and Harry Peters said, "Kurt, I couldn't say too much in the meeting since I'm stepping down, but after thinking about the overall situation we find ourselves in, I want you to know that I think you and Baker are doing the only smart thing there is to do. Getting rid of Jones is absolutely essential. Just wanted to give you my support, albeit in private."

"Thanks, Harry. I appreciate your candor and support. I promise I'll do everything in my power to make sure Mr. Jones disappears once and forever. I'll keep you posted."

The Bank jet began its descent into Charlotte Douglas International Airport. Lane, who had admitted to himself that his previous plan to sabotage Mr. Jones's jet had failed, was anxious to get to his office. From there, Lane knew it was time to implement another final and fatal attack on his sworn enemy, Mr. Jones.

Chapter Thirteen

The Connection

Jones and Mary were about half way up Highway 17 North when Jones pulled into a service center for gas and a pit stop. Jones had finally made up his mind about something he had been reluctant to do. Yes, he had no choice but to use one of his burner phones and call his connection at Treasury. It was risky at best, but Jones knew he had to have help in finding out who was trying to murder him. His Treasury contact might be able to supply him with valuable information that would put him on the right track. When they returned to their vehicle, Jones turned to Mary and stated, "I've decided to call my informant at Treasury. We have to have help."

Mary jumped straight up in her seat and asked, "Jones, have you thought this through?"

"Yes."

"Are you sure it's worth the risk?"

"No."

"What if they're tapping all incoming calls?" Silence.

"I'm not sure I agree," Mary nervously screeched.

Ignoring her, Jones picked up his burner phone from the seat and quietly replied, "Mary, we can argue about this forever and never agree. If you know someone else that I can possibly call for help, please don't hold back. We're in serious danger. I just survived a bomb attack. It's imperative we get information that we don't now know. I'm calling my informant, CLEPTO, at Treasury on the safe number he gave me back in the summer. Once I make the call, I'll destroy this burner phone. Then we'll get two new burner phones, and I'll call Richard with the new numbers."

"Okay, Jones. Obviously, you've made up your mind about calling CLEPTO without consulting me. Make it short and sweet. Be careful you don't give away our current location. This is too much cloak and dagger stuff for me. My nerves are quite threadbare.

Jones dialed the cell number. There was an immediate answer, "Hello. I'll call you back on my lunch break, about two o'clock." The phone went dead.

"Was that short enough," Jones quipped.

"Go to hell, Jones. This isn't funny. I'm scared to death."

Jones started the car, pulled back onto Highway 17, and once more, they headed north to Myrtle Beach.

At precisely two o'clock, Jones's burner phone rang. He answered with a soft, "Hello."

"Jones, I'm in the mall at Tysons Corner, so you'll probably hear background noise. Wanted to get out of the office to call you but wanted to be around people. Glad to know you survived the crash."

"Smart move. You never know who's listening. Bring me up to date with what's happening on your end."

"Yeah. Sure. No one here really knows if you're dead or alive, at least that's the line they're putting out. A couple of them really seem to believe you died in the crash. Hope you can keep it that way. Others think you're alive, but I don't know the reason. Your old boss at the Bank and the Federal Agency heads had a meeting two days ago in the Treasury SCIF. An Urgent Notice from Baker was hand delivered to all four, mandating that they attend. There seems to be no notes of the meeting, no minutes either, nothing. They suspect a mole, and they're terrified that you've been given access to financial data that proves their thievery. I'm scared, as well. Personally, I suspect Kurt Lane is right in the middle of it all."

"The crash was no accident, "Jones answered. "A bomb caused it. Maybe they all don't know it yet, but at least someone in that group is trying to kill me. I need your help finding out which one. Can you help me? Will you help me? I suspect Kurt Lane."

"You don't have to worry about me helping you. I'll do all I can. You can count on that. Listen carefully. Meet me in two days at the

Tysons Corner McDonald's at precisely 11:30 am. I'll be sitting at an outside table drinking a cup of coffee and smoking a cigarette from a pack of Winstons. We'll not use anyone's name and talk only about the weather and Carolina basketball. When I get up to leave, you'll find an almost empty pack of slightly crumpled cigarettes in my coffee cup. A thumb drive will be inside the cigarette package. It will be loaded with classified information you must use in order to save your life and maybe even our country. Got it?"

"Sure, I understand. Just one change. Mary will meet you at the table. She'll be wearing a reddish colored wig along with a pale blue UNC sweatshirt and jeans. Okay? Thanks."

"Fine. No problem. Look forward to meeting Mary. Bye."

Jones turned to Mary and asked, "Do you mind?"

"Why not. I'll make a perfect target for a sniper bullet."

"It's time to get rid of these phones and buy two new ones. Remind me to call Richard with our new numbers."

"Yes, Sir," Mary chided.

They arrived in Myrtle Beach a little after four in the afternoon. Jones headed straight to the North Myrtle Beach Hilton and parked the Tahoe.

"Come on. I know you'll want to stay here."

Jones and Mary checked in and went to their room. Before going to the bar by the pool, Mary and Jones added a little disguise. Mary put a baseball cap on over her wig and Jones donned large sunglasses. "This place never changes," Jones declared. "I've been coming here for years, and each time it seems to have been recently updated. Great place to bring a family. We'll blend right in."

"When in hell were you here with a family? Maybe we can rent a couple of kids. Haven't heard that story yet. Want to tell me now?"

"Cut out that crap. Don't try and make something out of everything I say. It's not the time for another negative conversation. We've got bigger fish to fry "

"Okay Mr. Jones. Whatever you say. You decide what we talk about, and then let me know. I'm good at following instructions."

"Damn it, Mary. Let it go, please."

Once they were settled by the pool bar, they ordered a couple of Tom Collins and relaxed in the late afternoon sun. Actually, the sun felt good on this late September day.

Around six o'clock they returned to their room, got cleaned up, dressed up, improved their disguises, hid the briefcase, and headed out to dinner. Jones had called Cagney's Eatery, located right on Highway 17, not too far from the Hilton.

After a quiet dinner with very few other diners, they made their way back to the Myrtle Beach Hilton, had a nightcap on the balcony bar and hit the sack. They had two big days ahead of them. Very big indeed. It was a matter of their lives or their deaths.

By the nine o'clock the next morning, Jones had put all of their bags in the SUV, Mary had grabbed pastries and two coffees from the free breakfast bar in the Hilton lobby, and they were ready to continue their trek northbound on Highway 17.

As Jones drove up the highway, he turned to Mary and declared, "If we stay on Highway 17, we'll pass right through New Ferry, North Carolina, the birthplace of the infamous Bank. New Ferry's only fifteen miles from the Fork, where EC, my grandfather lived. Since we still seem to be under the radar, I'd like to show you his Supermarket and his home. I went to see him there once during his eightieth birthday party celebration. It'll give you a perspective on where all of this mess actually started."

"It may soothe my nerves," Mary said. "I am interested to see all things EC. Certainly, we should take the time and go there. However, there's one other thing you missed. New Ferry, North Carolina, is where Melissa, my good friend and roommate at Dartmouth was born and reared, until she was two years old."

They crossed the North Carolina state line, and were breezing through Wilmington, when Jones pointed out a sign to Mary which read... Carolina Beach 3 Miles East.

"Mary, in May 1952 at the end of that road, a surf fisherman found EC's brown Packard stuck in the sand dunes. Inside he found Clara, EC's second wife, strangled with her own stockings, naked and spread eagle on the front seat. Her body had already begun to decompose in the warm spring sun. She had been abducted from her home at the Fork three days earlier. EC claimed he was asleep on the bed only ten feet from where she was kidnapped."

"Jones, do you have to be so damn graphic? That's horrible. Was the murder ever solved?"

"No. It's still one of North Carolina's most brutal unsolved murder cases," Jones answered. In another fifteen minutes, Jones turned left off Highway 17 North and drove toward Castle Hayne.

"Are you hungry yet?"

"Yes, I'm famished."

"Well, there's this famous hot dog store in Castle Hayne right outside of Wilmington. It's called Paul's Place. I guarantee that you can't eat just one."

"Sounds like the place to stop for lunch," Mary replied. "Count me in."

Once inside Paul's Place, an old remodeled gas station, Mary ordered one hotdog with mustard, chili, and onions. Jones ordered two the same way. In no time flat, Jones went back to the counter and ordered two more hotdogs, which they devoured immediately. They shared a cup of sweet iced tea.

"You couldn't eat these dogs every day, but two or three times a week would work for me," Jones remarked.

"Jones, you're just insane."

Once arriving in New Ferry, Jones and Mary had an interesting time riding around the small town. They tried to see if they could figure out where the infamous Bank, chartered there in 1952, had been located. Once they found New Ferry Shopping Center, Jones recalled that the Bank's first corporate office was in that center. Then they started searching for where they thought Melissa might have lived. Henderson Drive seemed vaguely familiar, based on photos Melissa had shared with Mary years before. Elated, Mary pointed to the back of an attractive home set far off Henderson Drive that fronted on Clyde Drive. *This has to be where Melissa lived,* thought Mary.

Once they finished looking around New Ferry, they drove on down the road about eleven miles to Groveland. It took only ten minutes to circle through town. It appeared to be a small, rural community. They saw the water tank that read Town of Perfect Water.

Mary asked, "There must be a story about the Town of Perfect Water. Must be something special."

"All I know about that is what Grandma Brenda told me a long time ago," Jones answered. "Around 1930, the North Carolina Department of Agriculture began testing the water supplies for all municipalities. The water had to meet certain requirements, relative to its purity, to determine if it was potable and safe for human consumption. If the impurity levels were too high, the water had to be treated with certain chemicals to bring the water into compliance."

"The water source for Groveland has long been derived from the Black Creek Aquifer located right there in Onslow County. Since the testing began in the early thirties, it has never been necessary to remove or add anything to the Groveland water supply, therefore giving Groveland the designation of the Town of Perfect Water."

Mary replied, "That's an absolutely unbelievable story. I wonder if it's still true."

"As far as I know. It surely passes the taste test," added Jones. "Iced tea and coffee brewed with water in Groveland is much better than what I've had anywhere else."

"That's simply amazing," Mary remarked.

After driving three more miles west, they saw what had been EC's Supermarket sitting right there in the middle of The Fork. It was in a terrible state of disrepair, and it had a sign above the door that read: Commotion - a Night Club! *What an appropriate name, Commotion,* Jones mused. "Why do you say that," asked Mary?

"Because this is where so much went down over the years. So much total commotion," Jones continued. "That real small house is where Clara was abducted right out of her bathroom window in the middle of the night. It was three days before they found her on Carolina Beach.

Mary commented, "I remember. You mentioned it earlier. That must have been horrible for EC's daughter, Elaine. What a tragic event, particularly for a five-year-old girl. Jones, who do you believe killed EC's wife? You must have an opinion, don't you?"

"Yeah, I have an idea of what happened to Clara. From all I've been told over the years, and that's a helluva lot, it seems quite logical that her abduction and subsequent murder were thought out well in advance. In other words, I believe it was premeditated."

As Jones cleared his throat, he continued, "In all probability, Clara's murder was directly connected to EC's affair with Katy Hoover, his employee. It had become way too obvious to Clara that something was going on between EC and Katy. Clara argued with EC about it the night before she was kidnapped."

"I believe that on the night Clara was abducted and murdered, she threatened EC's livelihood and personal freedom by insisting he quit screwing around with Katy. Clara promised EC that if he didn't stop seeing Katy, she would divulge everything she knew about his counterfeit money operation to the police. In my opinion, that very night with one phone call, EC put his premeditated plan to take Clara out into action."

"Who the hell did he call?" Mary asked excitedly. "Where was he when he actually called whomever he called?"

"Here's what I've been told, over and over, by several different people who were close to Clara. EC and Clara were on their regular Sunday night revenue run. It was something they did every week. They'd leave the Fork, drive around to all three of EC's drive-in movie theaters to pick up the week's cash. Then he'd stop by his appliance store in New Ferry and pick up its weekly receipts."

"So," Jones continued, "once EC was threatened that Sunday

night, most likely he used the phone at his appliance store to make that ominous call, when he went in to collect the week's returns. It only makes sense that EC called his two brothers that fateful night. They understood why he was calling, since they had worked out the details of Clara's possible disappearance with EC several weeks before."

"Did a lot of people believe EC had Clara murdered?" questioned Mary. "If your answer is yes, then why were EC and his brothers never brought in for questioning?"

"Yes, lots of folks believed and still believe EC was responsible for Clara's murder. EC and both of his brothers were questioned extensively about where they were and what they knew about her disappearance, but they were never designated persons of interest. No one ever became a person of interest. No one was ever charged or indicted."

"Why not?" Mary asked.

"The real reason no one ever talked back during those days was, EC and his wealthy business associates pretty much owned both the politicians and the law enforcement heads. In my opinion, Clara's murder was a complete cover-up from the beginning to the end."

"That's unbelievable," Mary added. "That's awful."

Jones replied, "Believe me, there are a great many folks in the area who feel the very same way today." "Anyway, as I was saying," Jones continued, "This is also where EC's counterfeit money operation was located. They printed the counterfeit $20's in his warehouse. It was located right there behind this old ramshackle store. The bogus bills were trucked to EC's appliance store in New Ferry and stored in the freezer lockers on the sales floor. Where the counterfeit money went from there is another long story."

"Damn, a real crime scene for sure," added Mary. "If I remember correctly, there's even more, right?"

Jones replied. "Yes, believe it or not, there were more crimes that originated at the Fork. First there was, as I already mentioned, EC's warehouse that was torched. They called it a friction fire. That's when the mortgage rubs up against the insurance policy and starts a blaze. Then a bit later, one of EC's friends asked if he would help him by getting his failing furniture store burned to the ground. EC was most accommodating. They called the furniture store fire---- arson."

"You can't make that stuff up," Mary exclaimed. "I guess if you have a propensity for crime, you just do whatever damn well you want to do in order to make money. Some of these locals had a hard time living the straight and narrow."

"You got that right," agreed Jones.

They looked across the road and saw a small brick ranch that EC built after he and Katy were married. It was the house the Feds raided on Easter Sunday morning in 1963, when they arrested EC the second time for counterfeiting money. The same house where Jones confronted EC on his eightieth birthday party. It was where Jones and EC had a major confrontation over Jones's mother.

"Is this where they had EC's homecoming celebration, when he was paroled from prison in 1967?" Mary asked.

"Yep, right over there in that open field where his drive-in movie was once located. That's where hundreds of people gathered to welcome EC home," Jones answered. "People who were actually there told me it was like the State Fair. A country band played. The locals dined on a catered pig-picking, along with all kinds of other country dishes.

"I never really understood why EC received so many free gifts that day," remarked Mary. "I mean, why did he get a new car and a new double-wide mobile home? All free? Was it a payoff, or was it payback or what? If so, who gave the gifts?"

"You're on the right track, my dear," Jones replied. "It's a fact that EC took the fall for many people, who were not only involved but also prospered from the counterfeit money operation. EC never ratted on a single one of them. I'd have to say the gifts were payback to EC for never squealing on anyone."

"Your last question brings up a real touchy subject for many folks. There has always been lots of speculation about who was and who was not involved in the counterfeiting deal. From what I've been told by very reliable sources, including Pete Hamilton, EC's cellmate, here's what I know for certain.

"Ralph Thompson, the heavy equipment dealer in Groveland, was definitely very active in the deal. So we're some of his business associates. Likewise, for Michael Banks, the first president of the Eastern National Bank, as well as his successor, Horace Felton. Several other bank employees like Barry Thomas and Clem Houston knew about the deal. Reginald Parker, a wealthy oil man/investor from Winston-Salem, knew about EC's bogus money deal, but he was not involved in any of the criminal activity of the operation. Hell, the Bank had to be folded into another regional bank to keep it from collapsing."

"Many of EC's male employees, like Nelson and Enoch Woodward, and others who worked at the appliance store and movie theaters, were right in the middle of most of his criminal activities. They, too, suffered bad consequences. There were others indicted along with EC, like Ed Spruce, the counterfeit paper man from Kinston, Earl Tardy from Virginia, and Fat Jake."

"Damn, Jones, you know just enough to be dangerous," quipped Mary. "Even today, it's still one very amazing tale. You should take a few million from your American Bank Corporation stock short sale and hire an executive producer to make a movie, as a HBO or Netflix series. Title it *Money to Burn*."

"Maybe I will. If I didn't know actual facts about my grandfather and his connections to the operation, it would be hard for me to believe any of this actually happened," offered Jones. "It's truly incredible."

Mary now had pieces of the puzzle necessary for her to fully understand the people and the places associated with Mr. Jones's early life.

Jones said, "Now you've seen and heard enough. Ready to head on to DC.?" "Sounds like a plan, my man," Mary answered. "Let's rock and roll."

Jones drove back to New Ferry and turned back on Highway 17 North headed towards New Bern. As they drove over the Trent River, Mary stared out the window at the river and thoughtfully said, "Jones, I've always found you to be somewhat of a mysterious man, one who reveals very little about himself. However, with what you shared with me in Melbourne at your Mom's grave, plus all you've told me about the Bank in New Ferry and about EC, I now feel we're much closer."

"So, we've finally bonded," replied Jones.

"Don't make a joke out of what I said, Jones. I'm dead serious about feeling much closer now," Mary quickly responded.

Bill Brown

Chapter Fourteen

The Drop

The next day well before 11 o'clock, Jones and Mary pulled into the very back of the McDonald's parking lot in Tysons Corner, Virginia. No doubt they were on time. They had decided to get there early and stake out the place, so they could see Jones's informant friend once he appeared. That way they could get the layout of the fast food joint and determine if everything met their smell test, as far as being safe was concerned.

Exactly twenty-five minutes after they parked their car, Jones saw his suspected ally from Treasury. He looked like the man who had tipped him off about the Guardian Society's meeting at the Greenbrier the year before. Jones realized he also appeared to be the same man he met at the White House, when the President ordered the Guardian Society to Cease and Desist.

When the man sat down at an outside table, he had a McCoffee in one hand and a red and white pack of Winstons in the other. When he immediately lit a cigarette from his Winston pack, Jones was sure he was the Treasury informant he had nicknamed CLEPTO.

Jones looked at Mary, gave her the high sign, kissed her on her cheek and said, "Good luck."

Mary slowly got out of the Tahoe and walked toward the table where CLEPTO was sitting. She was wearing jeans and a UNC sky-blue sweatshirt. Her red ponytail-wig was pulled through the opening of her baseball cap.

She made eye contact and CLEPTO immediately jumped up, extended his hand, and said, "Good morning."

Mary shook his hand and replied, "Good morning. Beautiful, don't you think?"

"Couldn't be nicer. Been here long? Hope I didn't keep you

waiting."

"Oh no. Everything's cool," Mary answered nervously.

Jones's Treasury mole kept the banter going by asking, "Your sweatshirt tells me you're a Carolina fan. Hope you bought season tickets for the UNC basketball games this year. Supposed to be a great one. Might make it to the Final Four again. They never made the Finals the years I was there. When were you there?"

Playing along, Mary responded, "It's about time. They haven't won a national championship since they defeated Michigan State in Detroit in 2009. Tar Heel fans are getting anxious. I'm a Dartmouth grad."

Suddenly, the informant jumped up, drank the last swallow of his coffee, put out his cigarette, placed the crumpled cigarette pack in the empty cup on the table and said, "Nice chatting with you. Gotta go. I've got a 12:30 tee time at Westwood Country Club. Go Heels!" And off he went.

Mary just sat there for a few minutes. After glancing around to see if anyone was watching her, she grabbed the coffee cup, removed the cigarette pack, stuck it her pocket, got up and headed toward the car. She dropped the empty cup in the trash barrel as she passed by.

Climbing into the Tahoe, she demanded, "Let's get the hell out of here, James Bond."

Jones started driving the SUV out of the parking lot and questioned Mary at the same time, "Did you get the thumb drive?"

"Yes. I mean, here's the cigarette pack." She took it from her pocket and handed it to Jones. Jones looked in the cigarette pack and found it. "Here it is," Jones exclaimed. He was ecstatic. As Jones headed the SUV toward Interstate 95, he mumbled something about Best Buy. "What'd you say? You're mumbling."

"Need to stop at a Best Buy. We can get the new burner phones there and we need to buy our own computer, so we can read this thumb drive. Probably should get extra thumb drives so we can copy this jewel. Need to have several backups."

"I can't wait to see what's on that thing," Mary whispered. "It's gotta be incredibly damaging information to a lot of people and companies. Probably to a lot of banks, too."

"We'd better hope so. It may be our only hope. We can most likely find what we need in Annapolis. Let's get going before the traffic gets too heavy."

They arrived in Annapolis mid-afternoon. Jones suggested they stay at the Annapolis Yacht Club on the sound. Mary disagreed, saying, "It's too high profile. As much time as you've spent there over the years, the chances are fairly good you'd run into someone who knows you. Let's just get a low-rent motel. Don't need to take any more chances than we already have. Remember the photos!"

"You're right, of course. Just wanted to stay there because it's so nice and convenient. Motel 6, here we come, again," groaned Jones.

They found a Motel 6, checked into their room, changed disguises, and then went right back out to go shopping. Mary had made a list of things they needed.

After locating the Chesapeake Bay Shopping Center, they found the Best Buy. They both went inside and straight to the computer section. Jones picked out a Mac laptop model.

Then he turned to the store clerk and asked, "Do you have thumb drives like this one?" He pulled the thumb drive out of his pocket and showed it to the clerk.

"Let me see, I believe we do, but they're in another section. I'll be right back. Wait here, please."

"No problem," uttered Jones. "What else is on the list, Mary?"

"Burner phones. We need at least two or three. I'll go and see if I can find them."

"Okay. I'll meet you at the front checkout in a few minutes."

The clerk came back with a box of thumb drives. "How many do you need?"

"I'll take the whole box, please. They are the same type, right?"

"Yes, Sir," the clerk responded. "I've got your computer here and these 64MB thumb drives. Follow me to the check out."

Mary was waiting up front. The clerk checked them out. Jones paid in cash he'd taken from the briefcase that he'd once again hidden in the ceiling tile of the motel room. Out the door they went. They had everything they needed to proceed to the next step.

Back at the motel, Jones unpacked the computer, set it up, and plugged it in. It would be charged by the time they came back from dinner.

They decided on a favorite casual spot for dinner. They opted for a Waffle Shoppe. Over eggs and waffles, Jones told Mary about his foray into the restaurant business. He explained how, early in his career, he became an equity partner and financier for the Flintstones Famous Food stores located on interstate highways in the southeast. They were partners with Texaco when the company wanted to determine if adding food service to their interstate gas operations would increase gasoline sales.

Jones told Mary, "Our group purchased thirteen mobile restaurants at a bankruptcy sale in Atlanta for a modest sum of money. The food units were strategically placed on Texaco properties on Interstates 75, 85, 20, and 40. After acquiring a licensing agreement from Hanna Barbera and Screen Gems, my partners and I staffed and opened all of the units."

"Over the next six months," Jones added, "with giant billboards placed on interstate highways, food sales in these stores really began to grow to such an extent that gas sales at these sites were experiencing fifty percent increases over the previous year. Texaco was so euphoric, they soon offered to build us fast food restaurants at any of their three hundred gasoline sites in the southeast."

"Texaco," according to Jones, "was so certain that they'd uncovered a financial 'genie,' they got involved in financing our expansion. New, built from scratch units were located off I-75 in Auburn, Alabama, off I-20 at Monteagle, Tennessee, and off I-40 at Greensboro, North Carolina. Business was so good that we flew to New York every other Thursday to meet with Honest Ed Justin at Screen

Gems, located at 711 Fifth Avenue, for updates. Everyone was seeing lots of dollar signs. Then one day out of the blue, Mr. Andrews, the executive Vice-President for Texaco Development in the Atlanta region, summoned my partners and me to Atlanta for a meeting. We met Mr. Andrews at a Holiday Inn restaurant near the airport. We walked in proudly, sat down, exchanged pleasantries, then he dropped the bomb!"

"He pulled an executive order from his coat pocket that he had just received from Texaco headquarters in New York. In part, it read, 'Cease all current development immediately. No exceptions. The energy crisis, caused by a shortage of fuel, will cripple all vehicular traffic, particularly on Interstate highways'."

"The jig was up."

Mary was really fascinated and intrigued by what Jones had just told her about his business venture destroyed by the "energy crisis."

"Jones," Mary stated. "you must have been so disappointed when the deal went down the tubes through no fault of your group. How did you get over that?"

"Thankfully," Jones answered. "I was able to write off most of my losses, but I felt awful for my partners who had put their hearts into the deal. With Texaco's commitment, we had all been on track to making a hell of a lot of money. It was a terrific shock. We were so surprised. We were not prepared for that kind of news."

By the time they got back to their motel, the computer battery had charged and the little green light was softly glowing. Jones sat down at the desk and logged in. His password was MONEY. He said, "Okay, show me what you got, big boy." He took out the thumb drive and inserted it into the USB port on the side of the computer. In just a few seconds, the file opened and what appeared on the screen shocked the hell out of Jones and Mary. In large red letters, the words read:

TOP SECRET CLASSIFIED & CONFIDENTIAL

Jones clicked on the file and the screen filled up with an Excel spread sheet. The chart listed individual names, addresses, and dollar amounts. It also showed company names, addresses, and dollar amounts. Jones immediately recognized many entities on the list. Mary saw several names she recognized and was shocked to see them implicated in what appeared to be the distribution data for a major heist. There were foreign addresses listed: London, Brussels, Madrid, Dublin, Tokyo, and even Luxembourg. It was stunning information. Jones scrolled down to the bottom of the file where there were total amounts. The US dollars column total was $17 TRIL-LION! The persons and companies listed on the spread sheet were obviously the recipients of the stolen US Treasury funds.

"Oh my God," screamed Mary. "Those bastards have robbed our country completely blind. Can you believe this, Jones? All these people should be put in prison for life."

"Prison. Hell, they should be shot for treason," Jones added. "Damnation, look at how much the Federal agency heads received. This is overwhelming." Both Mary and Jones continued reading the file. Jones was not surprised to see his Bank on the list nor the major insurance company that had insured all those worthless sub-prime mortgages.

Then Jones clicked on another file, and the screen showed a file titled:

TOP SECRET
THE GUARDIAN SOCIETY

The Guardian Society file showed a data sheet with the names, home addresses, phone numbers, and business addresses of one hundred members of the Guardian Society. They were the same members who tried to take over the country back in 2008. Their leader, from Seattle, Washington, got rich in the beverage business. He was an extremely progressive individual with beliefs including total amnesty, open borders, and full benefits for all illegal immigrants. Incredibly, many of the Guardian Society members' names were also on the previous spread sheet file, including Hollywood celebrities.

There was a footnote on at the bottom of this file written by Jones's informant CLEPTO at Treasury.

*** Our sources strongly suggest that The Guardian Society is reorganizing. You can see that they have named and branded their group. They're making a renewed effort to take advantage of what they perceive as an upcoming opportunity due to the continued financial disasters crippling the country. They will be meeting soon to lay out and ratify their plan of action. You have been forewarned.

Following the data was a three-paragraph narrative CLEPTO had added to the thumb driver.

He explained how the heads of both foreign and and global agencies like the Governor of the Bank of England, the Chancellor of the Exchequer, the Financial Services Authority, and the Financial Stability Board had unbelievable sway over decisions made in the US. The narrative went on to explain how the heads of the above-mentioned British agencies had monitored all meetings and calls concerning the potential prosecution of the British bank HSBC and its employees. They literally sent representatives to the meetings and/or had them listen in to all relative phone calls.

Furthermore, named British bank officials had confessed to a series of felonies in the subprime mortgage debacle. Additionally, and more importantly, they had also admitted their participation in a major international drug money laundering scheme. Even in light of all of their confessions, the British officials demanded that HSBC, and its employees go free.

Their justification was that "the matter" was under global jurisdiction; supposedly, the One World Government, therefore, no American or British laws were applicable. That false assumption based on the "International Immunity" status of the individuals involved determined the outcome. The mole suggested that was why none of the "too big to fail banks" were ever prosecuted. He also explained that none of the financial institutions' officers or employees would ever be indicted, and that no one would ever go to prison due to "their global immunity" status.

CLEPTO also added that Bill Baker, Ted Gomer, and Attorney General Edward Horne had caved to foreign pressure and dropped their plans to prosecute the British bank conglomerate (HSBC) and its principals. The fact is the DOJ and the already-mentioned Federal agency heads caved to the global demands of the heads of those British based "global" institutions.

*** One other footnote the informant added was the fact that most of the world was unaware of and didn't have the slightest idea about any of this hidden persuasion.

The fact was that the current Governor of the Bank of England, for the first time in over three hundred years, was a non-Brit. He was a Canadian, who had gained his financial training with Goldman-Sachs in New York.

"This is major, Mary. It's really big-time stuff. Now we can play hardball. We can use this information to save our lives, maybe, just maybe," Jones remarked.

"You don't sound too confident, my man. We've got to do better than that. Anyway, we've certainly got ammunition to back up our position," Mary replied.

Chapter Fifteen

The Last Leg

Both Mary and Jones were up early, ready to plow northward to their destination on Nantucket. They had agreed the night before to bypass New York City and head through to Boston, an additional five-hour drive. They both knew far too many people in the City to take any unnecessary chances of being spotted.

Mary suggested, "We probably need to wear different disguises each time we venture out in public, because the media is now putting out sketches of what we may look like disguised. We can't be too cautious."

"Good thinking, Mary," Jones replied.

"You remember what Thomas Wolfe said about his home town, Asheville, North Carolina?" Jones asked. "It was something like you can never go home again. I certainly hope he was wrong, because I really love New York City."

"I consider it my home," added Mary. "Not being able to go back would be devastating for me. We both have so many friends and business associates here. The energy in New York is contagious."

"We'll see," Jones added. "If we survive, we may want to live a more peaceful existence somewhere else. Let's try and stay positive. Tell me what exit to take in New York to head on up to Boston."

"Will do, Sir. Actually, I believe Interstate 95 takes us right into Boston. Probably the quickest way. I'll check that out before we get that far up the road."

"Good girl, navigator. You're doing a fine job."

After stopping for gas, Mary had Jones on course headed to Boston. They decided to stay at one more nondescript motel so as not to be seen by too many folks. The newspaper photos were beginning to make them much more nervous.

They talked about the people and companies on the thumb drive spread sheet. Overwhelmed by the enormity and the complexity of the governmental financial crimes, they wondered how so many people could be complicit and if they would ever have to pay a price for their criminal behavior.

Jones asked one question over and over again, "Can you believe that when the Secretary of the US Treasury and the Chairman of the Federal Reserve were asked on national TV, 'Where did all of the money go?' they blatantly refused to answer by saying, 'We'll never disclose who got how much money or where it all went.' Stunning!"

"I'm telling you, that's incomprehensible, totally unbelievable. Right here in the United States. All of the people on that list just pulled off the largest heist in American history. They stole $17 trillion dollars of taxpayers' money from our own Treasury, and no one is going to do anything about it. It's truly amazing -- the power of so much money."

"I'm totally shocked at some of the names on the list, both inside and outside of government," Mary added, "A couple of my clients are included. It's crazy."

"No, I can't believe it. But you won't believe what I figured out on the computer while you were napping the other day. Get this. Listen carefully. If you stack $17 trillion one-dollar bills in a pile, it would reach to the moon and back about five times. That's a distance of about a million miles. That also means the bills could circle the earth at the equator about forty-five times. Babe, that's a hell of a lot of dough in anybody's mixing bowl."

Mary's reaction was priceless, "Jones, you are a genius. With your brain power, we'll never lose our fight to survive."

There were many unanswered questions. Jones and Mary had lots of work to do.

They arrived in Boston about 3:30 that afternoon. It was raining like cats and dogs. The weather was totally miserable. In a matter of minutes, they both spotted a Motel 6, and Jones drove in. They checked into a first-floor room and put their bags away, and hid the brief case again. Then they went to the C-Store and bought beer and cigarettes, along with a couple more baseball caps and sunshades.

Jones popped the tops on a couple of beers, saying, "Here's a toast to our trip so far."

"Here. Here." Mary answered. They clicked their beer bottles together.

Jones, thinking out loud said, "Sure would be nice to have dinner at the Legal Seafood down on the waterfront tonight. What do you think? It'd bring back some great memories."

"I guess we could dress a little funky, put on new disguises and get away with going there. I can put on my wig and wear a cap. You can wear tinted sunglasses and your baseball cap. Most of those items are in the bag Richard brought to you. Anyway, that's what a lot of tourists look like who go there. Let's try it. We should fit right in."

"Are you sure?" Jones asked.

"Why not?" Mary retorted. "'You only go 'round once,' as they say. Let's do it."

About six-thirty, after they'd finished off the six pack of beer, they were on their way to Legal Seafood at Long Wharf. Time for more catch of the sea.

When they arrived, they saw that lots of other folks had decided to dine there that evening. Jones went to the check-in stand, found the maître d' and told him, "We need a table for two by the window, please. The name is Brown."

Looking back in total disgust, the maître d' started to speak when Jones stuffed a folded Benjamin in his shirt pocket. Recovering, the maître d' quickly said, "No problem, Mr. Brown. Give me a couple of minutes to get your table ready."

"Excellent."

Mary and Jones were seated ahead of many others waiting their turn in line. A few curse words were spoken as they followed the maître d' towards a table by the window.

Jones ordered a bottle of Chateau Montelena Chardonnay 2012

Bill Brown

to go with dinner. After a glass of wine, they ordered. Mary chose the Special of the Day, fresh flounder stuffed with crabmeat. Jones went all out for a platter of soft shell crabs. Neither was the least bit disappointed.

Jones spoke up, "Mary, remember the first night we came here? We had such a great time. I believe we even ran into mutual friends. It was a special evening."

"Certainly, I recall every moment from that night. It was the beginning of my infatuation with you. Then when we ran into the Cobbs, who were friends of both of ours, well, that was just too much."

Jones countered, "Then the second or third time we came here, I brought along that big-time Boston banker, hoping you would help me persuade him to sell American Bank Corporation his bank. He did, but it was only because of your contribution to the sales pitch that evening. Did I ever thank you properly?"

"Sure, you did. That's how I got this fabulous gold necklace from Barney's that I'm wearing. That's thanks enough," Mary purred.

"How about some of their famous lemon meringue pie? Been thinking about it all evening."

"I'll take a few bites of yours, if that's okay."

"Yeah, let's do it."

They finished their pie, Jones paid the tab, and they headed out the door.

All of a sudden without a word, Jones bolted towards the men's room, leaving Mary alone at the door. When Mary looked around, Jones was gone. Startled, she decided to head to the car. She immediately met a nice-looking, well dressed couple headed into Legal Seafood, but nothing registered with her at the time. The guy was tall, slim, with a touch of gray hair. The lady was blonde.

Several minutes passed before Jones joined Mary in the car. He jumped in, started the car, and began to drive.

"Damn, that was a close call. Two minutes later and I would

have been recognized. Too close for comfort."

"Please tell me what the hell you're talking about. Why'd you run off to the men's room? Are you sick?"

"No way. My food was great. Didn't you see them? We almost ran smack dab into them as they were entering the restaurant?"

"Yes, I saw a handsome couple. Who were they?"

"That was former Governor Matt Robbie of Massachusetts with his wife, Barbara. I think he's going to run again for President."

"So why did you run and hide? What are they to you?"

"When he was Governor, Matt Robbie saw to it that all of Massachusetts' state banking business was done exclusively with my Bank. He and I interacted on a regular basis. He would have recognized me in a minute, even with my sunglasses and baseball cap. I spotted him through the glass door. I knew I had to get out of his sight."

"Well, thankfully, I don't think they saw or recognized you. So, we should still be in the clear. Drive on, Mr. Jones."

Bill Brown

Chapter Sixteen

The Refuge

On a gorgeous late September afternoon, they were heading south and they were getting close to their final destination. In about thirty minutes they'd be picking up a ticket in Hyannis for the MV Eagle ferry. It would be a two hour-plus trip to Nantucket and on to 'Sconset.

"Thank God, we're almost there," Mary declared. "So far, so good. Hopefully, no one has spotted us yet. No thanks to the media. We're the modern-day Bonnie and Clyde."

"Let's not get too cocky. Don't want to end up like them, shot by the FBI. It's imperative we keep our guard up and stay extremely careful. We need to make good use of our disguises. If we play our cards right, we should have a good two months in 'Sconset to put a plan of action together without any disruption. This time of year, we should be the rare couple from 'off.'"

They rolled onto the ferry but decided to remain in their car. There they would be less visible. Mary decided to take a nap. Jones read the Boston Globe he had picked up that morning. Much to his chagrin, there was a follow up article on his plane crash. Authorities were still searching for his body. Thankfully, there were no photos in this Globe Edition.

Once the MV Eagle ferry passed the Brant Point lighthouse and docked in Nantucket Harbor, cars were started and began departing the ferry into the town of Nantucket. Jones drove down the ramp and headed in the direction Mary suggested.

"May as well pick up provisions while we're in town. We can stop at Nantucket's Wine and Spirits on the way out of town, near the Circle. Okay?"

"Good idea, Mary." replied Jones. I'll wait in the car while you go in and buy the groceries. No need to have people see us together any more than possible. Here's some cash," as he pulled a few hundred-dollar bills from his brief case.

"No problem. I'll just buy essentials to last us a few days. Be back in a few minutes." Mary soon returned with bags of necessities like coffee, cereal, bread, bacon and eggs, along with enough meat, fruit, and vegetables to last at least a week or more. She stashed all the groceries in the back seat of the SUV.

"Let's roll," proclaimed Mary as she jumped into the front seat.

On the way out of town, Jones pulled into the Island Shopping Center where the libations store was located. He jumped out of the SUV and hurried inside. In no time he returned with two bags of wine, along with bottles of Jack Daniels and Grey Goose Vodka.

"Need a drink?" he kidded.

"It must be five o'clock somewhere," Mary quipped.

Then it was full throttle as he turned right at the Circle and headed down Milestone Road to 'Sconset.

Once they were inside her sister's in-law's cottage on Baxter Road, they flopped down in the large family room overlooking the ocean. What a view. What a relief. There were shark images from the movie and book cover photos everywhere. It was obvious who owned this place.

Now Jones and Mary could celebrate no more long car drives any time soon, no more dinky motel rooms and fast food meals. They could hope for normalcy.

Jones declared, "I think we should keep the car in the garage with the door closed. Our temporary license plates might raise suspicions."

"Good thinking, Sherlock. Always one step ahead of the man with the net. I'm going to make up the bed and start prepping, so I can cook us a delicious and wholesome meal. Your job for the evening will be bartender." Jones left the room to move the SUV into the garage. He came back in, turned on the TV, and lay down on the sofa. He was asleep before the first commercial came on.

The spacious vintage cottage was crisp and clean. Large floor-to-ceiling windows served as the exterior wall facing the Atlantic Ocean. You could see where the beach erosion had created cliffs into the sand dunes. Hardwoods were the floors of choice in this home. Most of the upholstered furniture was an off-while color that blended well with the pecky cypress walls. The light fixtures in every room were simple, but exquisite. The kitchen was warm and inviting, with spacious seating around an open hearth. It had been perfectly designed for both cooking and company, not to mention for comfort and relaxation.

"Where's my drink?" Mary yelled from the kitchen. "I'm in here sweating over a hot stove, cooking us a wonderful meal, and I need a drink. Wake up, bartender. It's time for you to go to work."

Jones rolled off the sofa and stumbled over to the wet bar. "What time is it? How long did I sleep?"

"This isn't a game show. Stop the inquisition, please. About three hours."

"Once I get the casserole in the oven, we'll have about an hour before we eat. So bartender, I'd like a martini. Light on the vermouth, with olives, please."

"You're a slave driver, woman. Hell, I just woke up."

Jones handed Mary her drink as she entered the large room. "It feels so good to be in a real home, with more than one room, off the highway, and out of that car. What a relief. I feel better already." He was drinking a very strong Jack Daniels and water.

"Jones, I've been thinking about what type of story we need to come up with to tell anyone we come in contact with while we're here. It has to be something plausible, and one that explains who we are and why we're here. Something that is plausible, and a story that fits our image as a couple."

"Good thinking, barrister. I love it when your brain goes into overdrive. Let's see, maybe some connection to boating or fishing or both. It's something we both know a little bit about, and we shouldn't have any problem talking to anyone about either."

"Maybe we could come up with a tale about you being a boat captain and that we're in the charter boat business. Depending on whom we're talking to---we could say we offer sailboat cruises, or we offer charter fishing excursions. We can easily fake either one."

"That's a good line," Jones remarked. "If they ask where we keep our boat, we can say it's being repaired at the Hinckley service center in Oxford, Maryland, and that's why we're here. It's like we're sorta on vacation waiting until our Hinckley's ready, so we can charter it again. We must remember if we say we do charter fishing then we talk about a power boat, and if we say sailboat cruises then we talk about a sloop."

Mary chimed in saying, "We can say that the repairs most likely won't be completed until after the spring. That way we're covered time-wise, because we'll be out of here by then."

"Damn good story. We can add to it as needed. Want another drink?" "Sure, one more sounds good. Then it'll be time to eat."

Jones and Mary spent the next several days hanging out pretty close to the cottage. They trekked on the Bluff Walk, watched a lot of TV, and got lots of rest. They didn't drive the SUV for over a week. Eventually, cabin fever began to set in. So they talked about where they could go on the island without fear of being spotted. They both knew several people from New York who spent the holidays in Nantucket. They opted to stay away from obvious tourist attractions, like downtown Nantucket. Rather, they decided to frequent places where the locals hung out, both in 'Sconset and Nantucket.

On the first excursion out of the cottage that required their car, they went to Sea Grille at the Circle. It was a local hangout, for sure. It had a great bar, small and private, located in the rear of the restaurant, sort of a secluded area. However, Mary and Jones thought the best part was the food, which was always fresh and delicious.

A couple of days later they stumbled into the Hen House, a quaint little breakfast spot across the street from the Circle. It felt a lot like the Waffle Shoppes Jones frequented back in North Carolina. It was only open from six in the morning til two in the afternoon.

The pancakes, country ham, and rashers of bacon were the dishes that Jones went crazy about. He never thought for one moment he could find good Irish country cooking in Nantucket. They began to eat breakfast there two or three times a week.

Finally, one morning Jones asked the waitress, "Where do you buy this country ham? It tastes so much like country ham I used to eat in North Carolina." The waitress responded, "Let me ask the manager. I'll be right back."

"Jones, you're always asking questions about everything," Mary added. "You really do take the cake, but that's why I like you so much."

The waitress came back to the table and explained, "We buy the country ham from a company in Goldsboro, North Carolina. It's called the Wayco Ham Company. They ship it to us in cases by UPS. Our customers like it so much, we just keep ordering more."

"See there, Mary, I was right again," bragged Jones. "It's damn good country ham."

After a month passed, Mary suggested they broaden their horizons by exploring some of the other settlements around the island. Jones agreed that it'd be a great way to spend their days outside of the cottage and satisfy their curiosity at the same time. Mary volunteered to organize their explorations.

They spent a couple of days checking out the three light houses on the island. They went all the way to the far north end of the island to visit Great Point Lighthouse. It was built in 1784 but burned in 1816. It had been modernized with solar panels to keep the batteries charged. They spent another day checking out the Santaky Head Lighthouse in 'Sconset. It was built in 1850 and automated in 1965 and is still operational. It had recently been moved due to severe erosion.

Another day they had a long leisurely lunch at the 'Sconset Cafe near the Post Office. One day they visited the Nantucket Shipwreck and Lifesaving Museum. Another day they were taking photos of the Jethro Coffin House, the only surviving structure from the seventeenth century English settlement.

Because of Nantucket's origin as a whaling community and since Mary had read the book *The Essex*, they wanted to visit the Whaling Museum. However, they were afraid they might be recognized in such a close setting with so many visitors, even in the fall. One day, they slipped over to the Brant Point Lighthouse, built in 1784 and automated in the mid-sixties. It has the distinction of being destroyed eight times since its inception.

They drove out to The Wauwinet, a luxury hotel. It was a remote oceanside place with a couple of fabulous restaurants. They ate dinner by the fireplace in Topper's on more than one occasion. They loved the Retsyo Oysters on the half-shell, cultivated only three hundred yards away. Their wine selection had been awarded the Wine Spectator Grand Award numerous times. Jones and Mary took full advantage of this fact.

On most of their excursions, Jones had to take it a little slower than usual because his leg had not yet fully healed, and it required extra rest between longs periods of being on his feet. Mary and Jones never seemed to run out of things to say, talk about, or discuss in detail. One subject that always arose, especially around dinner time, was when and how were they going to get organized and come up with a counterattack, a way for them to survive. They kept avoiding the subject they both knew was imperative to their longevity. If the subject arose, Jones often ended it by saying, "Wait until we get somewhere safe and private for a couple of months, then we'll talk about it." *How could it be any more safe and private than Nantucket,* Mary thought.

Chapter Seventeen
The Nightmare

In late November, only days after enjoying a lovely and delicious Thanksgiving dinner with the Mayor of 'Sconset, at his home in Codfish Park, Mary and Jones decided to take a chance and head into town to dine with other new friends. They had reservations for drinks and dinner at The Pearl, an upscale, white tablecloth restaurant located in a two-story house on Federal Street in downtown Nantucket. It featured creative cocktails along with Asian- inspired seafood, including wok-fried lobster. Their dinner companions, the Brocks, were from Lime, Vermont. They were tenured professors at Dartmouth College, Mary's alma mater in Hanover, New Hampshire.

Jones and Mary had met the Brocks since arriving on the island in September. Mary, a '93 Dartmouth College graduate, immediately bonded with the academicians. After they returned to the cottage around midnight, Jones and Mary talked about how enjoyable it was to behave again like normal folks do, by going out to dinner with friends. After talking a bit about their evening and their exquisite meal, they went to bed.

About two hours later, Mary whispered, "Wake up, Jones. There's a car in the driveway. It's two- thirty in the morning. Who the hell could it be? Why are they here? We need to get the hell out of here. I've been thinking that for the past week."

Jones responded quietly, "Calm down. We haven't done anything wrong. Certainly nothing since we've been here. I'll go turn on the outside lights and see what happens. Stay here. I'll be right back."

"Are you crazy as hell? You'll let them know we're in here. No way, I have a better idea. Let's sneak out the ocean side door and make our way down to the beach. Then we'll call the Police. They should come and give those bastards something else to think about. Like being arrested. Agreed?"

"Agreed."

Jones and Mary pulled on their jeans and loafers, and then slipped out the back door, locking it behind them. Jones had a tough time moving because he was still incredibly sore from the crash. Navigating the many steps to the beach was brutal for him. About a hundred yards from the cottage, they stopped. Jones took out a burner phone and dialed 911. It was pitch black dark. The roar of the ocean was the only sound they could hear. The sky was black velvet dotted with thousands of tiny stars. When an officer answered, Jones handed the phone to Mary who blurted out, "There's a suspicious car on Baxter Road, driving in and out of different driveways with the lights turned off. Seems like they're trying to stake out an empty cottage, so they can break in."

The 911 operator asked, "What's your 10-20? Your location?

Mary responded, "We're on the beach about half way down Baxter Road. The car is stopped in our driveway at this very moment. Please come get them before something really bad happens."

"I've already dispatched a patrol car to the area. Stay in touch. If you notice any changes, call back. By the way, what's your name?"

Mary mumbled something like, "Janie Brown, that's my name." Then she handed the burner phone back to Jones.

While Mary was on the phone, Jones was thinking, we really need to get off this island now and find a safer place. He already had one in mind.

Mary and Jones made their way back up a set of stairs into a neighbor's yard, and then crossed over Baxter Road to the second row. From this vantage point they could still observe the car parked in their driveway.

When they looked back at the parked car, they saw two people, both wearing hoodies, get out and move toward the cottage. It looked like one of them was holding a pistol. One pulled on the roadside door, trying to open it. Then they ran around to the oceanside door and tried to open it. They even tried a couple of windows, all to no avail. As they scurried back to their car, the person with the pistol fired three shots in the air. He backed out of the driveway and began to move slowly up Baxter Road. Then the car stopped again in front of another cottage.

Mary, freaking out, whispered, "Jones, did you hear those gun shots? "Yes, I heard them," Jones whispered.

"What the hell are they doing? Do you think they're burglars or are they after us?"

Jones whispered back, "Don't know for sure, but if the Police aren't here soon, I'll call them again. This place is becoming a bit too risky for us to stay here much longer. Gun shots make me very nervous."

In fifteen minutes, which seemed like an eternity, Mary and Jones saw headlights coming up Baxter Road toward their position. They sure as hell hoped it was the cops. In a split second, they got their answer as the blue lights atop the patrol car began flashing in the night.

Immediately, the suspicious car they had been watching began to slowly move away, headed toward Ocean Avenue, still with no lights on. In a blink of an eye, the car was out of their sight.

The patrol car moved slowly past them as the cop flashed the external search light all about, through the privacy fences, first on one cottage and then another. Once the light even flashed their way, causing them to hit the ground.

Then, quite strangely, the patrol car lights went out, as well as the flashing blue light. Jones and Mary could no longer see the police car. *What the hell is going on,* Jones thought. Mary was thinking, *the way voices carry around water, we dare not talk for fear someone might hear us.*

Several minutes later, the blue lights on the Police car starting flashing again, as it moved toward Ocean Avenue. It didn't return.

Forty-five minutes later they crept back across Baxter Road and very quietly slipped into the cottage. Jones was finally able to get off his bad leg and lie down. His thigh, still very painful, reminded him of the accident. Both fell asleep on the bed in a matter of minutes.

The next morning around 9:30, Jones got up. He had decided it was time to go. He limped to the kitchen and made coffee, took a cup in to Mary, sat down on the bed and said, "Babe, I love you. I love being here with you. It's very peaceful, but it's become too dangerous. We don't know if what happened last night was a potential robbery, or if it means someone spotted us or got a tip that we're here. Maybe someone recognized us at the Mayor's house on Thanksgiving Day, or maybe someone saw us at The Pearl last night. Either way, it's time for us to go. Now. Today. Let's pack up and get the hell out here. We need to make the noon ferry." He got no resistance from Mary.

There was another reason they needed to leave Nantucket. It was almost December. Mary's extended family always traveled to 'Sconset for the Christmas holidays. They hadn't missed Christmas Stroll on Nantucket in years and for good reason. Every year since 1973, the merchants of Nantucket launch Christmas Stroll the first weekend in December. It is their way of keeping local shoppers from traveling to The Cape for Christmas shopping. In the forty years since the first Stroll, the event had grown exponentially and become a national event enjoyed by many. Huge discounts are offered shoppers, who receive tickets for each purchase. One half of the buyer's ticket stubs are put into a huge basket, and on the last day of the weekend, everyone gathers on Main Street at the Court House in front of the Christmas Tree to welcome the arrival of Santa and see whose tickets, drawn from the basket, win the prizes. One year Mary's brother-in-law actually won the top prize, when the other half of his ticket stub was pulled out of the cage. He was declared the winner, and the prize was fifteen thousand dollars.

So, no doubt it was time for Mary and Jones to leave this enchanted place, which is always so special at Christmas time. They knew they had to miss all local holiday celebrations like the ones they enjoyed a few years back. No mistake about it, they both were ready to get off the island. They needed a safer, more secluded place to hunker down long enough to put a plan together that might save their lives. It was past due.

Bill Brown

Chapter Eighteen

The Exit

While Chairman Kurt Lane and his Bank Board were trying to figure out what the hell was going on with their Bank, as well as what the hell was going on in the financial sector, Jones and Mary were making their own decisions. Both were very uneasy and agreed it was time to relocate.

On November twenty-eighth, Mary helped Jones pack the SUV. She scurried around trying to make sure they were leaving the cottage exactly like they found it. She even put their trash in the car. *No one will ever know we were here,* thought Mary.

Jones secured the computer in the back seat and placed the box of thumb drives in the glove compartment and locked it.

"We've got to make that noon ferry. Let's go," Jones urged Mary.

They were the very last vehicle to drive onto the ferry. They barely made it. The MV Eagle ferry left Straight Wharf dock at precisely twelve noon. Again, although disguised, they decided to stay in the car to avoid being seen by anyone who might connect them to their photos all over the media.

Two hours later, Jones drove off the ferry in Hyannis. He circled through a local burger store and ordered two large Cokes and two cheeseburgers with fries. They needed energy as they started on another eight-hour drive.

On the ferry ride they had discussed where they would go and how they could get there without being seen. The route they chose was around Boston to Albany, New York. From there they would drive on to Rochester, New York, where they'd spend the night. It was going to be a very long day.

They stopped for only half an hour to eat an early supper in Albany. They got gas and headed out again for Rochester.

When they finally reached Rochester, it was almost ten o'clock that night. Even in the dark, it was one ugly town. They found another Motel 6 that had "left the light on for them" and checked into a second-floor room. They both fell asleep watching the eleven o'clock news.

The next morning, they found an IHOP where they feasted on pancakes, sausage, and lots of coffee. After a great breakfast, it was time to get serious again. Today was the day they had to resume their cloak and dagger behavior. It was not something Mary particularly enjoyed.

Secretly, while on Nantucket, Jones had dreamed up a fairly clever plan to elude anyone who might think that they were still alive or who might be trying to follow them. It was an elaborate scheme of total mis-direction, involving his iPhone.

The night before they departed, Jones had totally erased everything from his cell phone: the numbers, the contacts, the files, everything as far as he knew. It was totally clean, completely blank.

Jones had decided they would return to a place they'd holed up once before. It was a remote, friendly hideaway situated in the foothills of eastern Tennessee. A place where they had made a great friend a few years back.

Jones had told Mary only what he had planned for their first day off the island and that he would reveal his plan to her on a daily basis. She had agreed. Today, he told her they would abandon their SUV by leaving it in the Rochester train depot parking lot. They then would take a train to Knoxville, Tennessee. But first, before leaving Rochester, Jones was heading to the local Old Dominion Freight transportation terminal. He was looking for a long hauler, an eighteen- wheeler, a tractor trailer that was headed south to Miami. It took about an hour before he found the terminal just west of town.

"Here's what we're looking for, the Old Dominion Freight Company. Just what the doctor ordered," Jones declared.

Mary sat up, looked out the window and asked, "Why this one? How do you know which truck to pick? How do you know which way they're headed?"

"I don't know. That's why I'm going to call the terminal and ask a few questions. Just need to know which truck is headed south."

"You've got some nerve. Then what?"

"It's simple. Once I know I have the right truck, I'll make sure I find a safe place for my iPhone. It's going to ride on a south bound truck all the way to Florida. I tossed my iPhone battery after Richard rescued me and brought the burner phones. I wanted to make sure that no one could track my iPhone. Now my cell phone has a new battery, so it should ping every cell tower it passes along the way. If the Feds are tracking my iPhone, they'll think we're headed south, and they'll probably conclude we're going back to Grand Cayman."

"Ingenious, Sherlock. You're one shrewd dude."

Jones made his call and gleaned the information he needed. He found the truck at the back of the loading zone. It was an Old Dominion truck with the dark green logo painted on the side of the trailer. Very carefully, he opened the back door of the eighteen-wheeler, jumped inside, and walked around several freight pallets until he got close to the front. There he placed his phone under the plastic covering the cargo. He thought it would be well concealed there. He jumped from the truck, closed the door, and headed back to the car.

"It's done. Let's go."

"Don't believe anyone from the terminal saw you. At least, I didn't see anybody."

"Great. Now on to the Main Street Train Station. It's right in downtown Rochester. Maybe we can catch the early train to Knox-ville."

"I looked it up on Google. It's an eighteen-hour train ride. We'll have to get a Pullman car. Can't sit up for that long of a trip."

"No problem. We can do that. I'm sure they'll be happy to take our money."

Upon arriving at the train depot, they parked the SUV as far away from the station as possible. Jones ripped off the paper license tag. It was quite a walk to the ticket office with their bags.

Mary reminded him, "Don't forget the thumb drives and computer and the cash stuffed in the briefcase. I have the other briefcase with the disguises and the passports and ID's."

"No way that I'd let that happen! What do they say? 'Don't leave home without them.' That's our life insurance," he said.

They purchased Pullman car tickets for the long ride to Knoxville, Tennessee, and sat waiting for the train.

Jones hugged Mary, who was acting a bit dejected, and said, "Cheer up, honey. Think of this as just another adventure. We'll be safely tucked away at Sugar Hollow in Butler, Tennessee, by this time tomorrow. Then we can rest, relax, eat out and start working on our overall survival plan. It's just the place for us for the next few weeks."

Mary sighed. "But I haven't talked to my parents since the crash nor to my sister. It just doesn't seem right, because I know they're worried and upset. Sooner or later I've got to call them. I really miss them."

"You certainly can call them, and you should, but please try to hold off at least until we get ready to leave Sugar Hollow. That'll give us enough time to formulate our plan. You know the Feds must be monitoring your parents' phone."

"I'll try to be patient. That's all I can promise," Mary replied.

They boarded the train, found their berth, moved in and settled down in the very small quarters. Jones muttered, "Gotta be damn good buddies to share this sardine can," The bar car was open for business, so off he went. It was time for a couple of real stiff drinks.

Mary curled up and went to sleep. When Mary awoke and saw no Jones, she headed to the bar. They chatted until they both realized how hungry they were. They reached the dining car just before it closed. Both ordered a small filet, salad, and, of course, red wine. They commented on how good their dinner was, considering it was train food.

That night they had no problem sleeping. The rails rocked them into a deep slumber.

Bill Brown

Chapter Nineteen

The Board Meeting

The Chairman of the American Bank Corporation, Kurt Lane, called the late November meeting of the bank's Board of Directors to order. The lavish boardroom was located on the top floor of the bank's corporate headquarters in downtown Charlotte, North Carolina. Lane immediately noticed several board members whispering among themselves. He had to rap the gavel a few more times to get their attention. Finally, they sat down.

Grim faces we're staring back at Lane, and rightfully so. Most of them had learned in the last few weeks just how many millions of dollars the bank had lost, and they feared personal liability as board members. They also knew the Bank was facing exposure to some very damaging claims, and it was quite likely that some of those claims were certain to surface soon. The claims would probably come not only from other shareholders, but also from Federal agencies governing the banking industry due to all the recent developments in the financial sector. The Bank had become a "Bad News Bank."

Kurt Lane began his opening remarks, "Ladies and Gentlemen, welcome. Thank you for making this meeting today. I'm sure some of you would rather be somewhere else, and I believe I'd fit in that category myself. I do realize we're all anxious about what's going on with our economy, and I know you have many questions that need answering. Please be patient as we try to sort out the terrible dilemma in which our bank has become embroiled. It's going to take some time to process all your inquiries, but I plan to stay here until all of you get your answers. However, before we get to that place on our agenda, there is another serious matter that has transpired since our last meeting. It needs our immediate attention. All of you need to be cognizant of all of the facts. I'll start at the beginning."

One of the larger shareholders stood up and remarked, "We've all read the papers and have seen the TV news about Mr. Jones's plane crash. There's no need to waste time explaining every detail about his testimony to the Senate Banking Committee. I believe we have more important matters to discuss and settle." Then he sat down. Lane heard "I agree" from several board members around the conference table.

The Chairman immediately detected signs of animosity among the board members. He knew, coming into this meeting, that he was going to have backlash about what had happened to the Bank, but he didn't expect it right off the bat. *Damn, this is going to get ugly,* he thought.

Another board member at the end of the conference table raised his hand and stated, "We warned you about buying that damn Wide Country Mortgage Company, but you insisted that you knew better and that it would make the Bank millions of dollars overnight."

Yet another board member sitting next to the Chairman added his two cents worth, "Then you went wild and crazy and bought the securities company, Murray Lane. How did those two deals work out for you and the Bank, Mr. Chairman? Got an answer for that?"

The Chairman could feel the heat rising in his neck. Fumbling around for an appropriate response to the last remarks, he stood up to speak, "There's no doubt that the Bank has been hit with a string of bad luck that has affected our stock value in a disastrous way. We can't panic. We must join together to devise a plan that will keep the Bank afloat until the market gets on a stronger footing."

Another member sarcastically tuned in with his comment, "I want to know what the hell you are going to do about all the litigation that, according to the Wall Street Journal, is coming our way from all directions. It's coming from the Federal government as well as the private sector.

Sounds overwhelming to me. What's your thinking?"

Kurt sat back down with his shoulders slumped and his hand to his forehead. "Look, I know it's bad, real bad. Hopefully, it won't get any worse. I realize that I need to own up to my part of the bank's dilemma, and I do assume that responsibility. I'm not going any damn where, and I'm not resigning. I'm staying until this Bank is back on its feet."

Holding a stack of papers above his head, another shareholder suggested, "All these are customer complaints. I've been told there are thousands of them. They indicate that we might need to consider another direction for our Bank. What's the old idiom, 'A new broom sweeps clean?'"

A wave of chuckles crossed the room. Kurt Lane continued to shuffle his papers as he listened. Then he made his next move.

"I understand that most of you know about Mr. Jones's plane crash from the media, and like most everyone, you assume that Mr. Jones died in the crash. What I know that you don't know is that last week Bill Baker from the Federal Reserve called an emergency meeting concerning this matter. He insisted that I attend along with Ms. Brand from FDIC, Gomer from the New York Fed, and Peters from Treasury."

"I'll be very frank. What was discussed at that session was urgent concerning not only our country, but also our Federal agencies and of course our Bank. Another item of interest that arose at that meeting was a possible sighting of Mr. Jones. Ms. Brand reported that someone from her New Orleans office thought he had spotted Jones and his friend, Mary Whitmore, having dinner at Antoine's. We all agreed it was just a report with no solid evidence." *I know better,* thought Lane.

The banker continued, "That in itself was not too worrisome, until yesterday afternoon. I received a call from one of our Boston branches. A Bank employee called his manager about another sighting of Mr. Jones. The employee spent the weekend on Nantucket. When he was returning on the ferry yesterday morning, he was sure he saw Mr. Jones and his girlfriend, Mary, in the Hyannis area, leaving the ferry. As I've already said, they were spotted by a person who works for our Bank. Ironic! Getting caught by one of your own." Kurt smiled at the thought.

"How did the guy know it was Jones," asked a board member, "in a car, driving off the ferry? Sounds doubtful to me."

"Hell, to date no one has proven that Jones is still alive," muttered another member.

The Chairman spoke again, "The fellow said they looked like the photos of the couple that he'd seen in the Boston Globe and New York Times, which had been doctored to include how they'd look disguised. Until the report about seeing the two of them in New Orleans, there hadn't been any mention of Jones surviving the accident. Mary hadn't been seen either, and Jones's villa in Grand Cayman is shuttered. I'm sure her family is berserk. Rumors have already surfaced speculating that Mary might have been on the flight. This is the second acknowledgement that someone has reported seeing Mr. Jones, since the crash in the Caymans back in September.

However, I wouldn't put too much credence in the sighting yet. A lot depends on whether or not we get more reports in the next few days."

"So what if he did survive?" the major shareholder asked. "If the Feds get him, his ass is grass for a damn long time and Mary's, too. That's between the Feds and Jones. Let them fight it out. We've got our own fish to fry."

"Not so fast," Kurt Lane remarked. "It's not that simple. We don't know how much Jones actually knows about the diversion of TARP funds from Treasury or the business that includes the Federal agencies, the Banking industry, not to mention our own Bank's business.

"What Bill Baker suggested at the meeting last week was horrifying. He truly believes there is a mole in one of the Federal agencies, probably Treasury, who may have given Jones a load of dangerous classified, top secret and confidential data that could bring down our entire government. Most of you know exactly what I'm talking about. That's why it's so vital to know if Jones is dead or alive!"

"What the hell are the Feds hiding?" asked one uninformed shareholder sitting at the end of the conference table. "For that matter, Mr. Chairman, what is our Bank hiding?"

A morbid pall fell over the boardroom.

The Chairman rapped his gavel on the table three times and stated firmly, "This meeting is adjourned. Thank you all for coming." He collected his files and walked out of the boardroom. Several board members looked at each other in amazement, while others began whispering among themselves. Others just left the room.

Had Kurt Lane just sealed his fate? Members questioned whether he would be strong enough to withstand any repercussions that might slam their Bank in the next several months. There was no way of knowing the answer to that speculation. However, Kurt Lane found out later there was serious conversation that day about having him replaced.

A number of big institutional shareholders were not at all pleased with what Kurt Lane had done with the Bank's funds during the peak of the economic crisis. They, along with other heavy hitters, were of the opinion that Lane thought he knew more than anyone else in the banking industry. They also believed that Lane was on an ego trip to show the world how important he and his Bank really were and that he had become quite offensive to many very important folks.

Things were not going as Kurt Lane thought they should, and he damn well didn't like that one bit. As a matter of fact, the more he thought about the board meeting, the more irritated he became. Too many negatives were affecting not only his Bank, but they were also having negative effects on him personally. As he took a step back and examined all of the variables, he determined immediately that there was one person responsible for all of his recent problems.

Mr. Jones! I'll fix that son of a bitch this time, you watch, thought Kurt.

The following morning Lane was in his spacious office at 6:00

a.m. sharp. Although he had a fabulous panoramic view of the Queen City from his desk, that morning he was focused only on what he knew he had to do. He didn't have to ask anyone who he could or should call. He knew precisely who to call. *No one knows that I had the bomb put on Jones's jet*, thought Lane. *It seems that attempt on Jones life failed. This one will not, he mused.*

Lane's Bank had had a long, tight-knit relationship with the "boys" down in Melbourne, Florida, going all the way back to the early seventies. They had collaborated on a number of situations over the years that proved mutually beneficial. Lane knew, unequivocally, that it was time he talked with Rocky Benito.

As he dialed Rocky's number, he was thinking, *my god, this is like a friggin' Mafia movie, me calling Rocky, the Rooster, Benito, to put a contract on someone.* Kurt remembered meeting Rocky once years ago. He visualized a short little man with dyed jet-black hair, who strutted around like a bantam rooster. His reputation was fierce and the notches on his belt were many and very convincing.

As Lane was identified by caller ID, Rocky answered in his thick English/Italian brogue. "Hello, Mr. Lane. You're up early this morning. I hear you're swimming in shark-infested waters. How bad is it?"

"Hi, Rocky. Thanks for taking my call," Lane replied. "Tell you the truth, it's as friggin' bad as it gets. The proverbial crap has hit the fan, and the only way to resolve the problem is to eliminate the problem."

"Okay, Mr. Lane, just tell me the location of the problem. Then we can go from there. You gotta know by now that we can help solve most any problem you may encounter. Just give me some details."

Lane cleared his throat and said, "I need four two-man 'hit squads' immediately. I want them sent to four different locations. One squad goes to Grand Cayman Island. Another squad goes to New York City, and another to the Boston/Nantucket area. I want the fourth squad to be on standby in Atlanta, Georgia, ready for immediate deployment to anywhere in the world, if called."

"Damn, Mr. Lane, your problem is obviously more serious than I ever expected," mused Rocky. Tell me more details, including your compensation plan."

"Hold on, Rocky, I'm getting to that. Here's the deal. I'm wiring you one million dollars. Give each squad one hundred thousand dollars up front. Whichever squad solves the problem gets another hundred thousand dollars. You keep the balance for your troubles. However, here's the kicker. Solve the problem now, this month, and I'll double the money."

"For Christ's sake, Mr. Lane. You gotta be friggin' desperate for sure. Send me names, photos, personal descriptions, copies of driver's licenses, phone numbers, and known addresses for each of the targets. Then we'll be ready to begin the elimination process. I promise you'll get your money's worth, and soon." "Rocky, I'm gonna hold you to that, I promise," muttered Lane. The phone went dead.

Bill Brown

Chapter Twenty
The Hideaway

Later the next morning, Jones and Mary departed the train in Knoxville, Tennessee. After gathering up all their belongings, Jones hailed a cab and asked the driver, "Can you drive us to Butler, Tennessee?"

"Yeah."

"How much will you charge?"

The driver checked his rate card and answered, "Hell yes, I can take you anywhere that you can afford. It's about a five hour round trip for me, plus my gas. The price would be five hundred dollars including tip, if you got it. You still want to go?"

Jones, smiling through his teeth, said, "Make it four hundred dollars and we've got a deal."

The cabbie laughed out loud and replied, "You're too tough, man. Let me get your bags in the trunk, and we'll head out. Okay?"

Jones stuck out his hand, "It's a deal. Let's shake on it."

The driver shook hands with Jones. They were headed to Sugar Hollow, the cozy corporate retreat in eastern Tennessee.

"Stop at the first Cracker Barrel restaurant you see, so we can get a real good country breakfast," Jones ordered. "We slept through breakfast on the train. We're starving."

Thirty minutes later the cab pulled into a Cracker Barrel. All three went inside and devoured large servings of eggs, bacon, country ham, grits, and biscuits. It was all simply delicious. Jones picked up the tab.

Jones got up from the table and said, "I'll be back in a couple of minutes." He stepped outside and sat down in one of the Kennedy-type rocking chairs at the far end of the porch. He pulled out his burner phone and dialed Sugar Hollow.

On the second ring, a familiar voice said, "Thanks for calling Sugar Hollow. May I help you? This is Marty."

Jones asked, "Is that you, Marty? This is Jones. You remember, Mary and Jones? From a few years ago"

"Oh, yes. Sure. Hello, Jones. Great to hear from you. Heard you were dead. Killed in a plane crash. Must have been just a rumor. How's my dear Mary?"

"We're both fine, thanks. Marty, I need a favor. We're in Knoxville, and we need a quiet private place to hang out for a few weeks. A place where no one will know or expect to find us. Can you rent us that little log cabin up on the hill? I promise we'll be no problem. There is just one condition, though. You must not tell anyone we're here. That means no one at all, including your boss the Doc. Can you do that?"

Marty spoke right up as she was always inclined to do, saying, "Yes, you can rent the little log cabin for as long as you need it. But only on one condition. You must not tell one damn soul you're here. That means no damn body. Can you do that?"

Jones almost fell out laughing. After composing himself, he spoke again, "Marty, there ain't but one like you. We'll be there in about two hours."

"Let me hang up and go get the cabin ready for you and Mary. You know which cabin, so I'll meet you there. Remember, mum's the word. Keep it under your arm."

"Marty, you're too damn good. See you soon."

Jones went back to the table and said, "Ready to go? Let's rock and roll."

The driver stood up and shook his head. He was really amused by Jones's personality and humor. Mary just rolled her eyes wildly.

They all left together and crawled into the cab.

About 3:30 in the afternoon, they arrived in Butler, Tennessee. On the ride over, Jones explained to the driver that their final destination was Sugar Hollow. The driver said he knew of the resort.

Twenty minutes later Jones and Mary were taking their bags

inside the little log cabin on the hill at Sugar Hollow. Jones gave the driver five hundred dollars. The cabbie bowed and scraped and hugged Jones before he left.

Two minutes later, Marty appeared on the scene.

Without speaking a word, Mary and Marty hugged tightly for a couple of minutes. Then Jones gave Marty a big bear hug.

"Y'all damn sure look alive to me. Who the hell put out that awful rumor that the two of you were dead. Disgusting, I'd say."

"Marty, it's so good to see you. So great to see someone who cares," Mary offered. "You're looking damn good yourself."

"I don't need to register, do I? Maybe you'll take cash in advance or whatever you want me to do," Jones said.

"Don't be ridiculous, man. Chill out. You're among friends. There's no paper work necessary. You can pay me in cash whenever you decide to leave. The rent is five hundred dollars a month and does not include any meals. You can rest assured, I'll make sure Dr. Surry gets all of it. You okay with that?"

"Certainly. I know we'll be here four to six weeks or more. You got us for Christmas and New Years. Hope the lodge isn't booked for the holidays. Is Surry planning to be here?" Jones asked.

"It's great you're going to be here. Don't believe you'll be bothered by too many guests. This time of year is not really our busy season. I wouldn't count on Surry being here for either holiday," Marty replied.

There's no problem on the food. We'll eat out most meals except when Mary wants to cook. Where's the closest grocery store and liquor store?" Jones asked.

"Just give me a list of items you want or need, plus some cash, and I'll pick them up for you."

"Marty, you're unbelievable," whispered Mary, as she hugged her again.

Jones handed Marty three hundred dollars, saying, "Take this money, and we'll call you with our order. Tell me when it's gone, and I'll give you more. Thanks, so much."

Mary and Jones went inside and checked out their new home for the next month or so. She put their baggage away, and Jones turned on the TV. Mary was checking the area promo package on the table, looking for a place to eat dinner.

"Looks like it's going to be Shirley's again. As I remember, it was bountiful. Remember what Surry said about saving room for dessert."

Their cabin was actually a real log cabin. It was both rustic, charming, and warm. It was well appointed with appropriate furnishings. Most of all, it was very private. The guests were tickled with their new abode. Jones was fascinated with the wagon wheel light fixture hanging in the den. They planned to enjoy every minute they were there.

Jones asked Mary, "Did you notice the changes Surry's made since we were last here? The Corporate Center has been completed. The road system is much better. Looks like he's added a couple of larger homes."

"Yes, I did notice that things are different. I'm dying to see all the renovations to the lodge." "Bad choice of words, my dear."

Mary threw up her hands in disgust.

They sat down at the kitchen table and made a list of things they'd ask Marty to pick up. It was quite a list with lots of wine and spirits included. Mary called Marty and read her the list. Marty said she'd bring the items by about ten o'clock tomorrow.

After a short nap, Mary called Marty again and asked if they could borrow a car. Of course, Marty agreed. She told Mary she could pick up the resort loaner car at the lodge. Jones and Mary got cleaned up and headed to Shirley's. As usual, they found the family style food delicious. The desserts were numerous and still out of sight, as well.

After returning to their cabin at Sugar Hollow that night, well fed and relaxed, they had little trouble getting a good night's sleep.

Chapter Twenty-One

The Conspiracy

In mid-December, only two weeks after his American Bank Corporation's Board of Directors meeting, Kurt Lane called Bill Baker at the Federal Reserve in DC and said, "We need to talk. Things are getting out of hand. If we don't put a cap on this soon, it's going to blow sky high. My shareholders are threatening a revolt. If that happens, we're finished."

Baker responded, "Sounds like we need to get everybody together again? Any ideas about what we need to do now?"

"Certainly. Look, Harry and Ms. Brand are not on the same page with us. I believe we can count on Gomer because he's looking to take Harry's place real soon. So why don't you and I talk first, and then bring Ted in at a later meeting. First of all, we need to come up with a deal that takes care of all of us. I've got some definite ideas."

Bill Baker, thinking out loud said, "Kurt, we have to be very careful. If anyone gets the slightest idea we have plotted against the masses, our days will be over immediately. That being said, why don't we meet somewhere in DC for lunch, just you and me. That way we can talk frankly with one another and not have to worry about what anyone might hear or think. Meet me at Old Ebbit's Grill on Fifteenth, Thursday at two o'clock. Most folks will be gone by then. I'll make a reservation for a booth in the back."

Bill Baker was already seated when Kurt Lane arrived at Ebbit's Grill a little after 2 pm, a storied restaurant in clubby surroundings. The place was half empty. Both men looked around the restaurant to see if they recognized anyone. They didn't see anyone of significance to them.

The waiter promptly came to take their lunch order, which began with a dry vodka martini for each. When the drinks arrived, they both ordered New England clam chowder and Caesar salads along with the cheese sampler for dessert.

Lane began the conversation by saying, "Bill, I'm glad that you agreed to meet me. Also, it makes things easier for me knowing we're on the same page. The real and certain danger that Mr. Jones and his girlfriend pose to us and our institutions is alarming."

"Make no mistake concerning how I feel about Mr. Jones," Baker responded. "As I've said before, he must be eradicated, taken out for good, this time. The sooner the better."

Sheepishly looking at Baker, Lane replied, "That's certainly re-assuring. The main reason I wanted to have lunch alone with you today is to bring you up to speed on what I have already set in motion. Since Jones's body has not yet been discovered, I'm almost certain he and Mary are alive. But since we're not absolutely sure Mr. Jones is alive, or where he may be if he is alive, I have instructed my contacts to dispatch a "hit squad" to Grand Cayman. They'll be in place by late this afternoon. Likewise, based on information I received from Harry, I instructed my contacts to dispatch another "hit squad" to the Boston/Nantucket area, and also one to New York, where Jones and Mary Whitmore lived and worked. I have a 'fourth team' that will be on hold in Atlanta until we determine Mr. Jones's precise location. Then, they'll be deployed and ordered to proceed."

"Damn Kurt, you don't waste any time, do you? Maybe we can take care of this matter sooner than I expected. Good job!" Baker said.

"Glad you approve," Kurt answered. "What have you decided the agencies need to do? When will that happen?"

"I've spoken briefly on the phone with Ted and Ms. Brand about a plan of action that's already in place. I opted to leave Harry out of the loop, because he'll be gone in just a couple of months.

Here's the crux of the matter. Listen carefully."

The Chairman of the Federal Reserve continued, "The agencies have to show the President, the Department of Justice, and the American people, for that matter, that we will not tolerate the kind of criminal activity that's been uncovered. All the banks, investment and bond houses, insurance companies, hedge fund operators, and the rating concerns that were involved must pay a heavy price. Initially, we'll allege all kinds of felony charges against each of them. We'll even charge some of the CEO's and Senior Officers."

"Hold on a minute, Bill. We've not discussed any type of action like this, much less agreed to anything like this. We need to talk this out."

"Calm down and let me finish. If we follow through on what I just outlined, then the world will think we're absolutely doing the right thing, not only for our agencies and our government, but also for the American taxpayers. In a nutshell, we'll be covering our asses."

Kurt interrupted again, asking, "Then what? Those kinds of charges could bring a lot of pain to all of those entities and to people you've just mentioned. Those types of charges don't just disappear, not once the DOJ gets involved. How are you gonna fix that?"

"It'll take a long time for all this to transpire. There'll be lots of screaming and yelling, but then it'll all settle down. Every law firm in New York and Washington will be ecstatic thinking about all of those fees they'll receive defending elite crooks. After about a year, we'll agree to reduce most of the really egregious charges. We'll even toss out some of the smaller cases. Then we'll get the DOJ to agree to major, I mean huge, fines in lieu of criminal charges against the financial institutions or their employees. Then it'll be over."

"What do you consider huge fines? Several million dollars for each defendant?"

Raising his hand, Baker said, "Hell no! I'm talking billions in fines. Gotta make it look like they're really being punished for crimes they committed. What no one will ever know is that over time, we'll announce payments of the fines by the different companies through the NYT and the WSJ. In reality, all the huge payments will simply be bookkeeping entries, since no money will actually change hands. Now, how do like that plan, my friend?"

"No wonder you're the head of the Federal Reserve. Your plan is ingenious. It looks like you're handling your end of the bargain. If I can take care of my end, I believe we'll have survived what could have been a major disaster for all of us," Lane said.

"One more thing, Kurt. I spoke with Senator Dowd. You know he's the Chair of the Senate Banking Committee. He was furious when he heard about Mr. Jones's crash, he called for an emergency meeting of his Committee that same day. He's pissed off that Mr. Jones defied his Committee's orders, not to mention that he made a mockery of the hearing. He wants revenge. He wants Mr. Jones to pay big time. Senator Dowd wants Mr. Jones incarcerated."

"I wonder what he plans to do. If Mr. Jones is dead, Senator Dowd can't do anything. That's the way I see it anyway."

"Here's the deal," Baker replied. "The Senator and I agreed on doing two things. He's going to issue a subpoena for Mr. Jones, to appear before the committee again in the near future. It'll be an open-ended subpoena with no specific date. That way, the committee can activate it when the appropriate time arrives.

Baker continued, "Then the Senator and I are going to influence the DOJ to issue a warrant for Jones's arrest, based on Congressional testimony of his admitted involvement with counterfeit money and bank fraud. Jones also violated the travel restrictions placed on him by the Senate. All of this makes him a fugitive. Then they can go after Mary with a warrant for aiding and abetting a fugitive. The warrants will be served in abstentia. That would further validate, in the minds of the general public, that we believe the two of them are most likely dead."

Lane stood up, shook Baker's hand, picked up the tab and said, "This is the most informative meeting I've attended in several years. Thank you for everything. We'll talk later."

Kurt Lane directed his chauffeured limousine to the Bank's corporate jet waiting for him at the Reagan General Aviation terminal. However, rather than flying back to North Carolina, he instructed his pilot to fly him to Melbourne, Florida. Lane had decided he needed a face-to-face meeting with Rocky "the Rooster" Benito. He wanted to make sure that Rocky realized how serious the situation really was, and how important it was to take out Mr. Jones and friends, once and for all. The sooner the better. Lane was ready to up the ante.

Rocky's cell phone rang three times before he could answer. "Hello, this is Rocky. What can I do for you today, Mr. Lane?"

"Rocky," said Lane. "Could you meet me at the Orlando Melbourne International Airport at 6 p.m. I'll be in the General Aviation Terminal. We can go somewhere close by and have dinner and talk."

"I've already made the 'hit squad' arrangements," Rocky replied. "You can't back out now!"

"I'm not backing out," Lane said forcefully. "It's time to turn up the heat on Mr. Jones. I'm coming there to up the ante, based on your performance. Interested?"

"I'll be there at six." Rocky's phone clicked dead.

About 6:15, the two men were in Rocky's car headed to San Remo Italian Restaurant on N. Harbor City Blvd. in Melbourne, a decades-old eatery a few blocks from the Atlantic Ocean. It was Rocky's favorite place for homemade Italian cuisine. Once inside, after Rocky spoke to half of the people dining there, he and Lane made their way upstairs to a back-corner table. It was private enough for them to talk serious business.

"How about some vino, Mr. Lane?" Rocky asked. "They have great reds. Perfect with their entrees."

"A great idea," Lane answered. "I'm starving for great pasta. Bring it on."

He continued, "Rocky, my situation has become quite serious. Even more so, since I phoned you. If you eliminate Mr. Jones and his woman friend within the next two weeks, I'll pay you five million dollars cash! You must get it done now. Understand?'

"Jesus Christ," Rocky replied. "You and your friends must be in some really serious trouble."

Lane responded quickly and adamantly, "Rocky, it is a matter of life and death and just not for me and my business colleagues. The future of our country hangs in the balance. It's your patriotic duty to get this contract executed as soon as possible. Get it done and you'll have the five million in cash, immediately."

Rocky reached across the table and said as he shook Lane's hand, "You got a deal my friend. Count on it!"

After finishing their dinners and several glasses of wine, both men knew they had no more to discuss. Lane told Rocky that he needed to get back to North Carolina before midnight.

Rocky obliged.

Chapter Twenty-Two
The Plan

Earlier, Jones and Mary had agreed that when they got settled into another safe place for any extended period of time, they would finally spend their daylight hours developing and fine-tuning a comprehensive plan for survival.

They both knew the time had come for them to do exactly that. They must devise a plan they could implement from wherever they might be. It was past time to get serious and get it done.

On the following Monday morning, Jones hooked up his computer and they got to work.

They created and an outline titled Name the Enemies. Then they listed them by entity. First was the Federal agencies and officials. Then the Bank and its representatives, followed by the Guardian Society and its members. Last came members of the Senate Banking Committee.

Then Jones typed his ideas, noting:

- Which is our biggest threat
- Which entity wants us dead
- Which has the most to lose
- Decide on plan to negate their actions
- Prioritize according to level of danger
- Develop plan to negate their possible responses
- Decide on a plan to negate their actions
- Prioritize according to their level of danger
- Develop actions to negate their possible responses

"Why don't we discuss an overview of what we need to do?" Mary suggested. "That way both of us can verbalize our thoughts, talk about them, and then put them in the computer.

What do you think?"

"That's a marvelous idea," Jones replied. "I'll go first, if that's okay with you."

"Sure. Let it rip."

Jones stood up, walked over to the window, looked outside at the wild turkeys near the tree line and then turned around and started speaking, very matter of factly, saying, "The people we're up against are playing hardball. They're playing for keeps. It's all or nothing with them. They have no choice but to take us down. However, that being said, we have no choice other than to do the exact same thing they're doing, or we're history."

Jones moved back to the kitchen area and sat down on a barstool. He continued, "Mary, it's imperative that we use every single tool that's available to us to destroy all these folks, and that's a mighty big task. I'm sure you'll agree with that."

"I agree. It's a damn big task. I just hope we're up to it." "Here are my thoughts on how we do that."

"First, we use extortion against the Feds. Second, we use ransom demands against the Bank. Third, we use blackmail against the Guardian Society, and fourth, we use bribery against the Senate Banking Committee!"

Mary, couldn't wait her turn, she exclaimed, "Jones, everything you just said is illegal as hell. I know that for a fact, because I'm a damn lawyer. Why do you insist on doing everything illegally?"

"Hell, Mary, I know you're a lawyer, and I know you know the law. But dealing with these bastards, legal doesn't mean a damn thing. Nothing! Look Mary, they're going to do all in their power, right or wrong, legal or illegal, to wipe us off the face of the earth. To kill us. We stand between their power, their freedom, and prison. You can damn well believe they've got no damn plans to serve time. We must do the very same thing!"

"I'm not sure that I'm strong enough to go through all of this. I'm already a nervous wreck. Can't you see what it's doing to me? I'm really scared, Jones."

"Mary, will you please let me finish my thought process about how we accomplish what I just proposed? Will you please listen and help me get it all organized?"

"Yes, go ahead."

Jones said, "I'm going to begin with the least threatening entity, as I see it. The Guardian Society is probably the least dangerous to us personally. But still, what bothers me the most about these freaks is based on the footnote my friend at Treasury put on the thumb drive about their reorganization. We don't need any interference from these creeps. So, during these days when our country is still vulnerable due to the financial crisis, we must help protect it from these barracudas."

"The Guardian Society has two weaknesses. The first would be exposure. Therefore, we threaten total exposure of all of their members and their contact information. Along with releasing that information, we would include a narrative explaining to the American public what they tried and almost succeeded in doing in 2008, when they tried to take over our government. All this would be very damaging to each of them; personally, professionally, and financially."

"Their second and maybe even greater weakness is criminal liability for the theft of US dollars. So what we do is threaten to divulge the amounts of money distributed on that Excel spreadsheet, and the members who received what amounts from the $17 trillion that was misdirected from our Federal Reserve. There is no way they can explain that away. Our thumb drive data backs that up."

"Basically, we blackmail them by demanding $25 million dollars to keep quiet about their identities and their 2008 theft. In all likelihood, they will not pay up, thinking that's kind of old news. Then we respond by contacting them again, raising our demand to $50 million and threatening to disclose their second weakness, which is how much money some of the members received. Chances are fifty-fifty they'll pay up. That's our leverage with them. Mary, you must have already figured it out by now. We're going to expose them in either case, if they pay up, or if they don't pay up. Why? Because what they're trying to do to the country now is as bad or worse as what the Feds have already done."

"Jones, you are amazing. What brain power. No wonder you're so rich."

Jones smiled, remembering all the threats of exposure and/or blackmail he had issued during the years of the Money to Burn scheme. Brain power or experience, he wondered. He was confident he had once again devised a great plan.

"May I proceed to the next group?" "Please. I can't wait to hear this one."

"The way we handle the Senate Banking Committee is we bribe them. We tell them we'll both come in without subpoenas and testify, if we are granted immunity from prosecution of any kind. We'll assure them that we have data that can bring the entire government to its knees, if it's made public. We won't ask them for any money. If they refuse to grant us immunity, we'll tell them we are prepared to expose every single member on their Banking Committee who showed up on the list of Senators receiving millions of dollars out of the stolen $17 trillion from the TARP or Federal Reserve funds that disappeared. I'd say our chances of being granted immunity would be a good bet. I mean, can you imagine how this information could impact the upcoming elections? And, of course, we will expose all of the Congressmen either way."

"Damn, Jones. You ain't taking no prisoners."

"You know the routine. 'Never wound a King, kill him.'" "Jones, I'm glad I'm on your side."

"Mary, help me get my ideas straight about the last two groups, the ones that have the most to lose. These are the ones we should be the most concerned about. We simply cannot lose to these killers."

"Go ahead. I'm all ears."

Jones continued, "Well, let's start with the Bank. Kurt Lane is probably the fall guy for the Feds. They're probably in lockstep. Most likely he is the one who had the fire bomb put on my plane. It was done at the same time that the mysterious note was put in my brief case."

"So, my plan is to demand a $50 million-dollar payment from the Bank. If the American Bank Corporation doesn't agree to pay this amount, we'll threaten to expose all we know about the Bank's illegal activities involving both Wide Country and Murray Lane Securities. Additionally, we can tell Lane we saw his Bank's name, as well as his own name on the list of financial institutions and bank CEO's that took part of the $17 trillion that was misappropriated from the TARP funds. My guess is he'll pay up, praying that either way we don't give him up."

"Now for the Feds, here is where we get really nasty," stated Jones. "We'll attempt to extort $100 million from this group. If they agree to pay, we'll tell them that we'll return all copies of the thumb drives, with all of the damaging financial data. We'll convince them we know how much money of the stolen $17 trillion each one of them accepted and where it is currently deposited."

"Additionally," Jones added, "if they refuse to pay our ransom demands, we'll release the information we have detailing their involvement, along with DOJ, in the absolute cave-in to the British authority, although HSBC had confessed. Remember, on the thumb drive, it verifies the acknowledged drug money laundering case against HSBC, the British banking conglomerate.

The Feds acquiesced to the purported Global Jurisdiction Authority and to the International Immunity Agreements trumped up by the Brits. The Feds and the DOJ agreed to dismiss all charges against HSBC and its employees in lieu of a substantial fine, which they most likely paid with laundered money! The American public would definitely rise up against these agencies both in the US and abroad, if the truth about this were to come out."

"Finally, we'll make all demands with taped messages delivered to the heads of these four groups via an International Courier. In every instance, our messages will reveal that we plan to provide thumb drives containing all of the damaging financial data to various media outlets if our demands are ignored. Those outlets include WSJ, NYT, WP, Fox News, LA Times, and CBS News. Of course, we'll send thumb drives to all these outlets regardless of their responses to our demands."

"The time line for either responses or payments will be twenty-four hours from delivery of the taped messages. We'll include wire transfer information for the Banque Internationale a Luxembourg account in the message, along with our encrypted email address. If we have to counter their email responses, we'll infer that we'll turn over the damning thumb drives to them, if our demands are fully met. Of course, we'll only return thumb drives to Bill Baker and Kurt Lane, and those will only contain a play-by-play account of last year's Super Bowl. You remember, when the Atlanta Falcons had an eighteen-point lead at halftime, and the Tom Brady and the New England Patriots made that miraculous comeback and won the game in overtime?"

With a sudden change in temperament, Jones continued, saying, "However, we have to think about the possible down side to all this. If any one or more of these groups refuse our demands and even refuse to counter, we must have a plan in place that determines our response.

Actually, based on my prior experience with the Guardian Society, I feel pretty good about them paying something, simply because they don't want the exposure. As for the Senate Banking Committee, if they deny our immunity, I fully plan to let the world know which members of Congress took how much tax payer money. I believe the two groups we really have to be concerned about are the Bank and the Feds. As for the Bank, in my opinion Kurt Lane will pay up immediately. Why? Because he, along with the Bank officers, are accustomed to doing these types of deals. For years, they've been bribing people, buying companies' silence, and threatening force whenever necessary. I'll bet they pay.

The Federal Reserve, however, is a different animal. They frighten me the most, mainly because of their innate power. Most people don't know or realize that the Federal Reserve is a non-governmental agency, totally independent from the US government. They make their own damn decisions, which is a damn scary thought. It would not surprise me if they ignore our demands. Furthermore, they may even call our bluff and refuse to pay anything. If this happens, we have two choices. First, we double down on our demands for payment, or second, we give the media the thumb drive data, take whatever money the others may have paid, and try to become invisible in Europe or Asia."

With a sigh of relief, Jones added, "Once we get all this formalized and exactly like it should be, we can develop our tactical plan. This will include who we get to make the tapes, how they're to be delivered, and the time-line we'll follow."

"Mary, can you help me get all of this organized and on our computer as soon as possible?"

Mary exclaimed, "Unbelievable! You've really thought this out, Jones. It's a masterful plan, and one I totally support. You know I'll do all in my power to help you execute it. Would you get me a glass of wine, while I get all this into the Mac?"

"A perfect answer. Glad to know we're on the same page! Hell yes. Let's have some vino."

Thanks to Marty, they had plenty of food on hand for several days and could hunker down and concentrate on their strategy and organization. They would revise one section, delete another, then add something new. They were dotting all the i's and crossing all the t's. They stayed focused, worked long days, ate, slept, and got back to work early in the mornings.

By Friday, two days before Christmas, they decided they'd celebrate and drive over to Johnson City. They planned to eat at the steakhouse they visited the last time they were at Sugar Hollow for the Storytelling Convention in Jonesville, Tennessee. They thought they needed a break and both were ready to get out of the cabin for a change. It would be their Christmas celebration.

However, the trip could happen only if Marty would let them borrow a car. As they expected, Marty brought them a loaner, all gassed up, along with directions and gift certificates to the Peerless

Restaurant. As if that weren't enough, she included some firewood for the cabin.

On Christmas morning, Jones was the first one out of bed. He built a nice roaring fire which popped and cracked so loudly that it woke Mary up.

"Please don't burn the cabin down. We'd have no private place to stay," Mary shouted from the bedroom. "Make some coffee, please. I'll make us a fabulous Christmas morning breakfast."

"The coffee is already made," Jones replied. "I'm waiting for the homemade biscuits and pancakes. And don't forget the grits."

"Lordy, are you trying to gain some weight? That menu is definitely not healthy. How about yogurt instead," Mary teased.

"Trying to run me off. That'll never happen. Let's compromise and have scrambled eggs and bacon. Deal?"

"Sounds delicious. Let me see what I can put together."

After cleaning up the dishes, Jones remarked, "It's strange not having a Christmas tree. I believe it's the first time I've never had one. However, I do have a Christmas present for you that I think you'll really like. I bet you'll be surprised."

"A present?" Mary asked. "I have not seen the first wrapped package. Where did you hide it? So sorry, but I haven't had time to get one for you."

"Don't worry about it. Come over here, so I can give it to you."

Mary walked over to the sofa and sat down next to Jones. "Okay, here I am. Where's my present?"

"Luxembourg," Jones answered. "When I sent Richard to Europe to take care of transferring all my funds to a tax haven, I sent him to Luxembourg. I instructed him to set up a couple of accounts for you, as well. Furthermore, I told him to split the investments between our two accounts. It's been done, and I can honestly say you now have the financial security you need and deserve. So, if something were to happen to me, you can continue living the lifestyle you enjoy."

Mary started crying. "Jones, you didn't have to do that. Really you shouldn't have done that. I can never reciprocate. It's just not right."

Jones scooted over next to Mary, put his arms around her, and told her in no uncertain terms how much he cared about her and how much he loved her. She just continued to sob.

Then he reached in his pants pocket and pulled out a tiny red box. Mary didn't even see him do that, since she was holding her hands over her crying eyes.

"Open your eyes, Mary. Here is a little something for you today. However, there's one condition you must agree to before you can have it."

Immediately, Mary realized the red ring box was from Harry Winston in New York. She looked up at Jones with tears on her cheeks. "What's the condition? What's the gift?" She asked quietly.

Jones opened the tiny ring box. He took out the beautiful, large, brilliant cut diamond ring that Mary had admired in the City for years and asked, "The condition is, will you marry me?"

Mary jumped right into Jones's lap, hugging him so tight that he couldn't breathe, saying, "Yes! Yes! Oh, my god, Yes! I love you so much."

Jones came up for air, grabbed Mary's hand, took her ring finger and slipped that gorgeous diamond on her finger!

Finally, Mary sat up, wiped the tears away and said, "Jones, you're the most loving, generous, and standup man I've ever known. I simply don't know how to thank you for all of this or how I can ever convince you of my love."

"You just did both. That's all you need to say," Jones replied.

Mary continued, "I'm overwhelmed and so excited. Can you believe it? We're getting married. Got a date in mind?"

"Let's celebrate with a few holiday drinks," Jones said. "We'll figure the date out later."

"Suits me. I need a drink to calm my nerves. This is the very best Christmas I've ever had. The best I'll ever have, I'm sure. Look at this incredibly big, beautiful diamond ring."

"Jones," Mary said very softly, "I need to call my folks today. It's only fair to let them know that I'm still alive and well. It would a great Christmas gift to them from both of us. Plus, I can tell them we're engaged. Please understand."

After brief consideration, Jones grabbed Mary's hand and said, "You're one hundred percent correct. Your folks need to know you're okay. It certainly will make their Christmas. Call them today. Call them whenever you want. Use your burner phone. Be sure and tell them that I'm going to take care of you, now and forever."

"Thanks for being so understanding. It means a lot to me. I'll call them this afternoon. It'll be so good to hear their voices again. I've missed them terribly."

Jones put more logs on the fire. They both gazed at the snow that had begun falling outside. Things were good. Things were very good, for the moment.

Later that day, they agreed to make reservations for a New Year's Eve dinner and an overnight stay in Bristol. That was going to be a great way to close out this extraordinary year. Jones said he'd tell Marty they'd like to use the rental car again.

Later that night, while Jones was snoring away, Mary sobbed quietly as she thought about her earlier talk with her mom. Initially, her mom was thankful to finally hear from her "missing" daughter. The past months, not knowing whether Mary was dead or alive, had taken a serious toll on Mary's mother. As for her dad, five years older than his wife, he was a total wreck. Mary spent a lot of time trying to convey to her parents exactly what the situation was so that they might understand and appreciate the circumstances. Mary told her parents about Jones and his Congressional testimony. She told them about the plane crash and why she and Jones were on the run. She explained why she had waited so long to call. Their chat had taken a very negative turn. Neither parent was too keen about Mary's relationship with Jones. When Mary told them she loved Jones and that they had just become engaged on Christmas Day, her mom started crying. It was not with tears of joy. Her father was so upset he hung up the other phone line.

But all of that was a total waste of time. They just didn't want to hear it. What Mary had thought would be a good Christmas Day present for them turned into a very disappointing conversation. Finally, Mary told her mom that she'd call her sister and explain everything to her, so Monica could in turn explain the total situation to them. Absolutely nothing seemed to suit her mom. Nothing at all. Mary hung up the phone with a very heavy and broken heart. *So much for my engagement celebration,* Mary thought.

Once the holidays were over, and their fear of running into any guests had subsided, Mary and Jones finally made it up to the Lodge. They were pleased with how much better it looked since their last visit. Marty showed them around and actually served them lunch in the remodeled bar. It was fun to be in the Lodge again, where they spent several hours visiting with Marty.

Over the next several weeks, Jones and Mary took things one day at a time. They interacted with Marty from time to time, and on other days they'd go hiking. Some days they'd just sit on the Lodge's back patio, watch the deer and wild turkeys in the meadow, talk, and have their late afternoon cocktails. On days when their cabin fever returned, they borrowed Marty's car and explored the surrounding areas.

Several days in January they were literally snowed-in at their log cabin. No way were they going anywhere. It wasn't safe to try and walk down the hill to the Lodge. However, Mary and Jones didn't seem to mind at all. They always had lots to say to one another, and when they ran short of words, they found other ways to enjoy each other's company.

Near the end of the month, they began to get a little antsy, a bit nervous, like when you know there's a great deal left to be done, and you just want to get it done and over with as soon as possible. That's where Jones and Mary were. What made their situation even more nerve- wracking was the knowledge that their lives depended on their plan. It would have to be precisely executed, if they were to have a future together.

In another month, they received news that blew their peaceful interlude to pieces.

Chapter Twenty-Three

The Disappearance.

In late February, Jones got a call from CLEPTO, his buddy at Treasury, who told him, "The Feds got a tip on your possible location. They've just received information on a call Mary made to her mom on Christmas Day. I've been told you might be in eastern Tennessee. Since they'd been tracking your iPhone, they still believed you went back to Grand Cayman by way of Miami. Now, they're pulling out all the stops, trying to determine if you're still alive. Once they believe you are alive, they'll be coming after you two from all directions. You better get all your business together in one bag and use the information I gave you now. Put a plan in place and take those bastards down, before they kill both you and me. They're a definite threat. It's real!"

The informant added one more comment, "Thought you should know that a bunch of us here at Treasury are going outside fishing next week. Some of the senior directors are planning to fly down to Melbourne, Florida, and charter a boat. It'll accommodate about fifteen people. Should be a lot of fun. I'll be out of touch for a couple of days. We'll talk when I get back."

The hair on Jones's neck was standing straight up. He knew he had to control his fear in front of Mary. *I don't like the sound of that last statement*, Jones thought.

His calm response was, "Thanks so much for the good news. Sounds like things are working in our favor. You've been a life saver, and I do appreciate it very much. So does Mary. My advice to you is to make sure you cover your own ass and watch your back. You are surrounded by a bunch of killers." Click, the connection went dead.

Jones sent Richard a text from one of his burner phone telling him they were leaving Sugar Hollow and driving to Cameron, Louisiana. Then, he added, they planned to sail back to Veracruz on the sail boat they left in Cameron. He added that if the sailboat wasn't there for some reason, he'd buy one. He also sent a second text saying he'd send more instructions later.

Within three days, Mary and Jones had packed up and persuaded Marty to drive them to Johnson City. There, they bought a used, nondescript pickup truck. After getting paper license tags, gas, a map, and a bucket of Bojangles fried chicken, they were ready to hit the road again. They said their goodbyes to Marty and headed south toward Cameron, Louisiana, but not before Jones gave Marty an envelope filled with twenty-five one hundred-dollar bills.

"Take out the rent I owe Sugar Hollow for the cabin. The rest is yours. It's for all the trouble we've put you through over the past two months and for taking the risk to helping us. We appreciate all you've done. Just remember, you've not seen or heard from us."

"I helped you because I believe in you. You don't need to pay me a dime, "Marty replied. "It was my pleasure spending time with you guys. Good luck and be careful."

Mary and Jones drove off in the pickup as tears came to Marty's eyes. Deep down inside, Marty was worried about her friends and for a very good reason.

Driving the thousand miles to Cameron gave Jones and Mary lots of time to talk about everything imaginable. They talked about the things they saw in the backwoods of Tennessee, Mississippi, and Alabama. They talked about Richard. They talked about their plan and their chances of surviving. Mary talked about her family, and how thrilled they were when she called them on Christmas Day. She said that they were overcome with emotion and glad to know she was still alive and well. But Mary lied when she told Jones they seemed pleased to hear about her engagement. They talked about the Luxembourg deal. Jones hinted he had another surprise for her later. Jones finally explained the threatening note he found in his brief case just before his plane crashed. He told her he thought the logo on the bottom of the note was meant to be a distraction, an attempt at misdirection.

Jones explained, "That note, with the cut-out letters, had the Federal Reserve Seal on the bottom of the page. It could have been photo-shopped, but most likely it was the genuine seal. Kurt Lane certainly had access to the Federal Reserve stationary. I believe he wanted me to think it was the Feds, who were trying to kill me. When, in fact, it was Lane. I'm sure of it!"

"Do you have any regrets about your testimony at the Senate Hearings?" Mary asked. "Do you wish that maybe you hadn't told them so much? It certainly brought the wrath of the Feds down on your head, and mine, too, for that matter."

Jones responded immediately, "I have no regrets other than how it has involved you. Look, you and I both know that much of the stuff I've done in the past was far from legal or ethical. I did whatever it took to get my Bank the deals it needed to rise to the top of the banking industry. It goes without saying that much of what I was asked to do, and actually did, was illegal and wrong. I know that I was a significant player in my Bank's success. I also admit that I was the one who was responsible for funneling millions upon millions of dollars of counterfeit money into the US financial system over the years."

Jones continued, "But somehow, to me at least, that pales in comparison to what those corrupt bastards have done to the US taxpayers, not to mention our country. I finally thought that things had gone too far, too damn far in my judgement. I thought it was time to let the world know, so maybe someone could help stop those thieving bastards from doing any more damage.

If I had any idea those crooks had planned to kill me from the very beginning, maybe I would have toned down my own self-incrimination. Honestly, I never imagined it would come down to this. Maybe I'm just too naive."

"That's about as far from the truth as anything you've ever spoken," Mary answered. "You? Naive? Not a chance in hell."

"You know, Jones," Mary continued, "I've been thinking about all of that damaging information on the thumb drives. With numerous members of Congress listed, plus several Agency heads, it makes me wonder what the hell else they're doing? Maybe all of the reports about the various scandals, plaguing this administration, are in fact, true. But what is so amazing to me is, where the hell was the FBI or the President when all of this went down? You'd think they had to know!"

"I agree. Which scandals are you referring to?" asked Jones. "Be specific."

"Okay, Jones," Mary answered. "Don't you remember hearing about the illegal gun purchase deal called Fast and Furious, where our DOJ bought $1.5 million in illegal firearms and sent them across the border into Mexico to be distributed? The Feds hoped the guns would be traced to the drug cartels, so they would then have evidence against the drug lords. Only problem was those guns were used against our own Border Patrol agents, killing several."

"Yes, sadly, I remember that story," Jones replied.

"There's more," Mary exclaimed. "One deal that really caught my attention back then was about a Russian company buying a major source of our uranium ore right here in America. How the hell did that get approved? Rumors floated around for months that lots of money passed hands between the Russian company that ended up with our uranium and one US politician in particular. You know, the one with the Foundation. Some estimates about the bribe money were in excess of $145 million funneled to the Foundation through Canada from the buyer. Can you believe that?"

"That's hard to fathom," added Jones. "Many got bought off on that deal. The hell with the money, what about our national security?"

"That same Foundation fronted the international 'Save Haiti' campaign that raised billions of dollars in donations worldwide to help the people of Haiti recover from a devastating earthquake,"

Mary continued. "It's been reported that most of the billions of dollars raised remained in the Foundation's coffers."

"Hell," Jones said, "I remember that I was in New York when a delegation from Haiti came to town and went before the United Nations demanding that the Foundation turn over the donated funds to Haiti. When nothing happened, that same delegation protested on the sidewalk in front of that politician's apartment on the Upper East side, days on end, demanding their money to no avail. Outrageous!"

"And then," Mary said, "there are all of those people who were connected to the Foundation, who died mysteriously over the years, yet no one was ever charged with any crime. It's simply amazing how things like that continue to unravel, but the seemingly 'bad guys' go scot-free and keep on raking in the cash. It never stops."

Mary continued, "Then there was the "Hush Money Fund", about fifteen million dollars of taxpayer money that was used to settle well over two hundred sexual assault claims against a whole bevy of Congressional officials, both Democrats and Republicans. You gotta wonder where the FBI was hiding when all of these crimes were being committed!"

"You add all of this to the Feds' heist," Jones replied, "and it makes it easy to understand and believe that 'Absolute power corrupts, absolutely.'"

"Amen," Mary said.

"Mary, changing the subject a bit, you won't believe what I left on the mantel in the cabin," Jones said. "I think it's funny as hell. Guess what it is?"

"I have no idea what you left," Mary responded. "Tell me so I can laugh, too."

"I left a note for the Feds," Jones responded, while laughing out loud. "The note reads, 'Catch us if you can! Bonnie & Clyde!' I put it in a small sealed envelope addressed to: "The Feds.'"

Mary doubled over laughing. She could not contain herself. "That's just too damn good, Jones," Mary muttered.

"A little levity, now and then, is good for your soul," declared Jones.

It took them a couple of days to reach Cameron, but they got good news immediately. "Their" sailboat was still there, just as they had left it. Jones went into the marina office, to settle up on the dockage fees with cash from his briefcase and gassed up while Mary began gathering supplies. They checked out at the counter and hauled their luggage and their bags of supplies to the sailboat. Once everything was aboard, Jones took the ropes from the pilings, pushed off from the dock, and they found themselves headed, once again, to Veracruz.

Later that night, Jones called Richard to fill him in on their new plan. Richard picked up on the third ring saying, "Yes Sir, Mr. Jones. How can I possibly help you at such a late hour? Could you please call back during business hours? They are 11 am to 3 pm Monday, Wednesday, and Friday."

Overwhelmed with laughter, Jones replied, " Shut up, you moron. I've got serious information for you. Get a pen and write this down."

"Give me a second. Let me grab a pen and paper. Okay. Shoot."

"We picked up the boat in Cameron. Fortunately, it was just as we left it. We parked our pickup in the lot behind the marina. I took the paper license plate and stuck it in my bag. The truck's barely visible. We bought supplies, got on the boat, and we're headed out to Veracruz. Should be there in three or four days. Once we arrive and get straight with the charter boat agent, we're going to take an AeroMexico flight over to Puerto Vallarta. It's a three-and-a-half-hour flight."

"You're going to the airport? You're going to get on a damn airplane? Are you friggin' mad? People are looking for both of you all over the friggin' Northern Hemisphere. You've gone absolutely crazy! Why Puerto Vallarta?"

Jones fired back, "Save your criticism for later. Just make sure you get all those things I've asked you to do taken care of before too many more days go by. Okay? Don't worry, Mary and I are using many various disguises."

"I have an old friend who spends considerable time there each year," Jones continued. "We met in Chapel Hill our sophomore year at UNC. She's an attractive lady named Reba Robinson. She owns a couple of condos down there and invites friends and family quite often. Both are open air and overlook the Pacific Ocean and the Bay, which are only two blocks away. Reba spends about six months a year there. She also rents them, whenever they're available. She agreed to lease one of the units to me for the next couple of months. I can't wait to to get there because, over the years, I've heard that it's absolutely beautiful. Here's how to contact me." Jones gave Reba's phone number and address to Richard but asked him not to call unless it was an extreme emergency.

"Leave the calling to me. I'll call you when we reach Veracruz, and I'll call again to let you know when we make it safely to Puerto Vallarta. See you later. Thanks for your support."

"Got it, Bossman."

About ten minutes later, Mary returned from the galley and said, "I've never heard about that 'attractive lady' before. Want to tell me about her?"

"Don't worry, Mary. We're just real good friends. Have been since our college days. Hell, Reba dated Tuffy, a good friend of mine down at the Zete House. Actually, they ended up married for a while. I can't wait until you meet her, because I think you'll both hit it off from the get-go."

"So, I don't have to worry about her at all, right? That makes me feel so relieved."

Jones pulled Mary into his arms and assured her she was the only woman he loved. They talked into the night under a full moon with a bottle or two of fine red wine. They both slept peacefully that night. Actually, they slept out under the stars until the sun reached the 10 am position in the sky. Jones, feeling the heat from the sun, jumped up and made a pot of coffee.

The next couple of days were most enjoyable. They were alone. There was no TV. There were no newspapers. Their troubles were far enough removed for the time being that it was possible for them to let their guards down and actually relax and enjoy one another. They cooked. They drank. They went swimming. They sailed. They made love. They talked about everything imaginable. That included the details of EC's counterfeit operation.

"Jones," Mary asked. "Tell me what EC's cellmate, Pete Hamilton, told you about EC's counterfeit money operation, and what they did with all of the $20 bogus bills they printed."

"It was an ingenious scheme," declared Jones.

"Here's what Pete told me. He said EC explained the total deal to him, while they were in prison. EC told Pete he got into the counterfeit money operation after the Sheriff's Department raided one of the local hunting camps frequented by Northern sportsmen. They confiscated slot machines, illegal whiskey, and a counterfeit machine with plates. According to Pete, the Deputy Sheriff gave the counterfeit plates to EC."

"As the story goes," added Jones, "EC met with a number of his business associates about printing counterfeit bills and several agreed to participate in this illegal deal. Some of the men involved were also involved with a new bank, chartered in New Ferry in October 1952."

"According to what EC told Pete," Jones continued, "EC set up the printing operation in his warehouse at the Fork. They found Ed Spruce in Kinston, who supplied the ink and the paper. They found and purchased a printing device in Chicago. EC got a man named Earl Tardy to head up the operation. Once they began, they started printing one-dollar bills. It soon became obvious that they had far to go before they'd have any bills looking good enough to spend. After several weeks of trial and error, they were finally able to print a few bills that looked authentic, almost."

"Do you believe all of that stuff, Jones?" Mary interrupted. "It sounds like a fairy tale to me."

"Damn, Mary, please let me finish my story," chided Jones.

"Sure, go ahead. I'm listening." said Mary.

"Pete told me that the whole dynamic of the counterfeit deal changed when EC decided to print twenty-dollar bills, especially when the twenty-dollar bills they printed looked like twenty-dollar bills should look."

"It was not long before EC had his 'boys' test these bogus bills in adjoining counties by buying small items in convenience stores. Not once were they even questioned. Then, again according to Pete, EC and his associates came up with the idea of putting the counterfeit bills into the new bank's 'old money' bags that were then sent to the Federal Reserve Bank in Richmond and burned. The new bank received a like amount of good money in return. With inside help, this scheme continued for quite a while. A great deal of money the bank received from the Federal Reserve was deposited in dummy accounts, all controlled by EC and his associates."

"Now, Jones, that part is almost more than I can believe," stated Mary. "Seems like someone at the Federal Reserve would have caught this somehow."

"I said they had inside help," Jones answered. "That's the only way they were able to get away with burning the counterfeit money at the Federal Reserve. Bank employees that were on the take, looked the other way, lots of times. Why? Because they were bought and paid for. It happens with great frequency in DC, even today. Once they burned a few million dollars of counterfeit money, EC, as Pete told it, came up with the very clever idea of where they could hide all the counterfeit twenties they planned to print later. EC figured that each time they printed one hundred thousand dollars of counterfeit money (5,000 bills), they could pack the bills into a briefcase and send one of EC's 'boys' to deposit the bogus cash in a safe deposit box at a cooperating bank. He'd get the access information and take it back to EC, who then entered that information, along with the bank's name and address, in his ledger book.

"They did this almost daily for several years. As a result, EC had millions upon millions of counterfeit twenties parked quite safely in bank safe deposit boxes all across the southeast and southwest. I know this is a fact because, as I told you earlier, I used a great deal of those counterfeit dollars in most of those bank safe deposit boxes, as leverage for acquiring or merging with hundreds of financial institutions for the Bank over the past thirty years."

"Did you ever see EC's ledger book showing where all of that money was hidden?" quizzed Mary. "That would have been a very important book."

"The answer is yes. You see, EC told Pete it was hidden on the bottom shelf in a Pepsi Cola display case in his supermarket. He wanted Pete to know where it was, so when Pete was paroled and went to the Fork to look after EC's family and business, he could use the information somehow. Once Pete and I hooked up, he gave me the ledger book with the provision that I'd share a percentage of the funds from each safe deposit box with him. That worked out quite nicely for both of us and the Bank. Hell, I knew from the ledger how much of EC's bogus money was in every bank that I wanted to buy. It was a piece of cake."

After four and a half days at sea with a steady wind and calm seas, Jones and Mary sailed the sloop into the harbor at Veracruz. It took a couple of hours to get all of their business completed and to settle up with the charter boat company. That bill was enormous, but Jones did some heavy negotiating and still had plenty of cash left. Then they jumped into a cab and headed to the airport. So far so good.

"Are you nervous about getting on a commercial flight, Jones?" Mary inquired as she climbed into the cab. "You think we might be recognized?"

"I'm not worried, especially since we made a few more changes in our appearances," Jones responded as he shut the cab door. "Time to get on with our lives and get to Puerto Vallarta. I'm looking forward to a few weeks of being off the grid, as they say."

"You got that right, my man. Can't wait to take off this ugly wig and let my hair down and just relax," Mary added. "Everybody needs a break now and then."

Bill Brown

Chapter Twenty-Four
The Side Trip

Upon arriving in the airport, Mary and Jones purchased their tickets and headed toward the departure gate. They ducked into a small cafe and ordered coffee and pastries. Both had made a modest attempt to change their appearances. Mary had cut her long, blonde, gorgeous hair relatively short, and she was sporting a Mexican-style ball cap. Jones had grown some facial hair, which really did alter his fresh-faced, altar-boy look. Both wore oversized sunglasses. They boarded without problems using another set of fake ID's that Marty helped them get before they left Tennessee. Obviously, they were being a little more cautious these days.

Once in the air, both loosened up a bit and resumed normal conversation.

Mary asked Jones, "Is Reba Robinson in Puerto Vallarta now? Does she know we're coming to her place today? Have you called her?"

"No. Yes. Yes. All of the above. This is usually the time of year she's in Mexico. Normally, she leaves the States around the year-end holiday season and heads south. I called her this morning to alert her of our arrival today. She told me that a serious family situation had required her to postpone her trip for awhile. She doesn't have any plans to return to Mexico any time soon. However, she seemed happy to know that we were on the way. Basically, we'll be on our own. She told me where to find the key and the best places to eat and drink."

"How long did you tell her we planned to stay in Puerto Vallarta?"

"I told her we'd like to stay a full two months, assuming everything goes according to our overall plan."

"Was she okay with that? Not a problem, I hope."

"None at all, as far as I know. No need to worry about that now." "Let's order a drink. It'll help us relax," Mary suggested.

"Great idea. Ring the bell. What are you going to order?"

"Hell, we're in Mexico or over Mexico. How about a Bacardi Rum and Coke?" "Make that two. Good selection, dear."

Between chatting, catnapping, and a couple of drinks, they were surprised how soon their plane began its descent into Puerto Vallarta.

"Touchdown. We're here. Wake up and smell the roses," Jones declared. "I'm awake. Leave me alone. Are we there?" Mary mumbled.

"Yes and right on time."

They collected their luggage from the baggage area, hailed a cab, and headed into town. Reba had informed Jones that her condos were right in the middle of all local activity, which meant they wouldn't need a rental car. Twenty minutes later, they arrived at Reba's address. Jones paid the cab driver and took their bags to the front door.

Jones found the "hidden" key and unlocked the door. Both walked inside and were pleasantly pleased at Reba's chic place, where they would be spending the next couple of months.

Mary spoke first, "This is divine. So warm and comfortable. I love the place already."

"You should have known that all my friends have great taste. It's a given that it would be quite nice."

Both climbed the stairs to the second floor and were immediately overwhelmed by the incredible view of the Pacific Ocean. It was breathtaking!

"Jones, will you buy us a villa like this? Please. It's all I'd ever want or need."

"You sure you want to live in Mexico? I don't believe you'd enjoy it here all year. Then we'd have to sell the unit and relocate somewhere that you'd feel more comfortable long term."

"You always throw cold water on my dreams. Can't a girl dream a little bit?"

"No problem. Dream all you want. I'll try and keep us grounded. One of us has to be the grownup."

"Go to hell, Jones. Why are you being so mean? We're finally in this gorgeous place, and you're acting like an old grump."

"I'm just teasing you. I'm feeling like my old self, I guess. Let's go down to the Square and find someplace to grab a bite to eat," Jones said, changing the subject. "I'm starving."

Two weeks had passed since Jones and Mary had arrived in Puerto Vallarta. They were both enjoying the leisure lifestyle and the privacy. Finally, they were in a place where they felt relatively safe and secure. Reba's condo was a godsend.

One morning over coffee, Mary offered, "I've thought a great deal about what we need to do going forward. I believe we must be certain about exactly when and where we initiate our plan. Precise logistics are extremely important to our overall success, and longevity."

"You are one hundred percent correct. What you just said is the operative word... logistics. Let's talk about the different options at length. Then we can decide which is the best choice and add that to our computer file," added Jones.

Over the next several days, they had many long conversations about their plan of attack. They talked about what they should do, where they should do it, and when to implement their plan. Quite often they'd be on opposite sides of the issue they were discussing, but more often than not, they'd come to the same conclusion at the end. That in itself was a good indication that their final plan would be the right one. At least they were doing all they could do to get it right.

Most days Jones and Mary worked on their plan until around five o'clock. Then they'd have a couple of cocktails and eat in, or they would walk down to the cafe for dinner and drinks. Many evenings they went to bed fairly early.

Finally, one morning Jones jumped out of bed, perked some coffee, turned on his computer, and called out to Mary, "Honey, get up. Coffee's made. Computer's on. Time to go back to work. Come on. We've got lots to do. We must get this plan polished off and ready to implement."

Mary, moaning out loud, said, "Come back to bed. I'll make it worth your while. We can work later. Never known you to pass up a good roll in the hay."

"Let's get our work done, and then we can make love the rest of the day. That's a better idea. Don't you think?"

"I can't believe you're rejecting my sexual advances. What a way to destroy a woman's self- confidence. Don't you realize how needy I must be?"

"Come on in here. Your coffee's getting cold. I'm already putting information in the computer. You need to look over my shoulder to make sure I'm getting it right."

"Okay. I'll be there in a minute, Mr. Romantic."

They spent the rest of the day going over the final details concerning the execution of their plan, where they would be when they launched their plan, and the exact date it would begin. They didn't leave anything to chance. They covered it all.

Finally, it was time to stop talking and time to take action. They remembered what CLEPTO had said about "taking them out before they take you out."

They needed to find a recording studio, where they could record the messages they planned to have delivered to the head of each enemy group. The tapes would spell out exactly what each must do in order to prevent Jones and Mary from publicly disclosing their corrupt and illegal actions. Jones agreed to search around and find the right studio, where they could be guaranteed absolute confidentially.

Both agreed that it would be more prudent if they hired and

used a third party to be the voice on the taped messages. Without either one of their voices on the tapes, no one could prove that they were still alive. They wanted a male voice, with very little accent, and solid clarity. They wanted to make certain the messages were audibly clear. Mary volunteered to interview voice candidates until she found the right one.

Jones deferred to Mary's concise knowledge of legal terminology, so he agreed that she should compose the content for the taped messages. Of course, he would have a great deal of input, but Mary would get the last word. However, Jones advised Mary to make the messages on the tapes short and to the point, with absolutely no ambiguity.

After a great deal of discussion and consternation, they agreed on who would receive the tapes. In most cases, it was only one head for each group. But for the FEDS, they agreed that all four Federal agency heads; Bill Baker, Ms. Brand, Harry Peters, and Ted Gomer should receive a tape. They hoped this would insure that the message would not get swept under the rug and covered up. They both agreed that sending one of the tapes to Kurt Lane at the Bank would be "sweet."

They then decided to enjoy the last month they had in Puerto Vallarta before launching their attack. That meant they'd be leaving Reba's villa around the first week in April. They needed to get out of Mexico, and they knew where they were going and why.

Bill Brown

Chapter Twenty-Five
The Grand Scheme

About two weeks after Kurt Lane and Bill Baker had lunch at Ebbit's Grill in DC, their combined plan of action was ready for execution. The time had come to use the total force of the US government to bring their financial calamity to an end.

Bill Baker called Kurt Lane and boasted, "The DOJ has totally bought into the idea of issuing warrants for Jones and Mary in Absentia. They issued the warrants without the slightest idea that they were being used to the max. Justice is providing credibility for all of our fraudulent subsequent actions. That development received major news media coverage everywhere."

"That's exactly what we wanted and needed," Lane remarked. "You couldn't have asked them to do more."

"Don't know if you saw this on the news, my friend," Baker offered. "but the DOJ action was followed by Senator Dowd's announcement at a national press conference that the Senate Banking Committee was issuing open-ended subpoenas for the two fugitives. Senator Dowd also announced the start of a major investigation into what actually caused the near-fatal collapse of the US banking and financial system."

"I saw it and it's incredible. Seems like everyone is following the same script," voiced the banker. "Does the Senator think Mr. Jones is alive, or is he just going along with the plan?"

"The Senator has a hunch that Jones is alive," Baker answered. "I think that the Senator may be right. What do you think?"

Lane responded, "I'm not sure. It bothers me that neither Jones nor Mary has been seen, dead or alive. That's almost too pat for me. Just doesn't seem right. But I've spent a great deal of time around Jones, and I know how he thinks. He's brilliant and he's a friggin' survivor. I'd bet he's alive, but I hope not for long."

"Did you hear about the note they found at a cabin in eastern Tennessee?" Baker asked. "It was addressed to 'The Feds.'"

Lane replied, "What note? I've not heard anything about any note. What did the note say? Who sent the damn note?"

"The note said 'Catch us if you can! Bonnie and Clyde.' It was in a small sealed envelope and left on the mantel in a cabin at Sugar Hollow Resort in Butler, Tennessee. We checked it for fingerprints, but it was wiped clean. The manager there is some woman named Marty, who claimed she didn't know anything. She said she had not seen anyone or had not heard anything about a Mr. Jones and his girlfriend."

"Lane asked, "Why did your folks even go there? How did they know to look there?"

"We monitored a call on Mary's parents' phone line," answered Baker. "We couldn't believe that she'd take a chance and call her parents, even on Christmas Day. But she did. It was a short phone conversation, but it placed the caller in Tennessee. My folks got the coordinates. Marty suggested it was a prank, based on information someone may have seen in the media."

"Probably so," mulled Lane, disgustingly. "Probably so, but someone made that call. That's enough proof for me to know that they're alive. However, we should keep our beliefs to ourselves. Don't want a full-scale manhunt on our hands that might disrupt our plan. Do you agree?"

"I agree," Baker replied.

One week later, the US Treasury Department referred charges, and prevailed on the DOJ to file criminal charges against the American Bank Corporation; Kurt Lane's bank, the largest bank in America. The Justice Department alleged the Bank and its top brass participated in criminal activity, which helped lead to the financial crisis of a few years back. The media went ballistic with this new litigation announcement. The bank's stock value hit rock bottom.

Two days later, the Federal Reserve announced it had also referred charges to the DOJ requesting that criminal charges be filed against seven of the biggest investment houses on Wall Street. They alleged not only fraud, but also money laundering. The market swings were incredible. The Volatility Index was outrageous.

By month's end, the DOJ filed a class action suit against a consortium of banks, both large and small. This development was a total surprise, and its repercussions were alarming. Some of the smaller banks just folded. They simply closed their doors overnight.

Two weeks later, the DOJ went after several foreign financial institutions based in Europe. The charges covered an array of criminal activity that fell under the felony classification. It certainly appeared that the DOJ had become an equal opportunity litigator. They were filing litigation cases against institutions of all sizes and types.

With all of the corrosive media coverage these announcements received, the general public was reacting in a very positive way. Many citizens actually believed the crooked financial companies were finally going to get what they deserved and would soon find themselves directly in the path of Lady Justice.

What the general public didn't know at that time were details of the $17 trillion heist. Participation in the heist and what benefits were received by whom were still well-guarded secrets. The four Federal agency heads and the top banker were going to do their part in making sure no one would ever know. However, secrets get shared, sooner or later. It always seems to happen.

During the ensuing weeks, many US financial companies and other institutions around the world felt that they had been broad-sided by litigation from the DOJ, and it was mind-boggling. The heads of all these financial entities were scrambling. They were all trying to cut deals. They would agree to almost anything in order to squash or at least minimize their exposure. Many of the charges against these defendants amounted to more than just a slap on the wrist, and convictions were what they all feared the most.

The very best legal teams that New York, Washington, and San Francisco had to offer were called into action. Their excessive and abhorrent hourly rates no longer mattered. The defendants only requirement was to get their client's charges dismissed or at least reduced to some more reasonable and workable settlement. The lawyers were in charge, and they were damn certain that they were going to make an absolute fortune off of their clients.

Most of the charges and allegations against these robber-barons of finance were answered in due time by their armies of lawyers. There were extensions, delays, postponements, discoveries, depositions, and general rebuttals filed daily. There seemed to be like competition as to which law firm could create the most paper work, or could drag litigation out the longest, or charge the highest fees. It was a highly unstable time in the country.

The financial institution hit the hardest by the DOJ was Kurt Lane's American Bank Corporation. It's alleged crimes had dictated a fine of more than $2 billion dollars. Although he had been forewarned by Bill Baker from the Fed, Kurt Lane was both frantic and furious. He believed they were ganging up on him and his Bank. He planned to have his legal team fight fire with fire to reduce his exposure. What infuriated him most was knowing that Mr. Jones, his former employee, was mainly responsible for the problems that he and his Bank were now facing.

I am going to kill that sonofabitch, if it's the last thing I do, thought Lane.

Chapter Twenty-Six

The Secret Group

The leader of the Guardian Society, who lived in Seattle, felt another opportunity was about to present itself in the midst of the continuing financial chaos and turmoil swirling about the country. He thought it prudent to call his top lieutenants together to discuss emerging possibilities. Perhaps they could come up with a formula providing an inside chance of accomplishing what they failed to achieve in 2008.

The summit took place in Las Vegas in early February, under the guise of R&R in case any government folks were monitoring their activities. He booked several rooms at the Bellagio, a premiere Vegas facility with a great casino and lots of beautiful women.

After the few senior members of the Guardian Society checked in, they gathered in the back of a small cafe off the main casino. Several ordered cocktails, the others just coffee. There was a certain degree of anxiety apparent among the participating members.

The leader stood and softly remarked, "Thank all of you for coming today. I'm sure it has been a bit inconvenient for most of you, but I felt compelled to call this meeting. As most of you must certainly realize, our country is struggling to stay afloat. It's a long way to fully recover from the financial bailout of 2008. The main Federal agencies that run our country are in such disarray that long term survival for many of them is doubtful. The obvious financial corruption prevalent among these groups is about to take our country down."

He continued, "Now, let me say, that in itself is a tragedy; but it's also a grand opportunity for us, for our Society. What we were missing, when we attempted to take control of the country in 2008, was that TOTAL corruption had not had time to permeate through the entire Federal agency system. Believe me, it now has consumed them all, and I do mean all of them."

"So what's your plan of action?" asked a member. "We must do something different from last time. This time our plan must be more aggressive, more decisive, and swifter in execution. No backing down. Never. That's the only way we can win."

"I like your straightforwardness. It's refreshing and very meaningful. Thank you. That's the kind of thinking we must have throughout our Guardian Society membership in order to proceed and prevail. Let's go around the table. Each one of you speak your mind to see if we can derive some kind of consensus on our plan of action. Let's go. Speak up."

All members at the table spoke their minds. Some of the remarks were repetitious, others were long and drawn out. But altogether, they were on the same page. The Leader suggested they think about everything they had just heard, overnight, and meet again for lunch tomorrow at noon. Same place. Everybody agreed.

Some of the members went back to their hotel rooms, while a few others drifted into the casino for a little gambling action. A couple of them ordered drinks and drifted to the Black Jack table. One well-heeled member proceeded to the Baccarat table for high stakes gambling. Each played well into the night.

At lunchtime the next day, each member filed into the cafe once more. Some were more alert than others. It was easy to tell who went to bed early and who had gambled the night away. The Baccarat player was bragging about how much money he had won. Not everyone bought his line of BS.

The Leader spoke, "Okay, listen up. We need to set a time-line for our overall plan. Let's declare our milestones and then draw up a list of demands. Once we get everything worked out, I'll call a meeting to present it to the full membership. I suggest we set our target date for April fifteenth."

The group worked steadily for the next few hours, trying to agree on an overall course of action. Some members were much more assertive than others and were adamant about taking control of the country by coup. Others favored a more diplomatic approach, using reason and dialogue as a means to their end, which was to stage a coup and take over the US government.

Around five o'clock, the group agreed on a set of demands for presentation to the full Guardian Society membership and for ratification in early March. Assuming ratification occurred, the demands would then be presented to the President of the United States on April fifteenth. The demands were tough, rigid, and non-negotiable. Acceptance of these demands by the President would most likely never occur. However, the Guardian Society members were depending on the financial stability of the country on that day to be so weak that he would have no choice.

Before adjourning the meeting, the leader stood up and began talking, "I thank all of you for your time and input over the last two days. I believe we can all say it was time well spent.

Another item of interest, I'd like to share with each of you, is a fact that should lend encouragement for the success of our cause."

He continued, "One thing that hurt our last effort was the involvement of that jerk from the American Bank Corp. I'm talking about the one they call Mr. Jones, the fellow who slipped unnoticed into our meeting at the Greenbriar. The next time we saw that bastard, he was sitting in the Oval Office, next to the President, when we were summoned there and received the Cease and Desist Order. Mr. Jones also warned Senator Dowd's Senate Banking Committee of our existence back in September."

The leader took a sip of his Perrier and spoke again, "The most recent news is that Mr. Jones, and possibly his girlfriend, did not survive his Citation X crash in the Caribbean last September. If that's true, we will not be bothered with that SOB when we make our move again this April. That's good news for our cause, as he helped put us down before. This information is not well known to the general public."

Continuing, the leader said, "I'm not sure we'll ever again see the conditions and circumstances so perfectly aligned for us to make our move. Our country is in a far worse place than it's been since the 1930's. If we're smart enough and execute our strategy precisely as explained, we'll have the opportunity to reshape the destiny of this country by drastically altering the country's direction. We'll make America safer and more prosperous, and we'll get America's finances corrected so that all Americans can realize the American Dream."

If Jones had overheard the Guardian Society's new plan at their Vegas meeting in February, he would have been horrified. It indicated they were up to their old tricks again. Luckily, he had been warned about it, after the fact by his friend CLEPTO, at Treasury, and he still had time to do something about stopping them in their tracks just like he had done before.

Chapter Twenty-Seven
The Launch

As Mary and Jones continued to refine their strategy and logistics, they were able to relax in the sun the last month they spent in Puerto Vallarta, Finally, the day came when they decided it was time to move forward with their plan.

Mary wrote Reba a note thanking her for the use of her villa and expressed how wonderful their stay had been. Jones left a bundle of hundred-dollar bills in an envelope for Reba on the kitchen table.

Meanwhile, Jones called Richard in Grand Cayman, using a burner phone.

Richard answered right away, "How are you, Mr. Jones? You and Mary all rested up and ready for a fight?"

"Ready as we'll ever get. How about you?"

"Kinda nervous, to tell you the truth. Tell me the plan. What are you going to do? What do you want me to do?

"Here's the plan. I'm going to buy a boat. Mary and I plan to leave here on April first, headed to the Papagayo Peninsula in Costa Rica. It'll take us a few days to get there. It's about a thousand miles. While we're on our boat trip, there's an important matter you must take care of right away."

Jones continued, "I want you to lease another Citation X jet. Put the documentation in one of my lesser known corporations. You can sign the papers as the Executive Vice-President. Get one exactly like I had, the one that crashed. Same color, if possible. If you have any problems finding a jet in the first week or so, call Jetcraft Corporation in Raleigh, NC. Most likely they'll be able to provide us with what we need."

"However, once you lease the jet, you'll need to hire two experienced pilots qualified to fly a Citation X. If anyone asks any questions, tell them that you have a big-time client in Costa Rica, who is working on a major international development deal. Your client requires the use of a private jet that can provide transatlantic travel. Tell them you have been negotiating this transaction over the last three months. Convince them the jet is an instrumental part of the contract. Tell them the time has come to close the deal, because you have finally come to an agreement on terms and conditions. The buyer has only one more condition. He wants you to fly the jet to Costa Rica and pick up two of his top employees. Then he wants you to fly them to London, where you will spend the evening and return the following day."

Richard interrupted, "Jones, how many months will it take you to drive that boat to Costa Rica? That's a damn long boat ride. Mary's gonna hate your ass."

"Don't worry about us. Just do as I ask you to do, and it'll all work out."

"Okay, Jones, but that jet plane story is some wild-ass tale. Were you drunk when you dreamed that up? Do you really believe anyone will buy that garbage? Who's the buyer?"

"The proposed buyer is Enrique Garcia, a billionaire developer who made a fortune by concentrating on resort and plantation development in Latin America. He is a great buddy of Mr. Carlos, what's his name, in Mexico. They spend lots of time together scheming and making money off less than reputable deals. Garcia put up half of the two hundred and fifty million dollars that Mr. Carlos, loaned to the New York Times at the height of the paper's financial crisis in 2009. They got a boat-load of warrants, which were later converted. Mr. Carlos increased his holdings to over sixteen per cent and became the largest shareholder of the New York Times Company. They both know the value of cheap labor and do they ever take advantage. What Garcia is developing on the Papagayo Peninsula in Costa Rica is beyond your imagination, but the labor costs for his projects are minimal. He is a 'something for nothing type' guy!"

"Sounds like a real nice amigo. Is this for real or is it just part of the fabricated story?"

"Of course, the truth is that you're taking the plane to Costa Rica to meet up with Mary and me," explained Jones. "Once we've connected, all three of us will board the Citation X, get the pilots to file a flight plan via New York for London, and take off. The story the pilots will be told is that the "buyer" wanted a test run for the jet. He wanted to see if the jet would serve his purpose of ferrying both investors and buyers from Europe to his Costa Rican developments on the Papagayo Peninsula, where he would close the deals. Mary and I are Garcia's top employees, and he wants us to participate in the test ride. The truth is that we don't plan on coming back anytime soon. Sound good?"

"Jones, you are a master of deceit. I just hope it works. What else do I need to know? Can I bring my girlfriend?"

"Girlfriend? Who is she? How long have you known her, and most importantly, can I trust her?" asked Jones.

"Hell yes, you can trust her," Richard replied. "Tina and I have been a serious item for going on six years now. I'm in love with her, and I think she feels the same about me. Believe me, you certainly don't have to worry about Tina. You guys'll love her once you meet her."

"I don't know, Richard," Jones replied. "Just wish I'd known about her before now."

"Look, Jones," Richard said very abruptly. "I'm not coming with you without Tina."

Jones gave Richard a sharp look and relented.

"Okay, you can bring Tina along and bring extra clothes. You may wind up in England more than one night. Also bring all the documents having to do with the business you took care of for me over there. I'll tell you the rest of the story when I see you in Costa Rica in about two weeks or so. Good luck."

"You're wishing me good luck? Damn, that scares me to death. See you soon, I hope."

Mr. Jones bought a used thirty-one-foot Bertram, a great sports fishing boat with a deep V hull. He and Mary planned to get aboard the Bertram in a couple of days and find their way to the Peninsula Papagayo in Costa Rica. It was going to be a damn long boat ride, for sure. It was time to get started.

Mary was on the dock untying the ropes. She was more than ready to get going. Jones was inside checking out and paying the bill.

As Jones came out of the marina, Mary yelled, "Let's go. It's time to get this ship headed south."

"I agree, Babe. Just hold on a minute. I want to get a newspaper."

After fetching a paper from the machine, Jones ran and jumped on the boat. He tossed the paper onto the table in the galley and went about helping Mary get the Bertram away from the dock and headed out to sea. Initially, they had to head almost due west in order to get beyond the point, so they could then set a southerly course toward Costa Rica.

The Pacific Ocean was a bit rough close to the shore, with too many cross-currents for a smooth ride. It didn't take Jones long to move the sports fishing boat a bit further away from the coastline. Even then, the swells were two to three feet high. Mary wasn't too excited about the conditions at hand.

An hour or so down the coast, the water became calmer and much more suitable for conversation. Mary no longer looked green. She was getting her sea legs.

Jones suggested, "How about a cold beer. I believe I've got everything under control now. Grab two bottles and join me."

"I'll be right there. Gotta get some dry clothes on. This spray is unbelievable."

"I'll wait here for you, but I'm really thirsty."

Five minutes later Mary delivered the beer saying, "You're a real taskmaster, aren't you? You certainly expect a lot from your subordinates."

"Wait a minute, Mary. I've never said or considered you were subordinate to me. That's total BS. I was just giving you a hard time about the beer. Damn, I'll get my own beer from now on."

"Sounds like an excellent idea," laughed Mary.

Changing the subject, Mary continued, "Can you believe the color of the water out here. It's so different from the color of the Atlantic, unless I'm colorblind. It's absolutely beautiful."

"You're not color blind. It's a very different color from the Atlantic. And yes, it is really a beautiful greenish-blue shade." Jones added. "What's on the menu for dinner tonight? Is there something I can cook?"

"Why don't we catch a couple of fish and cook them on the grill? I'll fix slaw and hush puppies. Just thinking about that makes me hungry."

Mr. Jones grinned and replied, "You gonna do the fishing? I've got to drive the boat. Unless you want to."

"No damn way am I going to drive this damn yacht. Never. Not me. Yes, I'll catch the fish, if you'll bait the hooks for me. Please "

"Okay, that's a deal. Open a small can of that tuna in the cabinet by the stove"

Mary continued, "There's one other thing that's so strange. I'm accustomed to going south on the water on the east coast and having the land mass on my right. Here it's the very opposite. We're headed south, and the land mass is on the left. That is very confusing to me."

Jones just laughed and took another swig of his beer.

They had been on the boat a few days when Jones began to hear a strange noise coming from the engine room. He checked it several times, but he never could put his finger on exactly what was making the racket. Also, the noise would come and go.

Early one morning as they were moving south again, the noise became louder and louder. It sounded like it was coming from the inboard engine compartment. Then Jones began to smell something that was burning or getting hot. It was a very strong odor. Mary came running out of the galley, where she was making breakfast and asked, "Do you smell gas? What is it? Are we going to catch on fire and blow up?"

"Christ, Mary. Calm down. Yes, I smell something burning. Gotta figure out where it's coming from."

About that time the motor made a strange sound, and the boat slowed down to nearly half its normal speed. Jones pulled back the cover over the port engine and the heat almost knocked him over. He had found the problem.

"I believe the motor's run hot. It's certainly smoking enough," Jones offered. "Better get to shore fast."

Jones looked at Mary and told her, "It's going to be all right. Luckily, this boat has two engines. We can get to shore with just the starboard engine. We're going to pull into Acapulco, which is about two hours south of here. We'll get the boat fixed there."

"Jones, how do you know so damn much about these boats? Have you owned one before? You're always so certain about what's going on with boats. I don't get it."

"There is a very good reason. I'll explain. I've always liked boating, even as a kid. But most of my early boating experience was with a small sailboat. Then I moved up to a larger sailboat. I became pretty adept at sailing. It wasn't until I got to college and hooked up with Donnie Barden, my roommate and DKE fraternity brother, that I learned about power boats. Everything I know about this boat and other power boats came straight from Donnie. He knows more about power boats than anyone I've ever met. I nicknamed him the 'Ancient Mariner.'"

Mary grinned, as if she understood.

Once they reached a marina in Acapulco, Jones secured the lines and went inside the marina office. He told the owner his problem and asked if he could help. The owner told Jones he'd call his boat mechanic and get him over right away.

Once the boat mechanic had taken a look at the Bertram motor, he told Jones, "The air intake hose on the port engine is clogged up. The motor overheated, and it cracked the engine block. Sorry to have to give you the bad news, but you're going to have to order a new head. Probably take two days before it gets here. I'd count on at least three days before she'll be ready to get back on the water."

"Damn, Damn", snorted Jones. "It's always something. Three days, that's not good at all."

The mechanic replied, "Just tell me what you want me to do. If you want me to fix the motor, I need to get busy ordering the parts. What's your answer?"

"How much money are we talking about here? The parts, your labor, and the shipping charges. Got any idea?"

"It'll kick two thousand dollars in the ass," the mechanic replied. "I'm sure. Twenty-five hundred max."

"Okay," Jones sighed. "Do whatever you have to do. The sooner the better. I'm gonna hold you to no more than twenty-five hundred dollars. Someone really knew what they were talking about when they said, 'Boats are a hole in the water, where you pour lots of money.'"

Mary came up to Jones and the mechanic and asked, "Will the boat be ready by tomorrow?"

"Dream on, my dear," said Jones. "Find us a nice hotel where we can stay a couple of nights. We can't sleep on the boat, while it's being repaired."

Mary walked back inside the marina. She asked the manager if he could recommend a couple of places to sleep and a couple of nice restaurants they could visit. He provided her with both. She started dialing her burner phone. She chose Emporio Acapulco, a nice hotel right on the beach.

Once Mary and Jones had checked into their hotel, they decided they'd take a short nap. Since they were stranded there for at least two days, they were eager to see as much of this famous resort city as possible.

Jones suggested, about half in jest, "You remember, I told you I came here in the summer right after my freshmen year at UNC. I know all the places to go, if you want to have some fun."

"You can stop right there. I don't need to hear any more about you and your fraternity brothers and your sexual escapades, when you were here. I'm surprised you didn't get a disease. I'll decide where we should go. How's that?"

"No mariachi bands? They were so much fun. You're just jealous."

Jones wanted to find Hungry Herman's, where he and his friends ate almost all their meals, when he was there years ago.

Mary suggested, "Why don't we try Tabasco Beach for breakfast tomorrow morning? I think we should dine here at the hotel tonight. Okay with you?"

"It's fine with me. That means we can go to the bar, have a couple of stiff drinks and then have dinner here. Sounds great."

The following night, after exploring the city all day, they got dressed up and disguised up and ventured out on the town. There were nightspots and restaurants everywhere. Finally, after hitting a few bars, they agreed to try ZIBU's for dinner. It was exactly what they were looking for----incredibly delicious seafood of all descriptions.

"Damn, that was good. Best soft-shell crab I've ever had," remarked Jones. "We gotta try their cherries jubilee." And they did.

After dinner they decided to go back to the hotel and have a short nightcap. They re-hashed all of the sights they had seen that day, including the cliffs where the divers plunge for money.

They decided to get up early and check on their boat, hoping it might be ready to go. The mechanic reiterated it'd be another day before the Bertram would be seaworthy.

Mary and Jones spent the morning going from one shop to another. Mary was having a ball. They had a taco lunch along with tequila, then headed back to the motel for a nap. They dined at the hotel that night.

The next morning, Jones packed up their things, including the briefcase of money they'd retrieved from its hiding place in the ceiling. Then they caught a cab back to the marina. The good news was that the Bertram had been repaired, and she was ready to head out to sea again. Jones was so excited he didn't mind paying the twenty-five-hundred-dollar repair bill. He even tipped the mechanic generously.

Once Jones had the boat headed south again, he ducked into the galley to grab a beer. On the table, he saw the newspaper he'd tossed in there a few days ago, when they were leaving the dock at Puerto Vallarta. He went back to the deck, took a swallow of his beer, and began scanning the articles. He turned to the second page of the newspaper, and the headline jumped out at him and smacked him in the mouth. BAM!!

"Jesus Christ! Oh, my lord! This can't be happening, Jones screamed at the top of his lungs."

Mary came flying up to the deck screaming, "What's the matter, Jones? What's wrong? Tell me right now."

"Look for yourself. Right there in the paper. Read that headline."

"Remains Washed Ashore in Melbourne, Florida identified As Those of US Treasury Agents"

Mary grabbed Jones with one hand, put her other hand over her heart and whispered, "Oh my god. It's already begun."

They both knew without reading the article that the body had to be that of CLEPTO, Jones's friend at Treasury. The informant who didn't make it back from the office fishing trip alive!

"I can't wait to hear the rest of that story," Mary sighed. "What kind of lies will they use to cover this up?"

"It just shows you what those bastards will do to keep their crimes from going public," Jones answered. "Believe me, they'll stop at nothing."

Bill Brown

Chapter Twenty-Eight
The Preparation

Meanwhile, back on Grand Cayman, Richard was on overload. Mr. Jones had given him too many instructions, too many tasks. Hell, he had only a couple of weeks to work everything out, before having to leave to meet Jones and Mary in Costa Rica.

First, he needed to start interviewing qualified and experienced jet pilots immediately. That was not going to be easy, finding two compatible guys that could work together from the beginning. Richard rang up Zee, a solutions company, and gave Erik Duke, the head of the company, his requirements. He agreed to pay extra for immediate service. Duke said he'd be back to him in a day with probable interview clients. Richard knew Duke, an ex-Navy Seal, would only send pilots who had cleared top secret background checks.

Next Richard decided against calling around to try and lease a Citation X and took Jones's advice. He called Jetcraft Corporation in Raleigh, NC. After about an hour on the phone with some guy named John, explaining in detail what he wanted, Richard struck a deal for a leased Citation X. Richard was relieved. John told Richard he'd call him in advance of delivering the jet.

Over the next three days, Richard met with six potential hires. The first two pilots he interviewed were not at all what he thought Jones would want. One was way too cocky and pretty much a wise guy. The other one had no personality and way too many personal problems.

The next day Richard found one pilot that had possibilities. He was about fifty years old and had thousands of hours flying international flights. He had been the captain in most jobs where he had been contracted. Two more interviews the following day were futile.

It took one more full day before Richard found another pilot he liked and respected. He was a little younger, but he exuded confidence and had a great deal of flying experience. He had lots of hours logged flying private jet aircraft all over the world. Richard informed Duke the terms of the pilot's employment and what their mission would be. He asked Duke to contract those two pilots as soon as possible. He didn't want them to get away. *Jones is going to love these two guys,* Richard thought.

Richard thought hiring two pilots was tough, until he told his live-in girlfriend of six years what he was getting ready to do. Their relationship had become quite serious, and Richard realized he certainly did not want to lose Tina. He flat out asked her to quit her job and go with him to London. She went berserk.

Tina Morales was born in Puerto Rico. She graduated from the University of Miami and moved to Grand Cayman seven years earlier. She was much younger than Richard, but that didn't matter to either of them.

Tina had worked her way up to become the Assistant Director of Tourism. The job fit her personality perfectly. She spent every day ensuring tourists who visited Grand Cayman could have a wonderful time. She had never met a stranger, was most attractive, effervescent, and smart---what a combination.

Tina's main objection to Richard's request was that they were not married, nor had they ever talked about it. She thought things were just great like they were. More importantly, she had a great job, lots of security, and she was making a very good living doing exactly what she loved doing every day. She wondered how could she leave all that, and what would happen to her if she left?

A week before Richard planned to leave for Costa Rica, he took Tina to dinner in Georgetown, hoping they could come to an understanding about the trip to London. He had not told her the whole story. She didn't know about Jones and Mary, much less their dangerous situation. In fact, she had never met them.

Once they were seated in their favorite neighborhood restaurant, Richard began the conversation, "Let's have a glass or two of wine before we order our meal. Does that suit you, Tina?"

"You say that every time we go out for dinner," replied Tina. "Of course, that's fine with me."

"Is it going to be red or white tonight?" asked Richard.

" I believe I'd rather have white tonight," Tina answered.

"White it is. I'll order a Russian River Chardonnay, just for you. You deserve it."

After they relaxed with a couple of glasses of wine, they agreed on what they'd order. Surprisingly, they both chose fresh pan-seared scallops and Caesar salads.

"We're fairly easy on the waiter tonight," Richard remarked, as he ordered two more glasses of wine.

After they had finished their perfectly prepared entrees, the conversation got serious.

"Look, Tina, I have a great opportunity to assist one of my clients in closing a big international business deal with a wealthy developer who lives in Costa Rica. The developer wants two of his assistants to take a private jet on a test flight to London. He wants them to determine if a leased Citation X jet would be suitable for ferrying both investors and buyers to his developments in and around the Papagayo Peninsula. If it suits, he will close the deal with my client immediately."

Richard continued, "Both assistants are Senior Vice Presidents of Enrique Garcia's development company. One is Mr. Jones. He is the Sales and Marketing person. The other is a young female attorney. Her name is Janie Brown. She's in charge of Investor Relations. They'll decide if the plane will service Enrique Garcia's needs. So be nice to them, please."

"I'm always nice to people, unless I have reason not to be."

"I know you are, Tina. Just be yourself."

"So why do you have to go? Why is it so important that I go with you? I don't understand. There must be something I'm missing."

How perceptive, Richard thought.

"Tina, if the deal closes, I'll receive a very large commission. Very large. Not to mention how excited my major client will be. Hell, to put it simply, I'll have enough money, so you can quit your job and we can go to London and stay for as long as we want. From there we could travel around Europe. Maybe we could lease a villa in Venice and live there for a while. How can you pass up that kind of offer?"

"Okay, I get the picture," Tina replied. "Why can't I just take a leave of absence or some vacation days? Why do you insist on me quitting my job? You've said absolutely nothing about us, our relationship, our future. Where does that fit in here? Can or will you please explain that?"

Richard squirmed in his seat, before he responded, "Tina, can't you read between the lines? Don't you see where I'm going with this? How about we get married in London or maybe Venice? Your choice."

"Damn, Richard. Is that a proposal? Are you asking me to marry you? Is that your question?" she asked.

"Hell, yes!" Richard replied. "Will you marry me? There, I've said it!"

"I hope you know what the hell you are doing," answered Tina, "because the answer is a great big fat YES! I love you, Richard. I really love you. When do we leave?"

Richard got out of his seat and grabbed Tina in a very long hug, saying, "I love you, too. We're going to be so happy together."

"When do we leave? Richard, you must give me all the details, so I'll know how to pack, what clothes to take, and all that kind of stuff. Can I pack two or three suitcases? Is that too many?"

"Just take enough to last a few days," Richard replied. "Whatever else you may need, we'll buy in Europe. How does that sound, Tina?"

"Best offer I've had in years," Tina said. "My dream come true, Richard. We're going to be so happy. Should I give my two weeks' notice yet?"

"Two weeks? Hell, Tina, we'll be leaving as soon as possible. Tell your boss tomorrow that you're resigning immediately. That's the only choice you have now."

Tina's lower lip curled up in total disgust as she spoke, "That's not the proper way to treat people, who have been so good to me. I'd feel awful doing that... not giving a notice."

"It's just the way things are, Tina. I know it's not the right thing to do, but you'll just have to quit, in order to go with me to Europe. That's it."

"Okay, Richard. I'll resign tomorrow, but I don't like it one bit. It just doesn't feel right to me."

"Hopefully, things will turn out for the best, and one day you'll look back and know that you did the right thing," Richard remarked, trying to make her feel more comfortable with his request and her decision.

Over the next few days Richard went full-blast trying to tie up all the loose ends, not just for Mr. Jones, but for himself as well. If they weren't coming back any time soon, he had to make sure he left things in good order. He listed Mr. Jones's villa for sale with an old realtor friend. He relocated the Fountain boat to another marina and put a price on it that he thought would bring a buyer quickly. Then he made sure all necessary documents were in order and in place for him to leave. He had to remember the disguise items Jones had mentioned. There were lots of items on his "to do" list and he was checking them off one at a time.

Richard's phone rang, as he walked into his office door. "Hello, this is Richard."

"Hi, Richard. It's John from Jetcraft Corporation in Raleigh, NC. I'm glad I caught up with you today. Just wanted to put you on notice that we'll be delivering your leased Citation X to Grand Cayman the day after tomorrow. Everything is in order. Zee's personal security pilots' backgrounds check out with us. Your payment method has been accepted, and all we need is your signature to close the deal. Will you be available to meet us in the General Aviation lobby about 2 pm?"

"Fantastic," Richard replied. "I'll be there. "I'm pleased you were able to accommodate me so quickly."

"Believe me, the pleasure is ours," John responded. "See you in two days. Goodbye".

Richard arranged for the pilots to meet him two days later at the General Aviation section of the airport. They had been there about thirty minutes, when they were informed that the Citation X was making its final approach for landing.

Once the jet arrived in front of the terminal, Richard and the two pilots went aboard to check it out. It was an exact replica of Jones's jet, which crashed back in September. It was the same color, the same year model, the same Series Class, and it had the same number of passenger seats.

Although unnecessary, the two pilots were given an instructional run-through by the Jetcraft representative, who had delivered the plane. Everything was in order, and Richard's pilots were comfortable that the jet was in perfect condition.

Richard found John, the Jetcraft representative, and they signed the contract. The deal was done.

Time to go to Costa Rica, Richard thought.

Chapter Twenty-Nine

The Hookup

The last night on the Bertram before reaching Costa Rica, Jones and Mary enjoyed grouper, which she had caught and grilled. To avoid negative conversation, Jones began by asking, "Mary, do you know anything about Costa Rica? Ever been there before?"

"Never."

"Would you like me to enlighten you a bit?"

"Sometimes you're so damn arrogant, Jones, that you become offensive," replied Mary. "Can't we just have a nice conversation without you sticking your head up your rear end? That would be much more enjoyable."

"Would you like me to enlighten you a bit?" She mimicked Jones's control tactics.

"Calm down, Babe," Jones said. "I was simply being my usual smart-ass self, just to get a reaction. Sorry to have offended you, my dear. Now, would you like to hear about Costa Rica?"

"Sure, Mr. Travel Guide. Enlighten me! Let's hear all about your new favorite country," retorted Mary. "Who knew I'd become an expert globetrotter--me, a lawyer--helping you avoid a contract on your life and becoming a target myself in the meantime. Too much, Jones, too much."

Jones took Mary's cue and deftly steered the conversation to neutral.

He began, "Well, it seems the Costa Rican government has finally realized the value of eco- tourism and is taking full advantage of that fact. Real estate has skyrocketed, and it's become a playground for rich foreigners.

"Since the country is partially located in the rain forest, Howler monkeys might wake you up each morning. We'll dock at the Marina Papagayo. The area is famous for its world-class beaches," Jones declared stiffly.

"Often we'll be greeted by natives with the phrase, 'Pura Vida," meaning 'Pure Life.' Expatriates live there to surf, chill out, smoke pot, and enjoy that 'Pure Life.' Developers are really raking in the dough."

"Thank you, Professor," mused Mary. "Now, I have my Masters in Central American Culture."

Jones poured them both another glass of Valley of the Moon Chardonnay and said, "Mary, I'd like to get serious for a moment and tell you what I've concluded relative to this whole Federal heist debacle. I want to tell you now, because I'm not sure Richard and his girlfriend are ready for what I'm about to say."

"Haven't seen you this serious in days," Mary replied. "This oughta be rich. Can't wait to hear your take on all of this."

"As you know, Mary," declared Jones, "over the past several weeks, I've taken a real close look at the financial data on the thumb drive we got from my friend, CLEPTO, at Treasury, and it just blows me away. During the years I spent in banking, I met and got to know several genuine high rollers, legitimate movers and shakers, and many extremely wealthy people. Because of those associations, I can understand the outrageous aspects of the robbery a little better than the average person on the street.

"Most Americans would scoff at the idea that anyone, much less our Federal agency heads and Congressmen, would or could steal such enormous amounts of money. Most Americans have no way of relating to the huge sums of cash that were stolen.

"However, in reviewing the data, the amounts of stolen money that were funneled to an array of recipients around the world is mind-boggling from two different perspectives. One is how much money some individuals received. Two is the number of different groups around the world that were included in the split. Several dozen Senators and Congressmen hauled in over one hundred million dollars each. To that category, add several members of our US

Federal agencies. The Guardian Society had numerous takers in the fifty-million-dollar class. American and international foundations were also enriched by millions upon millions of dollars. Many national and international corporations, including banking dynasties, were blessed with several billion dollars each. Even more surprising, there were a dozen or so foreign governments that wound up with billions of US dollars. It is inconceivable that this actually happened, but when you drop a few billion here and a few billion there, pretty soon you're talking trillions.

I have no doubt at all that this happened, especially when you see the net worth of so many members of Congress exceeding fifty or even one hundred million dollars. Yet their annual salaries are a bit less than two hundred thousand dollars a year. That just doesn't equate, at least not for me.

"Based on what I just said, the one interesting aspect of this charade that never occurred to me until after I really studied the data is the incredible number of people involved. That fact alone convinced me beyond any doubt that this whole heist is part and parcel of the New World Order or One World Order, whatever they now call their global classification. You know the group, the people that push for one world government, one world currency, and many other less than democratic principles; all in an effort to enhance and maintain their power, wealth, and elitism. Nothing else makes any sense. Nothing. Now, if I'm correct about this, and it actually is all about the New World Order, well, our country is in the most dangerous place it's been since Pearl Harbor. In other words, like then, these domestic traitors, along with their foreign accomplices, are not only planning America's demise, but they have already initiated an attack against our financial system, which when exposed, may very well bring our monetary structure to an end.

There is no doubt that replacing the US dollar as the universal currency has been their goal for years. The IMF has proposed that idea for sometime.

"Hell, they may be even making room for cryptocurrency, a

monetary network that takes place peer to peer, without any intermediary, exchanging digital currency. It could become a worldwide payment system that would be completely decentralized and without a central bank. It could possibly become a simple worldwide currency."

Jones, where are you getting all of this crazy information? Are you making this up?" Mary asked.

"Jones continued, ignoring Mary's question, "Somewhere in the back of my mind, something tells me this is somehow connected to the Wanta Fund debacle, and to the people who were involved. I've heard for years that one day that incredible financial scandal would be widely exposed."

"Wanta Fund?" Mary asked. "What the hell are you talking about? You've completely lost me with that one."

Jones responded, "I've picked up bits and pieces of this story over the years. I discovered a lot of this information in the book *Wanta! Black Swan, White Hat*. It goes like this. During the Reagan Administration, Leo Wanta, one of Reagan's special agents, was quite instrumental and heavily involved in the financial downfall and collapse of the Soviet Union. When Russia fell, Wanta amassed some twenty-seven trillion dollars in gold and cash. Wanta had agreed with Reagan that this fortune was scheduled to be returned to the US Treasury to reduce the national debt, to pay for a complete overhaul of the nation's infrastructure, as well as underwrite a nation-wide high speed rapid-rail transit system.

"However, with a change in Administrations, Wanta was abducted and illegally imprisoned in Switzerland. A year later he was transferred to the US, where he, on a trumped-up charge, was convicted of income tax evasion and sentenced to twenty years in a prison in Wisconsin. The twenty-seven trillion dollars remains in foreign banks, including the Bank of England. Many members of Congress on both sides of the aisle, even today, have huge bank balances in the Old Lady of Threadneedle Street, as the Bank of England is commonly called.

"A few years later, a large amount of the Wanta Fund, by sleight of hand and with the help of the Federal Reserve System, ended up in the Arco Trust Corporation in Texas. Doesn't take a rocket scientist to figure out that connection. Supposedly, some of the funds have been used to pay for assassinations, wars, bribery payoffs, and drug running---you name it. The next four administrators, who all had insatiable appetites for cash, kept the Wanta Fund and the Arco Trust at bay for their own benefit over the next twenty-eight years.

"For almost thirty years, Lee Wanta, now 78 years old, and some guy named Tom Heneghan, along with the sole help of the French government, have struggled diligently to get the twenty- seven trillion dollars back into the US. By now this fortune, still stashed in foreign banks and in the Arco Trust, has ballooned to over sixty trillion dollars! According to my sources, the Arco Trust account was just recently frozen by our government. Rumor has it that this money, after all of these years, is coming back to the US. If this happens, the repercussions may very well be devastating to many people that are involved. A great deal of this saga was written up in a book titled *PuppetGate*, by Lon Gibby who refers to Wanta's autobiography titled *Wanta! Black Swan, White Hat*, or something like that. I read that book and a bit later I stumbled across the official biography of Wanta titled *American Wanta Be Free* by Marilyn Barnewall. The information detailed in those three books, if even slightly true, paints an incredible mosaic of crime, avarice, greed, deception, international thievery, and elitism. What we're dealing with today is just a continuation of what came before with the Wanta Fund and the Puppet Masters, who are the same corrupt people with the same corrupt MO, only in another time. I really do believe that all of this is tied together. Should the American people ever get the complete story of this massive financial scam, you can look out for another American Revolution."

Mary, reeling from Jones's revelations, responded, "Jones, that is the most mind-numbing information I've ever heard. It's the most elucidating example of deductive reasoning or logical deduction that I've ever encountered in all my days of practicing law. I honestly believe you have uncovered the Holy Grail of the New World Order. There's no doubt in my mind that you are spot-on correct."

"All the more reason to bring these robber-barons to justice," offered Jones. "Well said, my dear," Mary answered.

"Are you going to share your theory with Richard and his friend," Mary asked.

"I'll tell them once this is all over, and we're all safe," declared Jones.

Finally, as Jones slowed the Bertram and steered it toward the shore, they arrived in Costa Rica. He docked the Bertram at the Marina Papagayo. It was seven am, the twelfth of April. He and Mary went inside the office, and Jones paid the docking fee for a month in advance. The briefcase that Richard brought Jones after the crash was still half full of money and coming in quite handy. Paying in cash seemed like a normal practice here, since no one said anything unusual. Mary asked where they might get a cab and was given a number to call. While she called the cab company, Jones went back to the boat and fetched their luggage.

The Peninsula Papagayo was without a doubt one of the most gorgeous properties Mr. Jones had ever seen. No wonder wealthy developers were interested in this large swath of land here on the Pacific Coast of Guanacaste Province. The Papagayo Four Seasons stuck in his mind. It was a spot he planned to bring Mary back to when all of this was finally over.

The cab arrived shortly. Jones tossed their luggage in the trunk, opened the door for Mary, and directed the driver, "Take us to the DHL office in Liberia. It's a few doors down from the Boyeros Hotel."

The driver responded, saying, "Yes, that's the one. It should be open by the time we get there. It'll take us about forty-five minutes. Is that satisfactory?"

Mary piped in, "That sounds perfecto. We'll want you to wait there for us, por favor. It'll take about fifteen minutes for us to take care of our business, if that's okay, Senor."

"What the hell's with all that Spanish?" Jones laughed. "You sound like a fool."

"Leave me alone, you old goat. I'm trying to be bilingual. You're just jealous."

"Don't believe you have the accent down exactly right, yet. But please keep trying, senorita." Arriving in Liberia, Jones spotted the DHL sign and ordered the driver to stop and wait for them.

Jones turned to Mary and asked, "How do you say DHL in Spanish?" as he started laughing out loud. The cab driver was amused, as well.

As they walked in, Jones was pulling the tapes from his briefcase and checking to see that he had all of them. Each one was labelled with the name and address of the intended recipient.

Mary moved over to the customer service counter and asked for assistance. She told the man behind the counter exactly what they wanted to do, and when she asked him to help, he agreed.

Jones spoke right up, "We want all these tapes delivered to the addresses as soon as possible. Guaranteed. No exceptions. No matter what it costs. They need to be sent in such a manner that the addressee must be the person to accept and sign for the package, however you do that."

The DHL agent responded, "Not to worry, Sir. We can do exactly as you have asked. We'll send them via International Courier, so not only will they be delivered on the day you have requested, but also, they'll be handed only to the person who can be identified as the addressee on the package. Sound good so far?"

"Excellent. Perfect," added Mary. "We'd like to make sure there is NO return address on any of the packages. Can you do that? The reason is logical. We will not be here long."

"I'm not sure about that. I'll have to ask my manager. Just a minute, I'll be right back." Jones commented, "I can't believe there would be a problem with that, can you?"

Mary answered, "Don't know if there is a problem. Let's just wait and see what he says. "

The DHL agent returned and said, "We can put this DHL location as the return address. Is that okay?"

Jones looked at Mary and said, "You're the lawyer. You decide."

"That'll be just fine. Now, how much is it going to cost to ship these seven tapes to New York City, Washington, DC, and Charlotte, North Carolina? Please make certain that they'll be sent as you stated via International Courier to arrive the day after tomorrow, guaranteed."

The DHL agent began entering the delivery addresses of all of the packages into his machine. Then he asked Jones to verify each address. Jones did as asked. Then the agent said, "The total will be four hundred and sixty-eight dollars. How would you like to pay for this service, Sir?"

Jones opened his wallet and pulled out five one hundred-dollar bills and handed them to the clerk.

Mary had a quick thought, *suppose that might be counterfeit money?*

The clerk gave Jones his change and asked him to sign the shipping order. Jones slid the paper over to Mary saying, "Sign this, I forgot my glasses."

Mary gave Jones a quizzical look, and then signed the shipping order....Janie Brown.

They got back in the cab and Jones told the driver, "We need to go to the Liberia International Airport General Aviation, or wherever the private jets land.

"No problem. You know it'll take about fifteen minutes. Okay?"

"Sure," offered Mary. "We're in no hurry. We just completed the most important task we've ever undertaken in our lives. I don't know whether I should cry, scream, or celebrate."

"It'll probably take some of all three before this is over," Jones declared. "We've got lots left to do."

The cab driver turned on his meter and drove off. Once arriving at the airport, he turned at the sign that read Private Aviation. When he saw the building with a sign that read OFFICIO, he pulled into a parking spot close to the door. Jones was looking out the window to see if he could spot his jet.

"There it is. Two planes over," Jones said. "See it Mary? Gosh, it looks just like the one that crashed."

"Yes, Jones, I can see the jet. Let's get going. The sooner we get the hell out of here, the better off we'll be."

After paying the cabbie, Jones said, "Let's go inside and find Richard. I hope he's got everything organized and ready to go. I'll get the bags."

"I'd bet he's all prepared and ready to go. He's always on time," Mary replied.

As they entered the lobby of the general aviation facility, Jones spotted Richard across the room. He was holding a cup of coffee and chatting up a young lady. She had shiny black hair, and she was quite shapely. Actually, she was very attractive, and at five foot-seven she was statuesque. *Sure like to see her naked,* Jones thought. *Then he slapped himself mentally for being such a horrible voyeur. Even with all the stress he was experiencing, his testosterone was still raging.* Richard, grinning, knew exactly what Jones was thinking.

Richard moved forward and spoke to Mary and Jones, "Guys, this is Tina Morales. We've been an item for more than six years. She was the Assistant Director of Tourism for Grand Cayman. I had to promise her the moon to get her to quit her job and come along, but she's here."

"Tina, this is Janie Brown and Mr. Jones. They represent Mr. Enrique Garcia, the wealthy developer, who wants them to advise him about about this plane. They'll be on our flight to London."

Everyone shook hands and made small talk. Richard suggested everyone visit the powder room and get ready to board. He stated that they'd be airborne in just a few minutes.

While the men went off to the restroom, Mary excused herself from Tina's presence for a minute, walked over to the corner of the room, and pulled a burner phone from her pocketbook. She sent a one-line text to her sister, saying, "In Costa Rica with Jones. Doing well. Will call tonight. Tell Mom."

In the men's room, Richard told Jones, "I took your advice and called the Jetcraft Corporation in Raleigh. I didn't realize they were the largest seller of private planes in the world. Do they ever have a fleet! I found the exact Citation you asked for, and I was able to lease it for a great price. Your name doesn't appear on any of the paperwork. So even if the authorities are checking in New York when we refuel, they'll not find any connection to you. By the way, how the hell did you know about Jetcraft?"

Jones replied, "The founder of the company is another one of my older DKE fraternity brothers. His buddies call him Bucko. He took over the Fixed Base Operations at the Raleigh airport in nineteen sixty-two and acquired his first four Lear Jets in 1970. The rest is history," explained Jones. "Great job, Richard."

"I told Tina and the two jet pilots that you and Mary were representing the developer. I didn't want to expose your full identifies for obvious reasons. If Tina knew the truth, she wouldn't have agreed to go with me to London. Thankfully, all three bought my story--- hook, line, and sinker."

"It's great to see you, Richard. I really appreciate all you've done for Mary and me. Setting up this trip is a big deal. Thanks for the cover story. I'll clue Mary in. You did the right thing,"

"Well, I tried to do what you asked me to do. So far, everything has worked out. Just hope it continues."

"By the way, where have you been hiding Tina for six years? She's dynamite!"

"Like to keep my personal life separate from my business life. Now they're merged," replied Richard.

"We better get going. It's time to for us to get out of Costa Rica. Mary and I just shipped the tapes before coming to the airport."

"Ten-four. Let's rock and roll, as y'all say."

Chapter Thirty

The Trip Abroad

About 8:15 am the Citation lifted off. After the pilots made their final adjustments, the aircraft was headed northeast. The captain told his passengers the flight would take eleven hours, barring any serious headwinds or inclement weather.

The captain continued, "It's about a 5,500-mile trip. This Citation X's flight range is only thirty-five hundred miles. We'll fly into Kennedy International in New York, which is approximately a five-hour trip, where we'll refuel and depart for London. That's a six-plus hour flight. We'll be landing at Gatwick International Airport about 10:30 pm., BST. It's a thirty-minute taxi ride to central London. Enjoy the flight."

"Well, at least it won't be after midnight when we get there," Mary said. "Maybe we'll have time for a nightcap, somewhere interesting before hitting the sack."

"Sounds like a great idea, Janie," Tina mused.

"Maybe a bite to eat as well."

"Don't count your chickens too early, girls," offered Richard. "Gotta get there first."

"Will you chill out, please," asked Jones.

"I'm trying to concentrate."

"Why so serious, Mr. Jones?" Richard uttered."What's on your mind? Thinking about the plane?" He was trying to keep the false story going.

"The interior is certainly first class and luxurious. What else could you ask for?" added Mary, who was also trying to keep the false narrative alive.

"The jet's perfect, so far, "agreed Jones. "Just need to relax and take it all in. We're gonna be on this plane for quite a while before we touchdown at Gatwick."

It wasn't long before the pilots reached their assigned cruising altitude and turned on the autopilot control system.

For the first few hours of the flight, Mary and Tina chatted up one another. They exchanged background stories in getting to know how they all met and came together. Tina still called Mary, 'Janie,' since she was the only one out of the four, who did not know the real story.

Mary did a great job at playing her part as the VP in charge of Investor Relations for the Costa Rican development company. It came quite natural for Mary, because she just expounded on what she had actually done over the years as an attorney on Wall Street.

When the cabin conversation included Jones, he was quick to continue their disguise by talking about his role as VP in charge of Sales and Marketing. He explained, "Enrique Garcia is about to close a big land deal on Peninsula Papagayo. If he does indeed buy this land, he's planned a multi-purpose, mixed-use development that would include hotels, residential homes, condos, townhouses, a golf course, and commercial spaces. To support this massive development, Garcia knows he'll need investors and buyers from other parts of the world.

Mainly, he thinks Europe is his best market. To get buyers and investors to his project, Garcia realizes that he must provide quick, easy, and convenient travel for these potential participants.

Therein lies his reason for checking out a private jet's ability to ferry these folks comfortably on transatlantic flights."

"In a nutshell, that's why we're making this test run," Mr. Jones added.

Tina spoke up, saying, "Jones you explained this so much better than Richard did. It makes sense. Now I know why we're going to London. Thank you."

"Wait a minute, Tina, "Richard objected. "I told you everything I knew at the time. Give me a break, please. I didn't know all those details about the development part Mr. Jones talked about. That's his job, not mine."

Mary responded, "Everybody just calm down. We're going to London, and we're gonna have a great time. Now, let's talk about something else."

The captain's voice came over the intercom, "Ladies and gentlemen, we have begun our descent into Kennedy International. In about fifteen minutes we'll be landing. So please fasten your seat belts until the plane comes to a complete stop. We'll only be refueling, so there is no reason to deplane. After thirty minutes or so on the ground, we'll be airborne again, headed for Gatwick International Airport outside of London. Thank you."

"That's means we're about half-way there," remarked Jones. "So far so good, wouldn't you say, Richard?"

"I agree whole heartedly," replied Richard. "The best is yet to come, I think."

Tina looked at Richard and gave him one of those "what the hell are you talking about?" kind of looks.

Mary just grinned at Jones.

Once the Citation was on the ground, Jones got up and opened the storage cabinet and the refrigerator. He handed everyone a bottle of water, a soda, a sandwich bag, and some cookies.

"It's lunch time in New York, so enjoy," Mary said. "Hopefully, our dinner in London tonight will be be a bit more upscale."

"There's nothing wrong with these snacks," Tina declared. "Best rare roast beef sandwich I've had today."

"About time for a nap," Richard suggested. "We'll move up to the front, once we take off for Gatwick. That way we'll all have a little more privacy. Be sure and wake me up at cocktail time."

"Good idea, Richard," added Jones. "Janie and I'll move to the back of the plane. Maybe take a nap. Maybe some conversation. Yes, wake me up for cocktails, too."

It wasn't long before the Citation, completely refueled, lifted off from Kennedy Airport. No Federal authorities knew the Citation X was leased to one of Mr. Jones's entities. Neither did they know that

Mr. Jones and Mary were onboard headed to Europe. London was their next stop. Just six or so more hours to a more secure environment.

Soon all four passengers were asleep. The pilots set their course as the jet climbed to its assigned cruising altitude of thirty-eight thousand feet. Shortly, the jet was traveling at five hundred miles per hour with a strong tailwind.

Three hours later, Jones woke up ready to talk to Mary about what they needed to do next. He shook Mary.

"What's up?" Mary asked. "How much longer before we land?"

"About another hour or so," responded Jones. "Wake up, we need to chat. Here is what I think we need to do once we land."

"Go ahead and tell me, Jones. I'm all ears," replied Mary, as she struggled to open her eyes.

"Once we get cleared inside the terminal at Gatwick, we need to get out our computer, and using our personal Hotspot, we need to check to make sure our secret email site is working. I expect we'll be getting "hot" messages in a day or so from the targets who received our tapes. Don't think it'll take long for them to respond.

Based on their responses to our demands, we'll reply accordingly. It'll probably take a couple of days for all of this to shake out. Once we know who agrees to pay, we'll confirm the amounts that have indeed been wired to our accounts in Luxembourg."

"Then what do we do?" Mary queried. "How do we get the money?"

"When we determine for sure the ransom money has been paid, we can access the funds at any time, according to the rules of the Luxembourg bank. They only charge a 1% fee to move money in or out of the account."

"What happens next? When do we send the thumb drives?" Mary inquired.

Jones answered, "Once we believe we've extracted all we might ever get from these corrupt institutions, we'll send the thumb drives, containing the damaging financial data, to all of the news media outlets we talked about earlier. We must make sure that the WSJ, NYT, LA Times, Washington Post, CNN, ABC, CBS, NBC, BBC, and Fox News all get a thumb drive."

"Then we send the thumb drives with last year's Super Bowl game to the Feds and to the Bank," added Mary. "They'll have absolute strokes, when they plug them into their computers."

Jones remarked quite seriously, "The day the media outlets release the thumb drive information to the public, an absolute financial storm will engulf the world. We must be ready for the repercussions."

The captain came on over the intercom and announced that they were beginning their descent into Gatwick International Airport. He stated that they would be on the ground in approximately thirty-one minutes.

All four passengers were feeling some relief.

Bill Brown

Chapter Thirty-One

The Clarification

Precisely at 10:30 pm BST, the Citation X pulled into its designated gate at Gatwick General Aviation Terminal. Once the foursome de-planed and found their way to the lobby, Jones opened his computer bag and logged onto the internet using his Iridium Hot Spot.

"There it is," he pointed to the computer screen for everyone to see. "The email site is alive and well." Tina did not understand.

"Richard, help me with these bags, so I can find our limo," Jones pleaded.

"No problem," said Richard. "I'll take care of the bags. You fetch the chauffeur."

Mary spoke up, "Does anyone know where we're going? Are we staying in London tonight?"

Richard chimed in, "I booked us rooms at the Stafford. A real nice hotel where we can check in, and then we'll meet later for drinks and a fine dinner. Sound good?"

"Sounds okay to me," offered Tina. "So glad we're not going out tonight, I'm exhausted."

Soon the two couples were in a chauffeured limousine, laughing about the steering wheel being on the "wrong," but right side of the vehicle.

Upon arriving at the Stafford, the bellmen took care of their luggage, while Richard checked them in. Then they were off to their respective suites in the ultra-private Mews.

Richard offered, "Let's meet at the American Bar in thirty minutes. It's open until one o'clock in the morning. We can have drinks plus something to eat."

Jones and Mary nodded in agreement. Richard and Tina made it to the bar first.

As they were being seated, Tina spoke directly to Richard, "I want you to damn well know that I'm not your average garden-variety fool. Furthermore, I damn sure don't like being treated like one. So why don't you and your two fake friends just cut out all of your lies and tell me what the hell is going on, now."

"There's no problem with that, Tina," Richard answered. "When Mr. Jones and Janie join us, we'll all explain everything you want to and should know. I promise."

Upon approaching the table, both Mr. Jones and Mary could sense the friction, the tense undercurrent.

"What's the problem?" Jones asked. "We don't need any bad vibes or bad blood or any negative thoughts between any of us. We're all one team, and we must all stand together in order to survive together."

Tina's facial color became very pale at Jones's remark.

Grasping the vibes from Tina, Mary interrupted, "Let me explain to Tina exactly what the deal is. If you will let me explain it, she'll understand the total situation."

Richard said, "Have at it, Mary. Don't leave anything out. Let's order drinks before you start."

Jones piped in, "Proceed, barrister. Do your stuff." He told the waiter, "I'll have a Jack on the rocks." The other three ordered dry martinis.

Mary began by explaining, "First of all, since neither Jones nor I knew anything about you, we really didn't know how much you might know about us or about Jones's plane crash. Jones and I trust Richard completely, and he was determined to bring you along. So we decided, just to be safe, to make up this total charade. Mary Whitmore is my real name. Jones and I have had a serious relationship over the past several years. I was a practicing attorney in New York, when I met Jones. He had an executive position in New York with a major bank, headquartered in North Carolina."

She explained in detail Jones's obsession with seeking revenge against the corrupt banking industry for what had happened to his mother.

Mary continued, "The broker/client relationship between Jones and Richard started way back in 1977. They've been trusted business associates and damn good friends for a very long time."

Mary gave Tina an overview of what had transpired with the US financial collapse in 2008, and what had transpired since. She explained that Mr. Jones had testified before the US Senate Banking Committee in September of last year.

She told Tina, "What Jones divulged in his testimony sent shock waves through most of the US Federal agencies. The results of Jones's testimony totally exposed to the world just how corrupt not only the US financial system is, but also the international banking system. Those powers want us dead! That's why we are on the run. That's why we're afraid for our lives, and now yours and Richards."

Then Mary told Tina about the crash of Jones's Citation X in the Caribbean back in September: how it had been taken down by a bomb, how Richard picked up Jones at the wreckage site before the rescue workers arrived, how they made it to Veracruz and then back to the US. She described their stay in Nantucket and their visit to Sugar Hollow in Tennessee. She explained how their sideways travel plans back to Veracruz, their stopover in Puerto Vallarta, and their arrival in Costa Rica were their way of escaping detection.

Mary said, "Richard deserves credit for everything he has done to help Jones and me survive. Really. He has honestly gone far beyond the call of duty. You've got to know how much Jones and I appreciate his friendship and his support. Jones needed him to tag along for his help, but he wouldn't come with us without you."

Mary assured Tina, "Richard has conveyed to us his love and admiration for you. You must realize it was only for the safety and well-being of all four of us that we had to concoct this wild- ass story as to why we needed to fly to England."

Finally, Mary briefly explained to Tina the actions the three of them had initiated and put in place to counteract the very real and dangerous threat against their lives. Tina was told about the tapes that had already been sent and the ransom demands that had been made. She also told Tina about the thumb drives that included information from CLEPTO on the theft of $17 trillion from the US Treasury. Mary further stated that all of this information would be sent to the US media.

"I honestly hope that you understand the necessity for the fake news narrative and that you will forgive Jones, Richard, and me for our part in deceiving you," Mary told Tina.

"From now on, please call me Mary. Please know and believe me when I say that Richard went along with the deception only because he was afraid you wouldn't come along, if you knew the real danger involved."

"One more thing," Mary said as she looked straight at Tina.

"It seems like we're both on the road to the altar. Congratulations."

With tears streaming down her face, Tina wiped her eyes and said, "This is overwhelming. It's mind-boggling. This is scary as hell. I just don't know what to say. I'm totally flabbergasted.

Yes, Thank you. But I'd sure like to get married before I get killed."

Richard reached over and grabbed Tina's hand, saying, "Please believe us. Please trust us. We're doing the only thing we think will save our lives and bring the corrupt Establishment to its knees. Tina, you've got to understand that I love you and need you to be one of the team."

Tina responded, "I'm really not as dumb as it may seem. As for the plane crash, I was on emergency leave visiting my sick mother in Puerto Rica when that occurred. Basically, I missed the ensuing newspaper articles with your photos. However, I did see or hear something on TV about it later, but it didn't register with me at all. For the six years or so that I have been with Richard, before all of this came up, I never not even once, heard him speak about a client. He's very tight-lipped about his business associates."

Jones interrupted, saying, "That's quite understandable. For the past ten or twelve years, I have been busy with my bank job, plus all of the time I spent in New York with Mary. I have had very little, if any, interaction with Richard, socially. The one exception was when I called him to help me with the short sale of my bank stock. Our friendship has been based on years of mutual trust. Regretfully, we've spent very little personal time together during our friendship and business association."

"Well," replied Tina, "When I first heard this tale from Richard, when he told me a Mr. Jones and a Janie Brown would be on the flight, neither name meant a damn thing to me. But later, on the flight from New York to England, my gut told me something just didn't add up. Your story was too pat, too perfect, and it made me suspicious. I finally realized that I was being spoofed, although I really didn't know why, but I did know something was off. You've got to know it's going to take some time for me to digest all this. I'm sure I'll have a thousand questions. Just be willing to give me time, all of you."

"That will not be a problem. Take all the time you need. You're one of us," Jones declared.

Richard quietly suggested, "Let's get appetizers, maybe some dessert, and call it a night. We've got a very busy day tomorrow. Meet you back here for breakfast at 9 am."

Midnight was approaching. Everyone nodded in agreement.

Once Mary and Jones were back in their suite, Mary said, "I promised to call my sister tonight and give her an update on our situation. It's only fair that she knows the truth about what's going on with me."

"That's fine with me," Jones answered. "I agree your sister should know you're okay and that we're in London. Tell her whatever you feel you should tell her."

"It's just that I miss my family so much, and I've put them through so much," Mary stated. "At least they should know part of what is going on. Hell, unless Mom told her, and I doubt she did, my sister doesn't even know that we're engaged, or that I have a beautiful diamond ring, and we're getting married."

"Mary, call her right now. Use one of the burner phones I picked up from the concierge," Jones said. "Talk as long as you want. Tell her as much as you care to tell her. Make sure you ask her to convey some or all of your conversation with her to your mother. It's the only right thing to do."

"Jones, thank you for your support," Mary whispered. "I really need it now."

With that, Mary went out of the bedroom onto the patio with a glass of wine, a pack of cigarettes, and Jones's phone. She dialed up her sister in New York where it was only 8 pm.

Mary's sister answered the phone on the second ring, "Hello."

"Monica, it's me, Mary, your sister calling," replied Mary. "Got a few minutes to chat?"

"Mary, where the hell are you?" her sister quizzed. "Still in Costa Rica? Sure, I've got plenty of time. Tell me the news, tell me everything. I'm so glad to hear your voice. We've been so worried. Are you okay? Are you safe? The news about you and Jones has been really scary. I'll shut up so you can talk. Go ahead, please."

"Calm down, Sis, I'm okay," Mary offered. "Jones and I are in London. We plan to be here for a while. We've devised a plan that we hope will exonerate us and put the criminals in jail. If it works, all of this cloak and dagger stuff will be over and done, but it's going to take a few more days, maybe another week or so. Right now, we feel safe. Just don't know how long it'll last."

"Well, I'm certainly thankful that you feel safe in England," Monica answered. "Why are you and Jones in so much danger? Who and why does anyone want to harm you? I don't understand that piece. Are you at liberty to tell me the reason why you and Jones are on the run? Why did you have to flee to England? To stay alive? I just can't imagine."

"Listen carefully and you'll understand, Sis," Mary said.

"We're about to expose the largest single heist of US Treasury dollars in the history of our country. We've got absolute, irrefutable evidence that several Federal agency heads, along with many US and International bankers, other corporate executives, and even members of Congress, colluded and participated in the theft of $17 trillion during the 2008-2009 economic crisis. We have their names, the amounts each received, and where their funds are deposited. You can certainly understand why they don't want this information made available to the public. That's why they want us dead."

"What?," Monica shouted into the phone. "They want you dead? They're trying to murder you and Jones? Go to the police. Get the authorities to help protect you now. Why haven't you already called the FBI? Call Scotland Yard! This makes no sense to me."

Mary answered firmly, "Monica, we've considered lots of options and going to the police is not one of them. We're on the wrong size of that equation until our evidence becomes public knowledge. Until then, we must continue to run and hide. Hopefully, this nightmare will be over in a few more days. We just have to keep our guard up for another week or two. Believe me, Monica, I'm ready to come home. I'm ready for things to get back to normal. Has Mom told you any of this?"

Monica interrupted, "Mom told me very little. She mostly said you were in trouble and that you were thinking about getting married. Then she clammed up. What can I do to help? Need a place to hide? If so, you can use the cottage on Nantucket. Do you need any money? Can I update Mom and Dad about this?"

"I tried to explain some of this to them, but they got real upset," offered Mary. "They really lost it when I told them that Jones had given me an engagement ring and that we're to be married. Tell them whatever you think they should know."

Mary continued, "No, we don't need any money, thanks. For your information, Jones and I spent almost two months in your in-law's cottage on Nantucket back in the fall. We left before Christmas Stroll began. We never saw one person we knew. I tried to leave the house like we found it, so no one would realize anyone had been there."

"Engaged? Really? When's the wedding?" asked Monica. "Congratulations. I can't wait to see Jones again. I'll be so happy for you once you get out of this mess. Want to get married on Nantucket? May I be in the wedding?"

"Monica," replied Mary. "I want you to be my Matron of Honor. Maybe we can get married in Nantucket, if you can fix it. You'll be the first to know when we set the date."

"That's really strange," Monica added. "When we were in Nantucket for Christmas Stroll and the holidays, I remember my father-in law mentioning something was out of place on the bar. He was adamant that he'd never purchased a California Chardonnay. Then one evening while we were dining at The Pearl, one of our 'Sconset neighbors mentioned that they had seen folks in our driveway back in late November, but they just thought we'd come earlier than usual."

"I've gotta go. Just wanted to let you know what we're up to and why. I'll keep you posted. Sorry about that odd bottle of wine. I love you. Tell Mom and Dad I love them so much, and I hope they understand," Mary replied hurriedly.

"I love you too, Mary," Monica responded. "I'll get Mom and Dad straight. You be safe and take care. Hope to see you soon. Text me anytime for any reason."

Mary put out her last cigarette and went back into the bedroom. Jones was fast asleep and snoring with the TV blaring. She decided to wait until morning to tell him about her conversation with Monica, which she prayed was not being monitored.

Chapter Thirty-Two

The Destination

Jones and Mary were already in the "coffee shoppe" sipping lattes when Richard and Tina arrived. *Tina's eyes are somewhat puffy, probably from crying most of the night. She must be scared to death. Bet Richard had a tough night as well*, Jones thought.

Once they'd ordered breakfast, Jones suggested they discuss their plans going forward. He began, "The tapes to the Federal agencies, the Bank, and the Senate Banking Committee will be delivered in New York, Washington, DC, and Charlotte, NC, tomorrow. It may take an extra day before the Guardian Society receives their tape. I expect that once they've all been heard and reviewed, all parties will be anxious to meet and decide how each individual group should and will respond. I don't expect we'll get any email responses until day after tomorrow."

"I agree," Richard added. "But we'd need to keep an eye on our secure email account just in case. Don't want to miss anything. They may surprise us and respond sometime late tomorrow afternoon."

"What's this secret email server you guys keep talking about?" asked Tina. "I don't have any idea how that works."

Mary spoke up immediately, "A secret email account is like the ones international hackers use. It is an account that is connected to a series of IPS addresses. They're all interconnected.

Supposedly, no one can actually determine the exact geographic location of who originates the email. It's part of the 'Dark Web'... which is used by terrorists to communicate with each other world-wide. Actually, it's a collection of websites that are on an encrypted network. They can't be accessed with conventional search engines or browsers. We're using a Tor browser to access our site. There are other tools available, but Tor is the best for us."

Jones said, "We gave the thieves our Dark Web email address to respond to the demands we outlined in the taped messages. Theoretically, they shouldn't be able to determine that we're in England."

"Sounds like a James Bond movie to me," quipped Tina. "Except I'm horrified."

The waitress brought their food, refilled their demure cups with coffee, and left them to enjoy.

Several minutes later Richard spoke up, "Since you probably won't have any responses today, I think we should gather up our belongings and head toward the Isle of Wight. We have a choice of ferries. One is a Hovercraft that gets us across the Solent in about ten minutes. We can board the Hovercraft in Southsea for the ten-minute trip over to Ryde on The Island. It's the last Hovercraft service operating anywhere. The other choice is the standard boat ferry that takes about thirty-five minutes."

"I agree wholeheartedly," remarked Jones. "Time to get settled in the furnished cottage Richard leased for us when he was here last month. My research shows the Isle of Wight is the second largest, most populated island off the coast of England, known for its boat and ship-building industry. It's bordered by the Solent River and the English Channel. But did you know it's about one hundred and fifty miles wide and about three hundred and fifty miles long and most of the Channel is less than six hundred feet deep? It is one of the world's busiest shipping lane. It was carved out back during the Ice Age ions ago."

"We already know all of that, Jones," Mary said. "But thanks for the geography lesson."

Jones continued, "I'm sure Richard found a special cottage for us in Bembridge. Hopefully, one on the Channel with a great view. We should be able to hide out there awhile, until all this financial mess shakes out. It should be safe. If we lay low and stay below the radar maybe no one will find us."

"That's a great point, Jones," replied Richard. "We can't be too careful. There is something that I never got around to telling you.

It happened when I was over here last month taking care of your financial business and renting the cottage in Bembridge. It was quite remarkable."

"Don't stop now. Tell me what the hell you're talking about. Is it good or bad?" Jones demanded.

"You'll have to decide that," Richard replied. "It happened the day I came over here to open your bank accounts at Lloyds Bank TBS. As you undoubtedly know, it's a British-based bank. I was waiting in the lobby to see the bank manager. When I looked up, I recognized Harry Peters, the US Treasury Secretary, coming out of the bank manager's office. I had seen him so many times on TV that I knew him right away. I was shocked and a bit frightened."

Mary, stunned, said, "What the hell was he doing over here? I'll be damned. Bet you my last dollar that he was hiding some of the government money they stole. Hope he didn't see you, Richard."

"Doubt he'd know Richard, even if he saw him," chimed in Jones. "Not too worried about that. Sorta proves what we've been saying all along. Those crooked bastards. Let's pay the bill here, check out, and head south."

Tina added, "You're not waiting on me. I'm ready to go and hide."

Several hours later, using Richard's fake passport, they rented a car and made it to the ferry port at Southsea. After turning in the rental car, Jones bought four tickets for the Hovercraft and they climbed aboard for the ten-minute ride. Once inside the ferry cabin, Richard spoke with the First Mate for several minutes before slipping him a Benjamin.

Upon landing in Ryde, everybody's curiosity was at an all-time high. What would it be like here? Most importantly, would they be safe?

"Let's hire a car to Bembridge," stated Richard.

Mary suggested, "We need to check out Bembridge before we go to the cottage. We need to get some sense of where everything is: stores, boutiques, restaurants, spirits, market. What do you say?"

"Great idea," tuned in Tina. "At some point I need to shop for a new night gown and some other items."

"You have too many clothes, as far as I'm concerned," Richard joked. "Naked is best."

Jones, laughing out loud said, "Easy Richard. You're wearing your feelings on your sleeve again."

"Speak for yourself, mate. You ain't fooling me, not one bit."

"Okay guys, that's enough for now," replied Mary. "Let's get going."

They grabbed a livery, threw their bags in the back, and instructed the driver to take them to Bembridge and give them a guided tour. He drove them to the center of the seaside community and pointed out different landmarks and places of interest along the way. It was a very informative ride. Jones paid him handsomely.

Their cottage in Bembridge was right on the street overlooking the English Channel. It was small with two bedrooms, two baths, a small den, and a smaller kitchen, but it was in the very best part of town. It was furnished with nice furniture, even a few English antiques, along with good chinaware, silverware, and cookware. There were flowers on the kitchen table next to a bottle of Mary's favorite wine. The leasing agent had done a remarkable job. Jones and Mary opted for the back bedroom which seemed a little more private to them. It didn't really matter to Richard and Tina. All four were just happy to be there, together and alive.

Once they were settled in, Mary called for Tina to meet her in the kitchen. Soon they were drafting a shopping list that included items they might want. The list was long and comprehensive: specialty foods and beverages, meat and vegetables, spirits, wines, desserts, paper supplies and more.

Jones gave Mary five hundred pounds and off she and Tina went intending to spend it all before returning home. Jones and Richard decided to chill out until the women came back with something strong to drink.

"Jones, where did you get those pounds?" Richard asked. "When and where did you make the exchange?"

"At the Stafford this morning before we left," replied Jones. "I also picked up several EU burner phones at the same time. Here is one for you. We need to operate with pounds for now, and no phone calls that could be traced."

Richard replied, "Got it. How do you think 'your enemies' will respond to the demands? Do you think any of the groups will actually pay the ransom or do you think they'll resist?"

Jones answered quickly, "They'll all pay up, if they think we'll cave. However, all of them might not believe we'll cave. I know that bastard, Lane, at the Bank will pay the ransom. He'll probably be the first to pay. I don't really know what the Senate Committee will do about granting us immunity, but they've been bribed before. The Senate Banking Committee will most likely be the hardest to deal with because I have undermined their authority by refusing to comply with their orders. I'm not too sure about the Guardian Society, but they may be the easiest to deal with and may pay the minimum amount based on our blackmail threat. But believe me, those four Federal agency heads will pay through the nose, and quickly, because they've got the most to lose. Plus, those crooks are accustomed to being extorted, and they damn well don't want to go to jail. They'll want some assurance that we don't take the money and run."

"Jones, you seem so confident about all of this. Aren't you the least bit worried or scared or pessimistic that this might not work out? How can you be so calm and so confident and so calculating? Don't you ever get nervous?"

"Richard, you gotta know that this ain't my first rodeo. This is what I've been doing for thirty years, dealing with a bunch of crooked, dishonest, and corrupt bastards, who'd sell out their own mothers for a buck. Believe me, I'm accustomed to dealing with thieves like these people. Hell, I guess you could say, I was one of them at one time. Some folks might still think so."

Richard replied, "It's sorta like the insurance ad 'We're in good hands.' Guess I need to rely on you and quit worrying."

Jones said, "You're damn right. You can bet your ass on it. But make no mistake, it's going to get real nasty, it's going to get real ugly, and it's going to get incredibly dangerous. I know these crooks."

Two hours later, the women returned, and their cabbie began honking his horn. Obviously, they needed help getting their purchases inside the cottage.

Richard jumped up, saying, "Let's go see if we can help those poor damsels in distress." "I'm right behind you," said Jones.

"I've never seen so much food," Richard said when he saw what was in the boot of the taxi. "Did you leave any for the rest of the island? We'll never eat all this stuff, but it should be fun trying."

"Did you find any decent clothing stores?" asked Jones.

"Yes, we found a couple of nice shops," Mary replied with a big smile.

Tina responded, "Just help us get all this inside. We can do without your smart-ass remarks. You'd be the first to complain, if there were no food or if we wore dirty clothes."

"Some of the pastries are out of this world, Jones," Mary added. "You're going to gain a few pounds while we're here. I'm gonna put some meat on your bones."

"Always wanted to be fat and sassy when I died," replied Jones.

"Damn, Jones. Ease up on the dark humor. It's more than we need right now," suggested Richard.

"I'm more interested in finding the bourbon," Jones exclaimed. "This old man needs a stiff drink. Maybe two or three."

"Make that two old men, who need a stiff drink or two or three," said Richard. "Please fix a vodka and tonic for me," Mary told Jones. "What would you like, Tina?" "I bought some dark rum. Just need a little Coke and ice, thanks."

After a couple of rounds of drinks, they all agreed that something akin to "comfort food" would be the best bill of fare. Tina ran off to the kitchen to season pork chops, put a cabbage head in a boiler of water, and wash sweet potatoes, so they'd be ready to slip into the oven about an hour before dinner time. *This is just what we all need,* Tina thought. *It's going to be delicious and so comforting.*

Over dinner, they speculated about how each group might respond to their "taped messages." Which group might cave first? Which group would resist the most? Who or what agency had the most to lose? The biggest unknown was how much ransom money they might be able to collect.

When they were talking about all that ransom money, Mary brought up a very interesting, but alarming fact.

"We need to realize that these corrupt bastards, with their backs to the wall and their personal freedom on the line, will stop at nothing to make this unpleasantness disappear. They could take a fraction of the amount of ransom money Jones is demanding and hire several contract killers to search us out and kill us. I guess what I'm trying to say is, we'd better be damn careful how we answer their email responses, once we receive them. If we do pull the string and ship those thumb drives to the US media outlets, we damn well better have a fool-proof plan for survival in place that very day."

"Well said," declared Jones. "You're a hundred percent correct about what they will and can do, and what we must do in formulating our survival plan. Starting right now, this should be top priority for us."

Richard stated, "I believe we agree about which group we should fear the most. It doesn't seem too logical that the Senate Banking folks will go to the trouble of having us killed. Neither will the Guardian Society people. The real SOB's we better be on guard against are Jones's old boss, banker Kurt Lane, and Bill Baker at the Federal Reserve. They're not just ruthless and corrupt, they're killers."

Mary warned the others, "We shouldn't get too cocky. I know

for sure there are Congressmen who would kill for the kind of money they stole. We can't or shouldn't write off anyone in any group. People do strange things when large sums of money hit the table, and they do even stranger things to maintain not only their power, but also their personal freedom."

"I'm a little late to the party," Tina offered. "So, I don't know all the details you guys are discussing. What I do know is that I've been living a very sheltered life, never realizing that these types of people actually exist and actually do these awful things, not just to their country but also to each other. This is difficult for me to comprehend."

Jones responded, "It's a crying shame that our government has become so corrupt. It appears that the only reason politicians go to Washington is to become rich and powerful. You remember what President Truman said, don't you? 'You can't get rich in politics unless you're a crook.'"

They don't seem to give a happy damn about our country. Once they get there, they spend most of their time making sure they get re-elected, so they can steal more money and gain more power. It's a vicious cycle that needs to be broken. Term limits would solve some of the problem, but good damn luck on that law ever getting passed."

Jones continued, "If we survive this nightmare, I have strong feelings about what we should consider doing to counteract the corruption and reprehensible behavior exemplified by those crooked bastards in DC. Yes, I definitely have some ideas that I believe would make an incredible difference. If properly executed, the right plan, along with all of the damaging information we plan to divulge to the voting public, would gain enormous support across the country. It could very likely change the total political dynamic in the next US elections. We'll talk about it later, when we're safe."

"Back to the matter at hand," Richard stated. "We'll need to keep a close eye on the secure email account, beginning now. When those tapes are delivered tomorrow morning, I expect all hell will break loose. No telling how many phone calls and meetings will spring from all this. But there's no doubt in my mind that the emails will start flying our way soon after."

Mary jumped up from the table. She started taking the dirty plates to the kitchen and said, "Jones and I will cleanup tonight. Come on, Jones. Get moving and give me a hand."

Tina could barely control her laughter. That remark to Jones just seemed so funny and unusual to her.

Maybe she and Richard could have that type of relationship someday, she thought. *Just maybe.*

Bill Brown

Chapter Thirty-Three

The Response

Bill Baker's private line rang early that morning. He picked up and heard Kurt Lane say, "Have your morning deliveries arrived yet? If not, get ready to sign for a package and then call me right away." He ended the call.

Bill Baker, still not fully awake, turned on his coffee maker. *What the hell was that all about,* he thought. Guess I'll just have to wait and see. Thirty minutes later, as he had just finished his second cup of coffee, an International Courier knocked on his door. The delivery person asked if he were Bill Baker, asked him to sign for the package, and then handed him the container.

Baker opened the parcel, noted the Costa Rican return address, and found the tape. He walked into his den, popped open the recorder on his desk, placed the tape into his tape player and hit the start button. As a very distinct voice began delivering the message in a clear and concise tone, Baker's heart began to pound, his blood began to boil, and his head began to throb.

Grabbing his chest, he fell back into the executive chair behind his desk wondering, Am I having a friggin' heart attack, or is this just a nightmare?

He managed to sit up, collect himself somewhat, and went back to the kitchen and poured himself another cup of coffee. Returning to the den, he played the tape again, which didn't make things any better. Actually, it made things worse. Baker was getting a message like he'd never ever received before. It was decisively threatening. It was demanding. It was horrifying for all the wrong reasons. The allegations were true, and Baker knew they were true. *Guilty as charged*, he mused.

Baker jumped up from his desk, grabbed his secure cell phone and dialed Kurt Lane in North Carolina. Lane picked up on the first ring and said, "We've both been playing along saying that Jones is dead, but we both know for certain the friggin' bastard is still alive. Can you believe this? What did your taped message say? What are Jones's demands?"

In a a very shaky voice, Baker answered, "No, I wanted to believe that the bastard didn't survive the plane crash, but he did and now he's coming after us all. How much did he ask you to pay? The guy's gone frigging crazy. He wants $100 million from the Feds wired to a foreign account, or he'll send the thumb drive data to every media outlet in America. What the hell are we going to do, Kurt? You were supposed to have taken care of this bastard long before things got this far?"

"Hold on a damn minute, Bill," Kurt responded. "This is no time to start pointing fingers. We're all in this mess together. I have already talked with Ms. Brand at FDIC, with Peters at Treasury and with Gomer at the NY Federal Reserve. They all got a taped message. I don't know if any other group received the same tape. Guess we'll find out soon enough. Look, Bill, we have to unite and take on this SOB together. Mr. Jones let my Bank off easy compared to the others. He's only demanding $50 million in ransom. I suggest you call an emergency meeting this afternoon at 2 pm in your office. We all must decide how we plan to respond. Remember, he gave us only twenty-four hours to reply to him by email. I'll contact the 'hit squads' again right now."

"Okay, Kurt. I agree. I'll call an emergency meeting at 2 pm today. Come on up to DC as soon as you can get here. See you then. I'll call the others right now."

Harry Peters was listening to the taped message Jones had sent, when Baker called.

"Hello, Bill, I bet I know why you're calling me. Hope you remember that I wanted no part of this damn deal. Now look at what the hell we got ourselves into. Got any ideas on how we manage to get out of this situation without going to jail? This is a serious problem, if you ask me. You got an extra $100 million dollars over there?"

"Shut the hell up, Harry. We've all got the same damn problem. One that will take all our best efforts and resources to resolve. So stop trying to blame everybody else and start thinking about how we can fix this mess. It's called super damage control. Get your ass to my office at 2 pm sharp today." Baker hung up the phone.

Ms. Brand's phone rang three times before she picked up. She dreaded what was coming.

"Good Morning, Bill. How nice of you to call. I'm sure you want me to help you undo this horrible mess you and Kurt have brought upon all of us. I'll remind you that I wanted no part of this deal. Remember?"

"Cut out the bull, Ms. Brand. Your sanctimonious attitude is nauseating. We've got a world of problems to solve and only twenty-four hours to respond. So, get over to my office today at 2 pm and plan to stay until we devise a way out of this dilemma. That's it. Goodbye!"

Baker had one more call to make. Ted Gomer had just finished listening to the taped message the second time when his phone rang.

"Hello, Bill. Looks like we got a major disaster on our hands. Where are we going to find the $100 million dollars Jones is asking us to pay? Do you believe he has the thumb drives?"

Baker responded, "So you are in favor of paying the ransom. That may be the best way out of this nightmare. Yes, I think it has to be Jones. Yes, I believe he has the thumb drives. He got them from the mole at Treasury, the one we had eliminated. You know, the remains that washed ashore on the beach in Melbourne. Everyone is meeting here at my office at 2 pm today. Come early."

Gomer replied, "Bill, you gotta fix this problem. I'm counting on becoming the next Treasury Secretary. We gotta keep all of this crap under wraps, or we'll all be ruined and probably go to prison. You have to do something about this today."

"No, Ted. WE have to do something about this today. We're all in this together. Don't forget that fact for one moment. See you shortly."

The emergency meeting in Baker's office began promptly at two o'clock. All five participants were present. Baker asked them to take their seats at the table. Then he closed and locked the door and sat down. The mood in the room was bleak, and the negative vibes were plentiful.

Baker began, "I appreciate all of you coming here on such short notice, but I'm sure each of you realize the gravity of the situation at hand. It's fairly obvious to me that we're not all in concert relative to the manner in which our problem needs to and must be solved. That being said, I am open to any suggestions or advice or resolutions that will get us out of this dilemma today. So, feel free to speak up with any new and viable ideas that may get the necessary results for all of us to keep our positions, our respective powers, and our fortunes."

The Federal Reserve Chairman continued, "We must understand the fact that we're at war. As with any war, first you have to identify the enemy, then you have to eliminate - *kill* - the enemy before the enemy kills you. That's where we are right now, this very moment. So speak up if you have any magical way we can solve this problem in a less violent way. It's urgent that we decide our method of attack. Now! Then we'll know how to respond to Mr. Jones's demands."

Peters was the first to respond, "It's unfortunate that we find ourselves in this most undesirable position. However, it's only fair to say that we all agreed to participate in a financial fiasco, most certainly knowing there could be very unpleasant repercussions if certain information were ever made public. Well, friends, that certain information is about to become headline news all over the world. How can we stop this oncoming freight train? I'm not sure about that, but I'm damn sure we can't afford to sit here on our hands and do nothing. What may or may not happen to us personally is one thing, but think about the possibility of the total collapse of our country. I urge you all to come to some kind of consensus plan that can be implemented immediately. Hopefully, one that will derail certain disaster for us and for America as well. That is, if any of us really care about America."

"I want to say something," Ms. Brand insisted. "I'm not the enemy here. I did the very same thing each of you did, so don't consider me the odd one out. We all took the dive and allowed greed to cloud our judgement, as we grabbed for all of that money. But hindsight is twenty-twenty and very seldom changes anything. I'm not an advocate of violence, never have been, and don't plan to start now. My idea of a solution to the problem is this---let's start a dialogue with Mr. Jones that suggests we may be willing to pay some amount of money to get those thumb drives back. We buy some time while we assemble a "posse" for the lack of a better word, to corral him and Mary and bring them to justice. Don't forget, they've committed a slew of felonies that would justify most any charges we'd level against them."

"That's total bull," growled Kurt Lane. "We ain't got any damn time to buy any damn time. Mr. Jones is a big enough bastard that he'll turn over the thumb drives to the media no matter what we agree to do, no matter how much money we pay. How do we fight that kind of bastard? It's got to be 'balls to the wall.' There's only one way. We must kill both of them. I've already hired four 'hit squads' to take them out. We tracked his iPhone to Miami and figured he might go back home. So, I sent one squad to Grand Cayman. Since Mr. Jones and Mary both lived and worked out of New York, I had one squad go to New York. According to what Baker told me about monitoring a text message from Mary to her sister, we tracked Jones's burner phone to Costa Rica. It appears that Jones now has some company---his broker friend, Richard and Richard's girlfriend, Tina. That's why I sent the 'hit squad' from Boston down there. We now know the tapes we all received were shipped from Costa Rica. The remaining 'hit squad' in Atlanta is ready to be deployed anywhere in the world on a moment's notice. In short, we have a very good chance of taking our enemies out, all four of them. Believe me, this is our best hope."

Lane continued, "I'm speaking only for my Bank and myself. What I've just said is our steadfast position, because we see no other way, no other viable solution. Furthermore, my Bank has already responded to Mr. Jones. It was a short and sweet email, simply agreeing to his demands for $50 million in ransom payment. We promised not to track down or harm Mr. Jones or Mary, if we receive the damaging thumb drives."

"Okay. So, we pay Mr. Jones," mused Ted Gomer. "So where do we get the money? How can we pull this off without the world finding out? This is not just a matter of writing a check. Wiring $100 million around the world leaves a paper trail a mile long. We better think long and hard about the best way we can achieve our desired results while limiting any unintended consequences. You all know that I'm in line to succeed Peters at Treasury next year, so it's damn important to me that we get this right. You guys take care of the killing fields, and I'll handle the payoff through the New York Federal Reserve Bank. I propose each agency put up $25 million. If that'll solve our problem, we can do that."

Then Baker stood up and replied, "What you guys don't know, something that I just found out about today, is this. Both Senator Dowd and that crazy bastard from Seattle, the founder of the Guardian Society which attempted a coup d'etat of our country in 2008, got a tape with certain demands from Mr. Jones. He told the Senator he'd come and testify, if he and Mary, along with Richard and Tina, were granted immunity from any and all prosecution. If they don't get immunity, he said he'd divulge names of the senators who took part in the $17 trillion heist on the TARP Fund.

"Mr. Jones also demanded $25 to $50 million from the Guardian Society for his silence about their activities. I think we can all agree that these two parties don't have the inclination or the capability to take care of Jones. It all comes down to this. The crazy sonofabitch has gone friggin' berserk, and he must be stopped. If not by us, by whom?"

After talking among themselves for another couple of hours, they finally decided to start drafting a comprehensive response to Mr. Jones's ransom demands. They bickered over wording of multiple email responses and were at an impasse, until Ms. Brand suggested that the email be composed by Baker and Peters and edited by Lane and Gomer. Her suggestion was approved, and they went about their business immediately.

Around eight-thirty that evening, after about six email drafts, the group agreed on the final version they wanted to send to Mr. Jones in response to his ridiculous demands. As they all huddled around Baker's computer, Baker hit the Send button on his computer screen. The email was now on its way to a clandestine server somewhere in the world. The email message was so vicious, so vile, so nasty, so undoubtedly disgusting, that Ms. Brand chose not to read the final version.

It's going to be most interesting to see how Jones reacts to this totally reprehensible communication, thought Baker.

"We've done all we can do for now," Peters said. "Kurt, looks like all our futures rest in your hands."

Bill Brown

Chapter Thirty-Four

The Resolution

Jones was the first one up. It was only 7 am on the Isle of Wight. He headed straight for his computer on the kitchen table. He turned it on and logged in. While he was waiting for it to boot up, he started making a pot of coffee. *Drank too much vino last night*, he remembered.

"Jackpot! Holy Toledo, we've hit the friggin' Jackpot!" Jones yelled as he clicked on the email account. There were three new messages from his targets, all responding to the tapes.

Immediately, Jones heard the others rattling around in their bedrooms, probably awakened by his shouts.

"What the hell is going on?" Richard asked as he came dragging into the kitchen. "Is the coffee ready yet? I need something strong to wake me up. Who the hell have you heard from, and what are they saying?"

"Surprisingly, Senator Dowd was the first one to respond. He states the Senate Banking Committee voted unanimously to grant Mary and me complete and total immunity from any and all prosecution. He says we must return to DC to testify in a closed-door inquiry. Mary can do the documents that we would need and get them recorded. We'd have to have written legal documents for our own protection."

"If it's legitimate, can't ask for any more than that," Richard replied. "Sounds like they have something to hide. Are they ever gonna get a friggin' shock when they all see many of their names in lights. It's going to get real ugly real quick. Mark my word, extremely dangerous."

"Who's cooking breakfast?" asked Mary as she entered the kitchen and poured a cup of coffee. "Tina cooked last night, so it seems fair that a man should fry up some bacon and eggs. Don't forget the pancakes, please. What are you hearing from those bastards, Jones?"

"I'll cook breakfast," Richard offered. "Jones is too busy manning the computer. How does everyone want their eggs? Scrambled or scrambled?"

Tina was the last of the sleepyheads to get up and make her way into the kitchen. She still looked half asleep when she spoke, "I dreamt that all Groups agreed to pay the ransom demands. Wishful thinking, I suppose."

"Not entirely," stated Jones. The Guardian Society responded that they'll wire us $25 million, if we remain silent. You can believe it or not, but Kurt Lane and his bank have agreed to our $50 million ransom payment demand. This is incredible. It's unbelievable. It fabulous."

"Calm down, Jones," warned Mary. "Remember, you haven't yet heard from the Feds, and they're the ones I fear the most. Be extremely careful how you respond to the emails you just received. How we answer them will have a direct bearing on the Feds' response. Let's just chill out for now, eat a hearty breakfast prepared by our own Chef Richard and talk about these things later."

"I bet you're a damn good attorney," Tina stated. "You think clearly, you stay calm, and you speak in a logical and matter-of-fact way. I'm glad you're on our side."

"Richard, when do we eat?" quizzed Jones as he looked up from his computer. "I'm starving. Better scramble a dozen eggs, and fry that whole package of sausage. I hope you're going to make pancakes. I'll fix another pot of coffee and move the computer to the table over by the sofa."

"Guys, if we keep eating like this, we'll all have to go to Weight Watchers before long," suggested Mary. "I guess the food and the booze help relieve the stress and fear we're all enduring."

"You mean I'm not the only one who's stressed out and scared to death?" Tina added. "I guess misery truly does love company. I hope I can be strong throughout all this. If I didn't love Richard so much, I'd be on the next plane to Grand Cayman."

"Okay, folks. It's time to eat," Richard announced. "Grab a plate and serve yourselves, and I'll finish the pancakes and bring them to the table. Here's the syrup and the Kerrygold butter is on the table. Freshly washed strawberries are in the bowl."

"I don't believe I could have waited another ten minutes. Richard, this looks and smells divine. Maybe you and Tina can take some of your ransom money and open up a gourmet restaurant somewhere in the United Kingdom, like in London, or Edinborough. What do you think?" asked Jones.

"He's just kidding, Tina. Don't pay Jones any damn mind," Mary suggested. "I believe we all have much more important things to consider than getting in the restaurant business. That's too much like work from what I've seen over the years. One of my restauranteur friends once told me that 'it was about ten percent glamour and ninety percent damn hard work."

They inhaled Richard's breakfast. They devoured the eggs, the sausage, and a second round of pancakes topped with strawberries. Everyone seemed replete.

About eight-thirty, after they finished eating and cleaning up the dishes, Jones's computer signaled the receipt of another email. This was the one they were waiting to see.

Jones jumped up from the kitchen table, knocked over his coffee cup, ran to his computer and clicked on the latest email received. He noticed it had been sent the previous evening and was unclear why it was just reaching his computer.

He immediately threw his arms up in the air and shouted, "This is it. This is the one. It's here! Oh, my god, it's awful. It's nasty. It's horrific. Those dirty bastards! They have defamed every ancestor I've ever had and yours, too, Mary. Jesus Christ, where'd they learn how to talk like that. This is killing me. It's almost inhumane."

"What are they saying," yelled Mary. "Tell us. Read it out loud, Jones. Come on, we want to hear all of it. Read it to us, now."

"No you don't," responded Jones in a dead serious voice. "It really is so despicable that I can't, in good conscience, read it aloud. It's that bad. I never thought they'd stoop this low. They've hit rock bottom with this kind of obscene trash."

"Just give us an overview," Richard suggested. "Leave out the gross parts. You have to let us know what they're saying and what they plan to do about our ransom demands. Go ahead, we're adults. You don't have to sugarcoat it."

"This is like a horror movie," Tina added. "How the hell is this going to end? And when?"

Mary walked over to Jones and started reading the email over his shoulder. "My god," she screamed. "Those filthy bastards. It's worse than you said. We can't let them get away with this kind of damn garbage. We need to respond right this minute. Tell the crooked bastards to go to hell. Tell them we're going to take them down. All of them."

"Whoa, hold on, Mary," Richard suggested. "Remember what you said about how we answer their responses. It's critical we do it right. Let's take a little time and digest what they're saying. Then we analyze it. Then we send them our well-crafted response."

Jones responded, "Richard, you're on the right track. Initially, I think they're trying to demean us. They're trying to make us incredibly angry with gross and obscene remarks, so we respond irrationally. As you suggested, we should chill out a bit. We need to talk about this in rational terms and keep our emotions and anger at bay. When we finally agree. we'll send them a response they'll never forget. Believe me, they'll soon realize their approach to this problem was inane, immature, and dead wrong. They'll regret their actions for the rest of their lives."

"Sounds like you already know what we should do from every angle," Mary confessed. "I'm sorry I went off, but their obscenities were just too much for me to handle."

"I'm glad I didn't read it," added Tina. "I'm going to agree with whatever you three decide to do. I'll clean up the dishes, while you work on our responses."

Richard asked Jones, "What's their deal? What are they saying. Just give me the highlights."

Jones replied, "First of all, they called Mary and me every kind of sorry, lowlife, and crooked piece of crap imaginable. Indirectly, they said the same things about our parents. Their expressions of vulgarity are barbaric. Really horrific. Secondly, they listed eleven different federal crimes that they allegedly will charge us with immediately. Finally, they adamantly stated that they will NOT pay one damn dime of ransom money, until they are in receipt of all copies of the thumb drives."

"Richard," Mary said. "It doesn't appear they have any idea of your involvement. Certainly, they'd have no idea at all about Tina. That's a good thing for all of us."

"I'm not sure I agree with that," Jones replied. "That does not sound like Kurt Lane at all. He blames me altogether for the Bank's problems. He'll never get over my short sale of the Bank stock. I'm certain he would have received intelligence on who helped me pull off the stock sale. It's no secret that it was done in the Caymans with Richard's firm. So, I'd say they know who Richard is and what he helped me do. That alone is enough to put Richard on their 'kill' list.

Plus, if they've been able to monitor any of our calls, they most likely know that Richard and Tina are involved."

"It gets worse by the minute," complained Tina. "You're right about one damn thing. If I'd known about all of this cloak and dagger crap, I would never have left home. But that doesn't diminish my feelings for Richard."

"Thanks," Richard uttered. "I understand your position. I love you and couldn't stand to leave you behind. I realize I've put you in grave danger, and I'm truly sorry."

"I definitely have some ideas about how we should react. Yes, some very definite ideas," Mary stated.

"First of all, let's all discuss what we want to accomplish in the end, then draft an email that will help us achieve our goals," suggested Jones. "That way everyone has an opportunity to contribute to the final plan. Okay?"

"Fine with me," Mary uttered. "About as democratic as you can get." Both Richard and Tina nodded in agreement.

"I say let's call their bluff," Richard said. "Don't back down one inch."

"How do we know they're bluffing?" Mary added. "We're dealing with some hard-ass crooks for sure."

"It's a chance I'm willing to take," replied Richard. "I vote we stand our ground."

Jones jumped into the conversation, "I believe we should up the ante. Demand more money due to their negative response. We should push back by shortening the time frame for alerting the media."

"We should throw them a curve," Tina unexpectedly offered. "Hit them with something they don't expect. Everybody knows about calling a bluff, upping an ante or reducing a time deadline. All good tactics, but they're responses they already expect. I believe we should throw something at them that is not already in the taped message."

"Brilliant, Tina," Richard said. "Great thinking. What do you have in mind?"

"Don't know yet," answered Tina. "Maybe some of you will come up with just the right idea to work perfectly."

"I agree you're on the right track, Tina," Mary replied. "Something they would not expect, based on what our taped messages contained. That's good."

No one said anything for about ten minutes. Tina finished clearing the dishes off the table. Richard made another pot of coffee. Jones went back to his computer. Mary said she was going to get dressed. It was 10 am BST on the Isle of Wight and 5 am DST in DC.

Jones was thinking, *if we decide to shorten the time frame, we must send the Feds our email response by twelve o'clock BST. Then we set a 6 p.m. deadline BST, for receiving all of the ransom money. That would not only shorten the time but increase the pressure for sure. It would give the Feds, the Bank, and the Guardian Society until 1 pm DST to wire the funds and meet our deadline.*

"Okay, Jones. What's up," Richard asked. "I can see your wheels spinning. Got it figured out yet? I believe we should get back to them by noon, BST, don't you?"

"Precisely, Richard. We're on the same page. Call the girls back in here and let's see if we can knock this deal out right now."

"Will do, Bossman," Richard said.

Once Mary and Tina came back to the table, Jones began, "See if you think this is a good response and one that not only you agree with, but also one you think will be effective in securing our safety and at the same time, forcing their hand."

"Go ahead," urged Mary. "You have our undivided attention."

Jones explained his thinking about the proposed email, "First of all, I want to keep it short, simple, concise, and non-ambiguous. There is no room for error. It'll begin with damning their reprehensible responses. Next, we'll list our new demands. Then, we'll drop the 'Tina surprise' on them." He continued, "Here is what it sounds like," as he began to read his composition:

> *Dear Feds,*
>
> *The disgusting and despicable expressions of vulgarity in the email response we received from you today only highlights your obvious desperation. The lack of good judgement on your part, in rejecting our fair and balanced demands, has only resulted in my raising the ante. The only amount that I will now accept from the Feds has risen to $150 million.*
>
> *Additionally, the time-frame for you to complete your response to my demands and to wire funds to Luxembourg has now been moved up and set at 6 pm London-time today. That would be 1 pm US-time today.*
>
> *There is one final thing relative to our discussions. You*

should fully understand and acknowledge that if you fail to meet my revised demands and my new deadline, you leave us with but one choice of action, which is as follows:

Rest assured that I'll not worry about wasting any more time sending the damaging thumb drives to all US media outlets listed on the taped messages. I'll simply deliver the damaging financial data on the thumb drives to the BBC, the British Broadcasting Corporation, in London. It would then be announced on their six-thirty World News Tonight program this very evening. The BBC headquarters is down the street from our current location.

Think about it, mates, your bloody names and nasty deeds are about to be revealed to the entire world!

Good luck and remember that crooks look really nice in stripes!'

Regards,
Mr. Jones

"What do you think about that?"

"Great! Ingenious! Brilliant" They all shouted at once. "Bravo!"

"Jones, you're a genius," charmed Mary. "My vote is to send it right this minute."

"Tina and I agree," said Richard. "It's fabulous. Send it on."

Jones took them at their word, checked it for errors, and sent the email to Bill Baker at his Federal Reserve email address. It was 11 AM in England.

By the time Baker arrived at his Federal Reserve office at 7 am, his computer was blinking and before he could login, his office phone began to ring. He reached for the phone as he sat down behind his desk. "Hello, it's Bill Baker speaking. May I hep you?"

"It's me, Bill," Kurt Lane answered. "Any news from Mr. Jones yet? Don't mean to rush you, but I need to know what's going on."

"Give me five minutes to get settled and check my computer, I'll see if he's responded yet. I'll call you right back."

"Okay, Bill. I'll await your call," replied Lane.

Baker logged in to his computer, clicked on the inbox, then opened the last email received. It was from Mr. Jones.

As Baker read the short and concise message, his face began turning red with anger. The more he read, the more irate he became. Even before he finished reading the email, he was dialing Kurt Lane's number.

"Hello, Bill. What you got?" Kurt asked. "Good news, I hope."

"Shut the hell up and listen, Kurt. We've come to the end of the road. Mr. Jones is calling our bluff. He's demanding more money, and worst of all, he's shortened the deadline until 6 pm tonight, London time. That's 1:00 pm our time."

So, the SOB's are in London," Kurt snorted. "I'll dispatch my last 'hit squad' from Atlanta there immediately. Can't believe they admitted they are in London. Is that all they said?"

"I have no idea where the SOB's might be. Hell, they could be right here in New York as far as I know. Obviously, we don't know squat. Listen to me, Kurt, there's more. Mr. Jones's message said if we don't wire all of the ransom funds by the 6:00 pm. London-time deadline tonight, they'll not waste time shipping the thumb drives to US media outlets. Instead, he said they'd just drop a thumb drive off at BBC headquarters in London in time to make the World News Tonight this evening."

"That bastard needs to die! Call a meeting, Bill. Right now!" screamed Lane. "We gotta make our move, now!"

"There is no time for a damn meeting," replied Baker. "We'll do a conference call. Stay on the line while I patch the others in. Hold on. I'll be right back."

Minutes later, all five parties were on a conference call, all talking at once.

Baker spoke up, "Everybody listen up. Mr. Jones has called our bluff, and we must send him the ransom money he demanded by six o'clock London-time today, or he's going to give the damaging thumb drive data to the BBC for airing tonight on their six-thir-ty news program. Any questions? His last remark stated that our bloody names and thieving deeds are about to be revealed to the whole world."

"Can't we do something to stop this crazy bastard from ruin-ing all our lives?" asked Harry Peters. "Certainly, we have the com-bined power to end this mess, don't we?"

"At the moment, unfortunately, Mr. Jones is in charge. We've got little choice, but to meet his demands and pay up now," suggested Ted Gomer. "I'm ready to do my part."

"I suggest we all do our part and get this done and behind us," said Ms. Brand. "This is nothing short of disastrous. I mean it's re-ally tragic."

Lane broke in, "I have already dispatched my last 'elimination team' to London. They'll be there about the time our deadline ex-pires. Don't know if they can find Mr. Jones, his woman, and their friends fast enough to take them out before they damage us, but we're sure as hell gonna try."

"Bottom line is, it's time to wire the money," Baker said. "I guess we'd better send Jones an email stating that we are in the process of complying with his last most recent demands. I don't like putting anything in writing, but I want Mr. Jones to understand that we will meet his demands. We should also remind him that he's to send us the thumb drives, as soon as he is in receipt of the funds. Guess we'll just have to trust Mr. Jones on that. Everyone agree with all this? Send me an email confirming your agreement to this activity, ASAP."

Everyone verbally concurred and agreed to send an email sim-ply stating 'Confirm' to Baker. All parties hung up.

Baker sent Mr. Jones an email stating, "Complying. Will meet 6 pm. London-BST deadline. Send thumb drives, immediately upon receipt."

It was only 9 am US/DST time. They had four hours to get their side of the deal done.

It was two in the afternoon when Jones's computer signaled another email arrival. Jones was just finishing his lunch, a ham and cheese sandwich on rye bread, when he heard his computer ding. He finished his pint and walked over to the table and checked the email.

He started screaming, "Bingo! Jackpot! Now, we're all friggin' rich! This is fantastic! Oh My god! I can't believe this! They're gonna to pay! They're gonna pay it all!

Holy Cow! I'd call this a Grand Slam!"

"I know you might not believe me, but I'm more excited about getting justice against those treasonous bastards than about all of that cash. Don't want to sound arrogant, but as most of you know, I already have plenty of money. I don't really need any more. I'm seeking justice, plain and simple. But make no mistake about it, I'm damned excited about all of you becoming wealthy."

The other three jumped up from their seats at the kitchen table and started yelling and screaming at one another. It was like they were speaking in unknown tongues, all of them. The excitement among this foursome was over the top. It was over the moon! If they didn't calm down a bit, they might get hurt. Thus far, they had exceeded anything that they had ever imagined.

"Where's the champagne?" Richard asked. "I'll find us some type of libation. We must celebrate like there ain't no tomorrow, but betting there is."

Mary and Jones were hugging and kissing and embracing to such an extent that Tina, jokingly said, "Get a room." They all joined in laughing out loud.

Richard came back with a bottle of champagne and four glasses. He popped the cork and poured everyone a glass full. They all clinked their glasses. The celebration had officially begun. "Now, all we have to do is wait until 6 pm and see if they deliver as agreed," Jones declared.

Bill Brown

Chapter Thirty-Five
The Thumb Drives

Four people on the Isle of Wight were thinking that this had to be the longest day in their lives. Would 6 o'clock ever arrive before they died of anxious anticipation? Their patience was wearing thin.

Eventually, Mary spoke up, "Jones, let's go for a walk. I can't stand sitting here in misery. A little fresh air should do us both good. Come on."

Jones jumped up, grabbed his phone and responded to Richard and Tina, "We'll be back before too long. Take it easy while we're out. Let's go, Mary."

Jones and Mary headed to the Bembridge waterfront. After several blocks they spotted a sidewalk bench and took a seat. They looked at one another as if to say, "what the hell are we doing here?"

Mary spoke first, "Jones, I didn't want to wake you the other night after I talked with my sister, but Monica and her husband are pulling for us. She was happy that we're engaged and getting married. Monica even asked me if she could be in our wedding. It was truly good for me to know that someone really cares about us and our well-being. Funny thing is, she asked if we needed any money or needed a place to hide. She even offered us the house on Nantucket before I had time to tell her we hid out there last fall. She even suggested we consider getting married there."

Mary continued, "Monica was horrified that we're on the run and can't wrap her brain around the fact that anyone is actually trying to kill us. She just doesn't understand but agreed to try and further explain as much of this mess to Mom and Dad as possible. Anyway, they're there for us anytime for any reason. She helped lift my spirits a bit."

"I'm glad your family has your back regardless of what has happened. As far as I'm concerned, there'll be no wedding unless Monica is the Matron of Honor. I think getting married on Nantucket would be a blast! Count me in."

"Jones, I love you. I pray we live long enough to plan our wedding on Nantucket. How many people can I invite? If I invite everybody we both know, will that be okay with you? Just tell me when. Please tell me we're going to get out of this mess alive."

"We will, better get going," Jones declared. "By the time we get back, it'll be time for cocktails. We'll celebrate our new fortune. A lot of money is about to come our way, and all four of us are going to share in the bounty that's about to change our lives forever. Richard and Tina are now part of our family. I wouldn't be here, if it weren't for Richard and you."

"By the way," Jones said as he handed Mary two small bank books. "Here are your account numbers and all related information, both here in Ryde and in Luxembourg. Keep this information somewhere safe."

Mary took the bank books and put them in her pocket. "Thank you, so much, Jones," she whispered. "I don't really know what to say except this wasn't necessary." Jones lovingly gave Mary the thumbs-up sign.

Mary composed herself, then she jumped up from the bench and said, "Jones, my dear, we're definitely on the same page. Let's go. I need a drink to celebrate our upcoming wedding and hopefully our soon-to-be enhanced net worth." They slowly walked back to the cottage.

It was 5 o'clock when Jones threw open the door to the flat and announced, "The bar is officially open. I'm having a double bourbon and water. What may I offer y'all? Just tell me what you'd like, and I'll fix you right up."

"Vodka martini, dry, straight up, with an olive," Mary responded. "Coming right up," Jones replied as he reached for the shaker.

"Jones, I'll mix Tina's and mine. Don't want to overwork the bartender just yet," Richard added. "Tina, what will it be?"

"I'd love a Cosmopolitan, please. Heavy on the vodka," Tina answered.

Richard cleared his throat and suggested, "We need to pace ourselves, until we get final verification that all of the ransom funds have been deposited. While we sip our cocktails, we can discuss preliminary plans for distribution of all that money. That piece of the puzzle is very important. However, most importantly we need to finalize our plan to get off this island." He mixed himself a double scotch and water.

"Great thinking ahead, Richard," Mary quipped. "Glad someone has his eyes on our future. If we do get all that money, we'll need a very secure plan as to how we access that money, how and where we choose to move it, and most importantly where in the name of god we can hide for a couple of years. Not to mention, how the hell do we get there."

Jones walked over to the bar and poured himself another bourbon on the rocks. Then he turned around, facing the other three, and stated, "That's good thinking by both of you. In addition to what you both said, we'll need to decide about the thumb drives. Who do we send them to? Where do we send them from? When do we send them? We must remember that when we let the thumb drives go, the world, as we know it, will in all probability turn upside down. That being the case, I'd suggest that whatever we plan to do with those thumb drives, we do it only after we've taken care of our new wealth in Luxembourg."

Jones continued, "So one thing we should consider immediately is---when do we go to Luxembourg? Or do we go somewhere else where we can take care of our financial business? My own opinion is that after we complete our wonderful celebration tonight, we make plans to leave here tomorrow morning and head to Brussels. That's right across the border from Luxembourg. We should be able to take care of all of our business there, both the money and the thumb drives. That's my only suggestion. I'm certain you three have your own ideas."

Tina spoke up, "I'm sure my opinion doesn't count for much, but I do agree. Based on all I've heard, we need to get the hell off of this island. We're too confined. We're like sitting ducks. I'm with Jones, we should leave tomorrow. We need to get back into a bigger world, for safety's sake."

"Well said, my dear," remarked Richard. "Believe me, your opinion does matter as much as anyone's. You have as much to lose as we all do. Our job from here on out is to survive until the villains are slain or imprisoned. What we do, we all do together. My vote is to leave first thing tomorrow for Brussels. Jones has picked the right place, the absolute best spot, for us to go."

"Before we get too busy celebrating," Mary began, "let's all agree right now about what we do tomorrow morning. I agree with everything that's been said already. So I suggest we all decide on what personal items we intend to take with us tomorrow, pack them tonight, and be ready to leave. I, too, agree with Jones about going to Brussels. We can do anything and everything we need to do there. As Tina said, we'll be off this island and in a bigger world."

Mary continued, "Now, what to do with the thumb drives. I say we send one to each of those US media outlets and one to the BBC, but not until we've taken care of our financial business in Luxembourg. That'll be the right time. Whether or not the corrupt bastards meet our demands, we're honor-bound to expose their evil and illegal activities to the world and let the chips fall where they may. That's my position, and I'm sticking to it."

Mary stood and concluded, "However, I'd like to say one more thing. I agree with what Jones brought up yesterday. If we do survive this battle, and we're able to find a secure place to live like normal folks again, I also have some very strong feelings about what we should and can do about getting rid of some of the shameful corruption in the upper echelons of our government. I just hope and pray we have the chance to discuss that real soon."

"Well, at least we know where everybody stands," added Richard. "So far I've heard no objections to leaving tomorrow, so that's what we'll do. Just need to decide if we're flying to Brussels or taking the train or driving. We can decide tomorrow. As for the thumb drives, I agree that we should send them to all the media outlets we mentioned. The corrupt bastards need to be exposed."

Jones emptied his glass of his last swallow and said, "I didn't plan to tell you what I'm getting ready to say until this ordeal was over, but I think I should warn you about what most likely will happen when all the damaging financial data hits the newsstands, the airwaves, and social media all over the world. It's not going to be pretty. It's going to be damn scary. It will change this world as we know it, overnight!"

"First of all, most financial markets around the world will collapse. The Dow, Nasdaq, S&P, and the London Exchange will plummet. Markets in Japan, Hong Kong, Toronto, Germany, and China will shut down immediately, due to plunging stock prices. Runs on banks around the world will force many financial institutions to close. The bottom will fall out of the Bond market. Governments will declare states of emergencies and shut down, and the US military will go on worldwide alert, as will other armies around the world."

"There will be riots in the streets all around the world, and many people will die because the local authorities will not be able to contain the unrest. In only a matter of days, people will be clamoring for food, water, cash, and guns. In a few more days, people will be killing for those same items. As bad as this sounds, that is not what we should fear the most."

"During this time of total international chaos, the world will be ripe for some foreign rogue nation like North Korea or Iran or Russia or even a terrorist group like ISIS, Al-Qaeda, the Taliban or HAMAS to make a move to force their ideology and control over the free world. This could happen in the blink of an eye, before any organized resistance can thwart their efforts.

"It would also be the perfect time for the International Monetary Fund nation members to finally vote to replace the US dollar as the world currency. Many of them have been advocating this move for many years. A surprising number of them have already made it clear that they have no use for the US dollar. They don't want it used as the world currency any longer. The proponents of a One World Order, which I have decided is what this entire debacle is about, would definitely back this monetary move. The BRICS, a group of nations (Brazil, Russia, India, China, and South Africa) are already using an alternative currency equivalent called SDR's, or Specific Draw Requests, for their trading transactions. The demise of the US dollar has already begun.

"If and when this happens, the first thing to fall like a rock will be the bond market and then the US economy will collapse. This is when the real United States has to stand up and restore some semblance of global order and maintain world peace. The question is not only can they, but also, will they? I realize that this is a very sobering conversation, but...."

As Jones was talking, his computer signaled that another email had arrived. Jones walked over to the table and clicked on the email. He checked his computer clock which read 5:55 pm.

The email was from the Banque Internationale a Luxembourg.

The message from his account manager was simple and straight-forward. Jones read it aloud. *"Mr. Jones,*

Your anticipated funds have arrived from three sources. The amounts are $25 million, $50 million, and $150 million, totaling $225 million. They have been certified and deposited in your accounts for immediate use. Congratulations! We appreciate your business. If I can be of any further service, please call.

Regards, Heinrich."

All four of them, Mary, Tina, Richard, and Jones, were totally speechless. They just sat there and looked at one another for moments on end. No one said anything. It was surreal, but also frightening.

Then Mary started screaming, followed by Tina's screams. Jones and Richard got up, shook hands, then embraced for a long couple of minutes. Then all four joined in a group hug. Tears flowed like water down their cheeks. Suddenly, they all seemed spent, exhausted. Relief mixed with fear began to spread over them. A whole range of emotions began to swirl in these four individuals. They had lived through months of fear, unrelenting pressure, undeniable stress, and total uncertainty. Slowly they were beginning to realize that this ordeal was close to its final outcome.

After a few minutes, things returned to a bare normal as the four began talking again. There were lots of comments, questions, speculative remarks, and declarations. They were aware they had to think about survival.

Finally, Richard spoke up and suggested that they grab a sandwich and a soda, pack up their belongings, and go to bed early. He reminded them of what they had to do the next day. There were no objections from anyone.

By 10 pm everyone was in bed, but not necessarily asleep. Millions of ideas were bouncing around in their brains. There was so much to think about, so little time to decide.

Around 2 am, Jones very quietly slipped out of bed and went into the kitchen. He couldn't sleep. Something was troubling him, but he couldn't put his finger on exactly what it was that woke him up. It wasn't a bad dream. It was something more. He was really worried. He decided to make coffee, go sit on the patio, and see if his mind would come clear.

After an hour and a couple of cups of strong coffee, Jones thought that maybe he had an answer to what was keeping him awake. He decided he was having a premonition, an epiphany, as some folks back home called it. But what was the message? That part was not totally clear, just that something major was about to happen. *I guess I'll know when it happens,* Jones thought. Then he went back to bed.

Jones wasn't the only person awake at two that morning.

When Richard and Tina went to their room, they knew they needed to talk. They needed to get things said. They needed to make decisions and their plans based on the outcome of events likely to unfold over the next few days.

Richard began, "Tina, I'm happy we're together. I'm glad you loved me enough to come with me without knowing all of the frightful details. I promise I'll do everything in my power to convince you that you made the right decision, even though things are terrifying right now. I love you dearly. There are so many things I want us to do, and so many places I want us to go. I truly believe we can be very happy together. We just have to survive this ordeal and things should get back to something that resembles normalcy. You gotta know that you have become part of the team, and that we're all in it together, no matter the outcome. Please try and remain strong and really believe that we'll all make it together."

Tina was having a hard time holding back the tears, tears of both joy and fear. She just couldn't help herself. Richard moved closer and held her tightly while she sobbed.

Finally, Tina spoke, "Richard, you must know how I feel about you, and how much I love you. But to be honest, I'm scared to death. I don't know what to do. Is it normal for me to be this frightened?"

After wiping away the tears, Tina continued, "Richard, I want to do the same things you want to do. I want to see the world with you, but will this crisis ever end, really end? Or will we be haunted by the Bank and the government forever? How can we ever get married under such a cloud? That's what has me worried more than I can say. I just don't understand how we can ever get away from this nightmare."

Richard interrupted, "Hold on, Tina. Don't go there. You're getting ahead of yourself. Things are not necessarily going to end up that way. Try and be positive. Look, we have the law on our side. It's the other side that's in the wrong. If, and I mean if, we survive along with Jones and Mary, we'll have immunity and we'll be exonerated, and the bad guys will go to prison. Then, we'll be able, due in part to a huge financial windfall, to go where we want to go, do what we want to do, and get married where and when we so choose.

That's what I believe and that should be our focus until it becomes a reality. Okay?"

"I'm sorry I'm not stronger," Tina admitted. "It's just a blessing that I have had you to lean on throughout this entire ordeal. Thank you for your love and your support."

"Come on Tina, we need to get some sleep," Richard stated. "Tomorrow's going to be a very busy day."

What Jones and the other three did not know as they tried to sleep was that Kurt Lane's "hit squad" was already in London with orders to take out Mr. Jones, Mary, and their associates.

When the two contract killers deplaned, they headed by taxi to the DHL office to retrieve their "hunting rifles," shipped over the day before. It was the only legal way to ship the firearms into England. Their pretext was they were going to use the rifles to go grouse hunting in Sussex. They picked up their long guns and headed into London's East End to find a cheap hotel room as a base for their operation.

Once they checked in, their top priority was to use the satellite data the Feds provided Lane to help them triangulate Mr. Jones's burner phone and establish his location. Later that evening, after several unsuccessful attempts using government high-tech wizardry, they hit the jackpot. Boom. They found him. Mr. Jones's location was in the English Channel on the Isle of Wight.

One man opened his phone, pulled up Google and entered "ferries to Isle of Wight" into Search. The search results showed a standard ferry that would take thirty minutes to cross the Solent.

The Hovercraft ferry would take only ten minutes. He pressed the link for schedules. It showed the first morning departure time for the Hovercraft at 6:30 am. *That's the ticket,* he thought.

The killers checked their rifles, loaded each one to the max, and stacked their gear by the door. They set the alarm clock for 4:30 am. All they had to do when they awoke was to make a reservation on the Hovercraft ferry to Ryde, call a hack to take them to the port at Southsea, and 'go hunting' with their long guns once they arrived

Bill Brown
on the Isle of Wight.

Chapter Thirty-Six

The Finale

It was barely seven o'clock in the morning, and Richard's phone was ringing again. It was the third time in the last minute. Richard rolled over and looked at Tina in disbelief.

"What the hell?" Tina mused. "Somebody's playing games."

Richard picked up his phone and answered, "Hello, Richard here. Speak louder, please. I can't hear you very well."

"Hello mate," a voice yelled. "It's me, your friend from the ferry. Can you hear me now?"

"Yes, now I can hear you. What's up?"

"They're here. Those guys you described as gangster looking. The ones you asked me to call you about, if I ever saw them. There are two of them. They look like thugs."

"Okay. Tell me what you know. Where are they now?"

"The ones you called the 'bad guys' just got off the Hovercraft. They're damn sure not Brits. They look like Americans, but real nasty lookin' fellas. They look kinda scary, I think."

"They're the 'ones' I've been expecting. Thanks for the call and the warning. I owe you. I'll put you in my will," exclaimed Richard.

The man from the ferry continued, "They're carrying funny looking cases. Long and narrow. They look a bit like rifle cases, if you know what I mean."

Richard answered, "I'm afraid I know all too well what you mean. Which way did they head? Did they say anything?"

"Yeah, they talked about coming here to hunt. Wanted to know how to get Bembridge to meet their guide. I knew they were lying to me. I gave them the wrong directions, away from the cottage, where you said you're staying."

"Mate, you're a saint. Thanks for everything. Goodbye."

Richard turned to Tina and said, "They're here. Get your stuff. We're leaving. Now."

Tina responded, "How the hell did they find us this quickly? Something doesn't add up. Actually, it smells to high heaven. Richard, better go tell Jones now."

"Yes, I will right now, but get your belongings together. We all need be out of here ASAP."

"Okay. Ready in five minutes. Wake up Jones and Mary."

Richard dialed Jones. His line was busy.

Richard closed his phone and yelled at Tina, "Damn it. Can you believe that. His line rings busy. Unbelievable. Who the hell is he talking to now?"

Richard's phone rings again. "Damn, this is outrageous. Hello."

"Richard, this is Jones. Pack up your stuff. We gotta leave right now."

"I just tried to call you, Jones, but your line rang busy. Why?"

"Someone just rang my phone three consecutive times and never said a word. I believe we've been located somehow. How the hell did they get my burner phone number? We need the answer to that question."

"I know they're here," barked Richard. "The mate from the ferry I told you about just called and informed me that two American men just got off the Hovercraft. They're packing long guns, pretending to be hunters."

"Damn, how the hell did they know where to find us?" asked Jones. "I guess they probably got my burner phone number from my buddy's file at Treasury. That's the scary thing. Richard, we gotta get off of this damn island right now."

"You're not waiting on Tina and me, Bossman. Let's go. I'll call a hack right this minute. I'll tell the driver to pull in the back alley. The safer the better."

Jones replied, "We gotta take the Hovercraft. It's the quickest way off this island and back to the mainland. We should have a better chance of surviving there. It leaves every hour on the hour from Ryde. I put the pilots up at the Stafford and paid them to hang around awhile. I'll call and instruct them to meet us at Gatwick in two and a half hours and have the jet ready to depart. If we can get to Gatwick, we can take the Citation to most anywhere from there today. Meet you in the den in five minutes."

"Ten-four, my friend. Never really wanted to die on the Isle of Wight." The foursome met six minutes later, carrying their bags.

Richard asked Jones, "You're sure you've got all the thumb drives?"

"Yes," Jones answered. "I've got the thumb drives in my brief case which is attached to my wrist. Can't afford to lose our life insurance. We need to get the hell out of this part of the world. The Citation X is still at Gatwick and the pilots are meeting us there in two and a half hours."

Richard asked the others, "Does anyone have second thoughts about sending the thumb drives to the media outlets once we get to Brussels?"

"No," was their response.

"I damn sure won't want to change my mind, "Mary answered very abruptly. "Those bastards need to be arrested and locked up for life."

Smiling, Jones said, "I'm glad we're all on the same page about this, but right now we need to be concerned about getting out of here and off of this damn island. We've got to move our money and find a safe, secure place before these thumb drives are released. The Hovercraft's next departure for the mainland is in fifteen minutes. Bembridge is about eight miles from Ryde where we came over on the Hovercraft. That hack needs to get here and damn quick. No time to waste, if we plan to make it."

Richard said, "I told the driver just that. He swore he'd be here in five minutes. I also told him the quicker he got us to the Hovercraft, the bigger his tip. Like a two-hundred-dollar tip."

"I'd sure like a shot of vodka," stated Mary.

"It would calm my nerves." "I need more than that. Maybe a

double shot," uttered Tina.

"We'll all deserve a drink, if we get there in time," Jones added.

The hack arrived and drove to the alley exit as requested. Jones and Richard threw their bags in the trunk as Mary and Tina climbed into the back seat.

"Come on, Richard," yelled Jones. "Crawl in the back seat. I'll get in the front with the driver."

Suddenly, a shot rang out as the exterior passenger-side mirror on the hack shattered and fell to the pavement.

"Get the hell out of here, "Jones screamed at the driver. "Everybody keep your heads down." *A little too close for comfort*, Jones thought.

"What in the name of god is going on?" cried Tina. "Who's shooting at us?"

Mary responded, "It doesn't take a rocket scientist to know those bastards want us dead."

The driver stomped on the gas, and they sped away as the tires screeched. Two more gun-shots rang out, but luckily they missed their mark.

Jones told the driver, "Take a back way to the port in Ryde, please take it and hurry."

"Why are you being shot at? Who wants you dead? This is a bit too dramatic for me. I didn't agree to this kind of danger," squealed the driver.

"Shut the hell up and drive the damn hack," screamed Richard. "You're getting well paid for this trip, that is, if we make it in time. Just step on it."

"Okay, I'm doing the best I can do under the circumstances. I'm not used to being shot at. Here is where we turn to go the back way. Hold on, it's going to get very bumpy."

Five minutes later Jones yelled, "There's the port. I see the water and the ferries. We just might make it in time."

Richard pulled out two one hundred-dollar bills and handed them to Jones. Jones placed them on the driver's leg.

"Hurry. Drop us off at the entrance to the Hovercraft," Jones demanded. "We'll jump out so you can keep on going. Take another way back to town, go home, and hide your car tonight because those bastards will be looking to find out where you took us. Now, hurry up. Thanks."

The hack driver said, "There's only one entrance and one ticket booth for both of the ferries. That's where I'll drop you off."

"Ladies, as soon as we reach the entrance, run quickly to the ferry. I'll get the tickets while Richard gets our bags. Don't waste any time and don't look back. It's a life or death situation."

The cabbie shouted, "Here we are! Jump out! I got you here in time. Great. Good luck. I'm going home to hide." He screeched away.

As Jones was buying the tickets, Richard passed him with their bags, headed to the entrance right behind Mary and Tina.

"Come on Jones," Richard yelled. "Hurry up. Hurry up, now!"

As Jones ran to the ferry entrance with the tickets, he screamed at the other three, "This way damn it! This way. You're all going the wrong bloody way! Come on this way, now. Hurry. Get aboard here, now. Hurry!"

The Hovercraft motors began to hum as the air pushed the craft upward above the water. Its skirt filled with air as it started moving away from The Island. When the Hovercraft ferry reached fifty yards offshore, there was an enormous noise, followed by an incredible explosion. The Hovercraft disintegrated into a thousand pieces!

NOBODY could have survived that disaster! NOBODY!

The port at Ryde on the Isle of Wight was suddenly thrown into total chaos. Sirens were screeching! Fog horns were blasting! Boats were scattering! People were screaming, yelling, and crying! Body parts and burning debris were floating in the Channel.

Although the standard ferry was not scheduled to depart from the shore for another fifteen minutes, the Harbor Master ordered it to leave immediately.

TBC.....

49605399R00143

Made in the USA
Columbia, SC
24 January 2019